I0731036

T.M. CROMER

Pints & Potions Copyright © 2021 T.M. Cromer

ISBN: 978-1-7352032-5-6 (EPUB)
ISBN: 978-1-956941-02-9 (LARGE PRINT)
ISBN: 978-1-956941-01-2 (HARDBACK)
ISBN: 978-1-956941-03-6 (PAPERBACK)

Cover Design: Deranged Doctor Design
Edits: Precise Editing Group & Postscript Writing Services

To Sarah Hegger:
Thank you for always being available to brainstorm and help tweak the important things!

To my Irish beta team:
Thank you for all your hard work and for making sure I have all the lingo down pat. My heart is always with you on your beautiful Emerald Isle.

To Marion R.:
Thank you for helping me tweak Cian's speech. You have my deepest gratitude, to be sure. ;)

"You need to hurry up, Piper. You're going to miss your flight. Although—"

"Don't say it," she snapped. She was currently lying, belly down, across the top of her overstuffed suitcase in order to make the edges meet. "I think I'm going to be over the weight limit."

"Take everything out but the sexy underwear," advised her cousin and best friend, Liz Thorne-Xuereb. "Or let me cast a spell to lighten the case."

"I don't have any sexy underwear." Piper willfully ignored the spell comment. She'd be damned if she would use magic for anything she didn't classify as an emergency. To do otherwise would be an abuse of power as far as she was concerned. Of course, her attitude wasn't popular among her family, who used magic with the speed of a ravenous chocoholic consuming bonbons.

Damn, she could really go for lemon-buttercream chocolates to temper her traveling anxiety right about now.

"*At all?*" Liz screeched, pulling Piper back into the conversation. Her cousin was clearly appalled that a single woman wouldn't have the basics.

Heat crept up Piper's neck. "Well, I *do*, but not packed. It's *Ireland*, Liz. People dress in layers over there."

"Sure, but eventually they have to strip down—if you know what I mean. And thermal long johns aren't a turn-on. What happens when you meet a hot Irishman and take him back to your hotel?"

"It's a B&B, and I won't be bringing any men back to my room. In case you failed to remember, I'm on a dating hiatus for a while. It's called *vacation* for a reason."

"Need I remind you that I found Rafe while on vacation?"

"Rafe found you, and he was in Paris on *business*."

Liz shrugged as she rummaged through Piper's dresser, no doubt looking for sexy articles of clothing. "You say tomato, I say tomahto."

"I'm pretty sure you stole that line from him. Regardless, I've sworn off men."

"Irish women are hot, too. Really, anyone with an Irish accent would do."

"You *know* what I mean. And while I'm open to just about anything, it's doubtful I'll switch sides this late in the game. Seriously, I just need a break from dating." Piper snatched the underwear out of Liz's hands as she tried to add it to the suitcase. "Stop, or you really will make me late."

"Let's compromise. Take four matching sets."

"One."

"Three."

"Two and no thongs. I hate those things. They're little more than ass floss."

"Deal." Liz grinned triumphantly. "But if things get hot and heavy, I want a sex tape."

"Okay, *eww,* because you're my damned cousin. You're

getting as bad as Mackenzie. Next thing you know, you'll be telling me you're into bondage." When Liz flushed the color of a ripe beet, Piper laughed. "I didn't know you had it in you!"

"It was only handcuffs," Liz retorted.

Piper arched her freshly waxed brows.

"All right, a blindfold, too. But that's all."

"Who was sporting the cuffs and blindfold? You or Rafe?"

"Rafe."

Tickled by the new carefree side of her cousin, Piper hugged Liz. "I'm so glad you found him. You deserved so much better than Franco."

"I still can't believe he stole my magic. Who *does* that?"

"Well, thankfully Rafe discovered his plan in time." She rounded up the last of her toiletries.

Liz cleared her throat, and Piper suspected it still stung her cousin's heart that her now-deceased boyfriend had tried to use her for nefarious purposes. "Enough with all the maudlin BS. Let's get this show on the road. Promise you'll FaceTime me from a pub while you're sharing a drink with a local hottie."

Struggling against a laugh, Piper said, "I'm telling Rafe that he's not satisfying your urges if you're thinking about my sex life and hot Irishmen."

"Believe me, my woman's urges are completely taken care of —on every level." Rafe's sexy, slightly accented drawl came from the doorway and startled both of them.

Again, Liz flushed, and Piper was positive he spoke the truth. She sighed with the smallest hint of envy. Hair so dark it looked black in this light, midnight-colored eyes, and six feet of sinewy body, Rafe was every woman's walking fantasy. However, he'd only had eyes for Liz from the day they recon-nected a handful of years after their Paris meeting.

Feeling a bit warm herself, Piper returned to the bathroom to retrieve the last of her travel necessities. Once her carry-on was packed, she allowed Rafe to take both cases to the car. When he was out of earshot, she turned to Liz.

"You have to be the luckiest woman on the planet. Promise me I get him in your will should anything happen to you."

"Nope. I have a stipulation that he must mourn me forever. He's not allowed to find comfort with another woman."

"Now you're just being selfish."

They shared a laugh and headed out to join Rafe for the short ride to the airport.

After they arrived at the terminal, Rafe unloaded the cases from the truck and escorted Piper inside. "Remember, no taking candy from strangers. And any guy you're interested in has to provide you with a full name, date of birth, and some form of ID so I can scry and check him out. That way, we can avoid an incident like the last one."

Rafe was referring to Piper's god-awful taste in men. Her radar was defective and had failed to pick up on the fact her ex-boyfriend—a mortal one at that—was engaged with a baby on the way.

"Got it," Piper responded with a grin and a hug. "Thanks, Rafe."

"Be safe and call us when you get settled. Liz and I want to know when you arrive, okay? Although, why you don't teleport is beyond me." He grinned when she groaned.

"Not you too!"

Rafe shrugged, glanced around, and lowered his voice to say, "Don't use the name Thorne. Lie if you have to. It isn't safe to bandy about that name when you're on your own, even in this day and age."

"I'll be plain old Piper Kelly. I plan to vacation like a normal person. And I promise to let you both know when I arrive."

Rafe shook his head. "This bizarre need of yours to be 'normal' baffles me. We're magical beings. You should embrace your heritage."

It was an old argument between her family and her. It seemed Rafe had taken their side. No one would ever understand. In a family full of the most powerful witches on the planet, Piper got lost. Not bothering to answer, she kissed his cheek and hugged Liz.

Two and a half hours later, Piper was boarded and on her way to Ireland for her much-needed dream vacation. Two weeks in the Emerald Isle with nothing to do but enjoy the countryside, eat fish and chips, and listen to Irish folk bands play in local pubs. No corporate headaches, no IT problems popping up from employees who could barely sign into their email accounts. Most importantly, no running into her ex-boyfriend at work or his pregnant wife at their hometown supermarket.

Piper would take the time to lick her wounds and formulate a new plan for a family of her own. Perhaps it was time to rule out a lifelong mate and go with artificial insemination. That way, she would be able to pick a sperm donor based on genetics and brains instead of waiting for Mr. Wrong to come along for what seemed like the millionth time. Goddess willing, by this time next year, she would be a mom. It didn't get more normal than that, right?

The idea had a soft smile forming on her lips. The thought of holding her own newborn close and rocking him or her to sleep made Piper's heart ache with longing. All she'd ever wanted was a family to love. At thirty-three, her biological clock wasn't only ticking; it was setting off alarms on an hourly basis.

But first, she'd take one last vacation before her world would be forever altered by a baby. Afterwards, her life wouldn't be her own, and she intended to live it up on this holiday while she still could.

CIAN O'MALLEY DIDN'T MISS MUCH. EARLY ON HE'D TRAINED himself to gauge the energy of the pub's patrons and work the room. That gift had come in handy at times he needed it the most. From his position on stage, he noted the stranger among the standard Friday-night crowd. He caught sight of the black-haired beauty the moment she stepped into his pub. Her rich-honey eyes were bright with excitement, and he immediately recognized that she wasn't from around these parts. Mainly because he knew almost everyone who was. He also recognized the magical glow around her. With such a bright, blinding aura, she had to be a witch—a powerful one at that. If he was mistaken, he'd eat his microphone.

As he picked out a lively tune and sang about a love gone wrong in a way only the Irish could, he tracked her with his eyes. Before this night was out, he intended to not only know her name but also steal a kiss from those glossy, beguiling lips of hers.

His sister Bridget served the stranger a Guinness, and he nearly laughed at the face the woman made upon taking her first sip. A pint of plain wasn't for the faint of heart. But he had to give her credit for trying the dark brew.

The noise of the room abruptly faded away, and her American accent drifted to where he sat. As he transitioned from one song to the next, he watched his new obsession laugh and flirt with some of the other male patrons. Yeah, he'd be settling up with those plonkers later for making time with the woman Cian had mentally claimed for his own.

Soon enough, his set was finished, and he made his way through the swell of customers and friends slapping him on the back. When he was less than five feet from her, the dark-haired siren turned her merry eyes upon him. It was as if lightning struck. His entire body sizzled and Cian found it impossible to catch his breath. His only consolation was her own dumb-struck expression. She felt the connection as well.

Good to know he wasn't the only fool for love.

That stray thought brought him up short, but he quickly brushed it away. He didn't do love or anything remotely leading to commitment. Burn me once, and all that shite.

"Well, hello, darlin'. I see you've been enjoyin' yerself in me pub." He laid the accent on thick because American women turned to mush after hearing his honeyed Irish tongue.

With sparkling eyes, she asked, "Your pub? So you're *the* O'Malley in Lucky O'Malley's Pub?"

"One of them. Cian O'Malley at your service, darlin'. And whom do I have the pleasure of speakin' with in turn?"

"Piper Kelly."

"Ah, to be sure, you must be a good Irish *cailín* with a name like Kelly."

Her laughter was as golden as her aura. The sound reached in and grabbed him by the nads, making him lose all sense of up or down.

"Does this—" she made a swirling gesture with her hand around his mouth "—actually work to help you pick up women?"

He placed his palm flat over his heart. "You wound me, darlin'. You surely do."

"Uh-huh." She sounded doubtful, but his soon-to-be lover had a twinkle in her eye, which clearly indicated she liked his suffering.

"Put a man out of his misery and run away with me, why don't ya?"

"I'm sure your wife wouldn't appreciate that." She gestured with her thumb over her shoulder to Bridget, who stood behind the bar, giving him the evil eye.

"Bridget isn't my wife, love. She's my sister. And the look she's gracing us with, is because she's vexed I'm passing time with you, and not servin' up these louts hangin' about me bar."

"Pull on your wellies, lads," Bridget called out. "It's about to get deep in here because Cian intends to rabbit on in hopes of catching a ride!"

"Ride?" Piper questioned just before taking a sip of her pint.

He mentally debated the merits of honesty when the ginger-haired Seamus, sitting on the stool beside her, spoke up and beat him to the punch. "Shag. Cian's hopin' to shag ya."

Guinness sprayed the air as Piper choked on her drink. Seamus earned a dark glare from Cian as he snatched up a dry bar towel to mop the beer from his face.

"Dry up this mess and don't be annoying me, Seamus, or you'll be finding yourself out on your arse," Cian growled and threw down the damp towel.

"Jaysus, Cian! Don't be hasty," Seamus exclaimed, rushing to comply. "It was Bridget who said it."

"And it was *you* who were repeating it, you feckin' eejit."

"Is this always the way you woo women?" Piper asked with laughter heavy in her voice.

Her grin was as bright as the noon sun on a clear summer day, and Cian found himself soaking up its warmth.

"If we're being honest, no. I'm much more smooth and charming."

"Good to know you weren't banking on your looks alone."

Although they were in a crowded place, Cian only had eyes for this lone woman. The tilt of her head and the half smile still lingering on her lips fascinated him. She was, without a doubt, flirting in return. Ah, the sight of her sped up his heart. It truly did.

"Love, I have a bet with a few of me friends." He laid it on thick, but he was savvy enough to recognize she was enjoying their exchange. "It's a well-known fact that me boyos look up to me in these parts."

"Uh-huh." She sounded cynical but amused. "So what's this bet?"

"Well, it's more of a tradition, really," he lied. "I'm forced to kiss all the new colleens who stroll into me pub."

"*Forced* to?"

"Yeah, and if I can win a kiss from the fairest of women—that be you—I'd be a living legend in these parts."

"Still not seeing where the bet part of this comes in."

"I bet me boyos that you'd take mercy on me and bestow the kiss to end all kisses."

"Interesting. When exactly did you make this bet? Since I've been here, you've been on stage or in front of me."

Cian could see his sister's smirk from the corner of his eye. The patrons of the pub had grown quiet to watch the interplay between Piper and him.

"She has you there, Cian!" someone hollered.

"It's implied," Cian informed her without missing a beat, ignoring his heckler.

Her left brow practically shot to her hairline and she bit one corner of the plump lip he was dying to sample.

"One taste, darlin'. That's all I'm hoping for. Then I can die a happy man," he said softly.

"Who am I to stand in the way of tradition?"

He wasn't sure he heard her correctly, but he didn't give her a chance to change her mind. Swooping in, hands cupping her exquisite face, he claimed his prize. When their lips connected, warning bells sounded in his brain. This long-legged dream of a woman was dangerous to his well-being.

Her arms went around his neck, and her fingers wound their way through his hair. Her light caress on his scalp sent desire racing through his entire body like a runaway train. He tightened his hold and had his eyes been open, he'd have closed them in ecstasy. Hoots and catcalls sounded around them, but Cian was damned if he could sever their connection.

That was *until* a cold blast of water from his right side dampened his ardor.

"Bridget, you she-devil!" he swore.

"Stop mauling the customers and get back to strumming. We have a pub to entertain."

"Oh, you can be sure we were entertained, *mo ghrá!*" A male voice called out from a table in the far back reaches of the pub.

"I'm not your love, Ruairí O'Connor. And you'd best be remembering your manners in my pub."

"You'd be my everything if you give me a chance, Bridg," Ruairí returned.

"Pfft." She rolled her eyes. "Right. You say that to me and every other woman within a hundred-kilometre radius." Bridget winked in Piper's direction. "Don't believe any of these wankers, girl. They delight in pulling your leg. My brother Cian is the worst of the lot. You're the fifth woman he's hit on this week."

Piper turned disappointed eyes on him but didn't look surprised.

Cian felt a tightening in his chest and scowled at his sister from where he stood behind Piper. "Now, don't be spreading tales, Bridget. You'll have my darlin' Piper believing the worst of us." He swept aside the hair from Piper's neck and leaned in to whisper. "Ignore her. She's out to kick a man in the bollocks on her best day. Will you stick around for my next set? I'll dedicate a song to you."

"It's been a long day. Maybe next time," she demurred, apology heavy in her voice.

Although it sounded as if she'd like nothing better than to hang out for another beer and to flirt with him, she also looked like she was on her last leg.

"Are you stayin' local?"

She nodded. "For a few days."

"Good. I'll walk you back to your hotel."

"No need, I'm only right next door at the B&B."

"Humor me."

The steely tone caused her to frown and most likely had her wondering where his charming Irish accent had gone. She was clever enough to realize he laid it on a little thicker for the tourists, and Cian surmised it was why she didn't say anything.

"You can trust him to walk you to your room, Piper," Bridget assured her as she drew another Guinness from the tap. "He knows if he disappears on me, there'll be the devil to pay." Addressing Cian, Bridget warned, "Five minutes. Any longer, and I'll come for you myself."

Seamus snorted and said, "Five minutes? More than three be one too many for Cian."

Cian shoved him off the barstool.

Seamus had the reflexes of a cat, and the man didn't spill a drop of his beer. "What? I was meaning to get into the gal's—"

Cian clamped a hand over Seamus's mouth. "I know what you were meaning. You'd do well to shut your pie hole, Seamus McCleary." He released his drunk friend with a second none-too-gentle shove. "He's cut off."

"Ya got a mean streak as wide as—"

"Not another word, Seamus," Cian growled.

"You've wasted two of your five minutes, Brother."

"Come on, love. I don't want you to be a witness to murder."

Cian placed his hand on Piper's lower back and guided her toward the door. A current of sorts passed between them, surprising him, and he sent her a sharp glance to see if she'd experienced the same.

She appeared unfazed.

A simple touch had never set him off before. Dry-mouthed, he held his own council and silently walked with her toward the building next door.

"You handled that well," she said as he strolled beside her.

Thrown by her cool sarcasm, he stopped and stared. His

laughter, when it started, was deep and boomed out across the night. The sound carried and seemed to echo forever. He couldn't remember the last time he'd laughed that hard.

Cian reached for her hand and placed a lingering kiss on her fingertips. "Come, let's get you home."

2

Piper woke with a song in her heart. She stretched and grinned.

Ireland!

Her welcome yesterday had been more than she could've hoped for.

Cian was delicious. With his shaggy, sandy-brown hair, dancing green eyes, and tall, muscular—but not overly so—build added to a keen intelligence and a devil-may-care attitude, he had checked off every single one of Piper's heretofore unknown boxes.

He'd been the perfect gentleman when he walked her to her lodgings. He'd insisted on checking out the premises, which surprised and thrilled her. Last night, she'd figured it was another of his flirty games, but once he'd declared the all-clear, he had graced her with a light kiss on her cheek and disappeared.

Apparently chivalry wasn't quite dead yet.

She'd practically danced all the way upstairs to her room, reliving their mini make-out session in the pub.

Damn, the man could kiss.

She'd forgotten where she was the minute his lips touched hers and had gotten carried away. Cian had too. She'd felt it in his touch and the budding erection pressing against the soft swell of her belly. If it hadn't been for Bridget's timely interruption, they'd have gone up in flames.

Piper toyed with the idea of stopping by today in the hopes of seeing him again. But first things first, she needed a shower and a cup of coffee—not necessarily in that order.

She stumbled into the bathroom and groaned at her reflection. Yesterday's forgotten makeup made her resemble a demented raccoon. So as not to terrify the other occupants of the B&B should they run into her, she scrubbed her face clean, pulled her unruly hair into a topknot, and dragged a large cardigan sweater over her pajamas.

Halfway down the stairs the wonderful aroma of fresh-brewed coffee and perfectly cooked food drifted to her. For the second time that morning, she grinned. This trip was going to be incredible. And if she skipped down the last of the stairs in her eagerness to get to those mouth-watering smells, well, no one was around to bear witness.

She sailed around the corner and buried her nose directly into a burly, unyielding chest. Pain set her eyes to watering, and although Piper wanted to cuss up a storm, she muttered, "I'm sorry" instead.

"No need to apologize, darlin'. I understand your eagerness to see me again. I'm feelin' the same way, myself. Anytime you want to sniff my chest, I won't deny you, to be sure."

The delicious sound of Cian's amused voice jerked her head up.

O'Malley's Black Cat Inn!

Of course! Either he was part owner, or he was related to the owners.

She'd been too tired to make the connection before.

Piper eyed him; irritated he looked so well rested and gorgeous this early while she was a complete mess. Maybe she should rethink shunning magic long enough to utilize a glamour spell.

A cup of coffee appeared before her. "Cut the girl a break, Cian. We don't want her running for the closest airport," Bridget scolded.

Piper took a huge sniff of the coffee and groaned her appreciation for Bridget's thoughtfulness. "Besides, I'm in love with your sister."

Cian, in the process of drinking his own morning brew, spit it out in a perfect imitation of her reaction to Seamus's comment last night.

Bridget's laughter triggered her own.

He scowled and caught the hand towel his sister threw in his direction. "You're proving what I've long known to be true," he muttered.

"Oh? And what's that?" Piper asked as she followed the delectable smells the rest of the way into the kitchen.

"That all women are evil and out to break my poor wee heart," he hollered after her retreating back.

She took a seat at the counter and, to hide her grin, she bit into the toast Bridget had placed in front of her. Piper loved their verbal judo. Cian challenged her in a way she'd never been before, and it was fun. Although she only just met the man, he had a warm, flirty quality about him that made her feel she'd known him a lifetime. His easy, uncomplicated manner attracted her on every level. Life was much easier with a drama-free man.

The thought brought her up short. She shouldn't be thinking about long term with Cian. He lived an ocean away and, according to his sister, he had a wandering eye.

Speaking of his eyes, she couldn't seem to look away and was drowning in those sparkling emerald depths.

"What do you have planned today, Piper?" Bridget's voice had a slight edge, and it was enough to break the staring contest between Cian and Piper.

"Since this is my first trip to Ireland, I thought I'd hit all the touristy places." Piper started devouring the scrumptious meal. "Do you have any suggestions? Any must-sees?"

Cian leaned around her and snatched a piece of toast from her plate. "I happen to be a brilliant tour guide."

"You have work to do today, you feckin' skiver. Don't even dream of leaving it all on my shoulders." His sister shot him a dark look.

"Bridg, we can't neglect our guest now, can we?"

Piper's lips twitched as she observed Bridget's irate reaction. It seemed her hostess's temperament was as fiery as her red hair. If looks could kill, her brother would be dead and buried in the family cemetery.

"I'm not going to be your excuse to get out of work, Cian." Piper finished off the last of her breakfast and put her empty plate by the sink.

"But you have to see the real Ireland, love. You won't find that in some tourist's book." Cian put an arm around her and steered her toward the stairs. "Now go get dressed, and I'll soothe my sister's ruffled feathers."

A glance back showed Bridget wasn't as put out as she'd first appeared.

Cian's wide shoulders blocked Piper's view of the kitchen as he closed the distance between them. With his lips pressed to the shell of her ear, he said, "Or if you'd rather see something native, you don't need to get dressed. I can join you in your room, and we can have a grand time here, to be sure."

"Keep it in your pants, player. I'll be down in ten minutes."

"You aren't doing anything to make me believe you aren't a cruel woman, Piper me love."

"And you aren't doing anything to make me believe you aren't a horny man out to score, Cian *me love*," she mocked and headed upstairs.

"I never said I wasn't a horny man," he called up after her.

"Lay off before you scare her, you eejit," Bridget scolded when Piper was out of earshot.

"Do you really need my help today?" Cian asked over his shoulder, all kidding aside.

"No, I'm just having powerful fun watching you get shot down." She smiled and patted his cheek. "Make sure you bring some johnnies with you. The woman doesn't need to end up with a babe for your carelessness."

Oddly enough, the idea of impregnating the lovely Piper didn't upset him. Instead, the image of her cradling a dark-haired babe to her breast spread warmth through his chest. With any other woman, he'd already be breaking out in a fine sweat. Perhaps he should utilize Bridget's excuse and leave Piper to her own devices. He'd known the woman less than twelve hours, for St. Peter's sake! Why was he picturing her with his child?

"You okay?"

He started from where he'd been staring at the empty staircase. "Yeah. Just woolgathering."

"I like her." Bridget nodded to the stairs. "She doesn't put on airs. Not like the last one."

He dismissed her comment with a shrug and helped finish cleaning the kitchen. "If you need a night off, I can call in Ruairí to help me at the pub tonight."

"It's shameful you'd believe for one moment that I would

allow him to run my business. He's the enemy, Cian, and don't you forget it."

"Oh, give over, Bridg. That bloody war has been done for decades. You're the only one still holding on to it."

"Someone has to remember why the O'Malleys lost their power, brother. You and the others may be fine without, but I'm not."

"All I'm saying—"

"I know what you're saying. I just don't happen to agree with you. An O'Connor will never be welcome behind my counter or within my home. It's bad enough I have to serve him."

"Business is business. We can't afford to be picky. Our finances are nearly non-existent, Bridg," Cian said grimly.

She grimaced. "We used the last batch of Granny O'Malley's potion when we made the new brew. We're likely to lose everything when this last store of beer is gone."

"We'll have to become like normal folk, but we'll make it work."

"Normal," she sneered. "We're meant to be great witches who rule our island, you bloody eejit."

Cian cast a nervous glance toward the stairs. "Shhh. Do you want to let the whole of America know what we are? 'Cause that's what'll happen if our guests overhear you."

"She's our only boarder until Wednesday, and if you haven't figured out by now that she's a witch, you've not the sense the Goddess graced a mule." She shoved by him and grabbed a light jacket from the hook. "Find Carrick and tell him to get his lazy arse over to the pub. You'll have to trade shifts for the day."

"I knew last night Piper was a witch. For the record, you get bossier with every year that passes."

"Shut your mouth or I'll serve over bossy."

He ignored her threat. Not that Bridget wouldn't carry through, but she had a soft spot for Cian and he wasn't opposed to exploiting it now and again. "Carrick might have a problem. He won't want to leave Aedan alone with a sitter tonight."

His sister stopped on her way to the door. "What's wrong with Aedan?"

"He's having the terrors during the day now."

Cian's young nephew had been experiencing paralyzing night terrors in the eight months since he'd witnessed his mother's death. He swore evil monsters were trying to steal his soul. No amount of therapy had helped him conquer his fear that someone was after him or that his father might die in a fiery car crash like his mother had. More recently, the boy had started seeing his demons during the daylight hours.

"Carrick said just yesterday Aedan ran inside, terrified out of his wee mind. Said it took him a good hour to get the boy to calm."

Bridget's worried gaze met his. "Then Carrick needs to stay home and take care of his own. I suppose you'll have to call Ruairí and have him cover. I'll have no choice but to put up with him for a day."

Color crept into her cheeks and she avoided his questioning look. For sure, the relationship between Bridget and Ruairí was volatile, but Cian was at a loss as to why. His sister avoided being alone with their neighbor for reasons other than what she pretended, but she refused to divulge the real truth. Cian knew her personal grievance with Ruairí went back at least fifteen years or more.

"Ma might come if I call her," he said softly.

"I want her less than I want an O'Connor in my place."

"When are you going to tell me what happened?"

"Never, because it's ancient history on all accounts. Our mother is an evil person, Cian. You know this. Why would you ever think of bringing her back here?"

"She's not, Bridg. She was good to us once."

"Right. When Da was alive. After he disappeared, she became a miserable feckin' bitch. No thanks, she can stay in whatever hole she crawled into." Bridget shot a quick glance toward the stairs before turning her attention on him. She had a wary look. "If you insist on playing tour-guide today, be careful. You still have powerful enemies wandering about."

3

Piper was excited in a way she hadn't been in a long while. If she stopped long enough to think about it, she experienced a pang of guilt. Maybe if she'd been more attentive to previous boyfriends and less involved with her job or hobbies, she wouldn't still be alone at this point of her life. And there was still the problem of her inability to choose a good guy. It's like she was a beacon to all the lazy-good-for-nothing cheaters on the planet.

Of course, none of them had looked like Cian or possessed a smidgeon of his charm. She refused to think she was setting herself up for heartache. Accepting him as her tour guide was as far as this flirtation went.

Or so she kept telling herself as she flew down the stairs, was ushered out to his car, and fought back her answering grin when he flashed his pearly whites her way.

"Where to?" he asked, as if he were at her disposal and would cater to her every whim.

It was a heady sensation, and she almost forgot herself as she stared at his brain-cell-scattering face. He had the kind of handsomeness that was seen on movie stars and that made women go a little nuts in their desire to be with them. More than good looking, he was compelling, and his dazzling grin was hypnotic.

After giving herself a mental smack, Piper dug inside her backpack and pulled out a notebook. "I made a list of places I should see while I'm here."

Cian glanced down at the paper and shook his head. "Of course, you did. Now put that back in your bag and tell me which way your *heart* tells you to go."

Her gaze locked with his, and she wanted to get lost in those emerald depths for all eternity. She almost said her heart was pointing to him, but she didn't want to sound like an idiot or be a love-at-first-sight statistic like the rest of the Thornes. There was such a thing as free will and she damned well intended to use it.

"Abandoned mansions are a thing of mine," she finally confessed.

When Cian started the car and shot her a quizzical look, Piper elaborated. "I enjoy the history. I like to wander through the ruins and guess what the old place might've contained by way of furniture, people, and dramatic circumstances."

The slight smile on his face spoke of understanding. Piper was drawn to that half-smile. Maybe even more so than to his wide, engaging grin. Because although she wanted to be the recipient of that grin, she also liked the realness when he dropped his practiced charm.

A short drive later, they pulled off the road onto a dirt drive. Cian put the vehicle in park, climbed out, and walked around to Piper's side to assist her. Nerves ate at her belly when she got her first good look around her.

The area was desolate and had a neglected, abandoned air about it. The grass came up mid-thigh, and overgrown trees obstructed the view down the lane.

"There's nothing here." Her voice came out tentative and shaky due to her sudden awareness of their isolation.

"Piper me love, you have an adventurer's heart." Cian took her hand in his and brushed her fingertips with his lips. "Consider this your first Irish adventure."

"I thought that was last night's kiss," she muttered.

He stopped short and spun back around. His brows shot up and a delighted grin took up residence on his face. "Our kiss was quite the adventure. Care to take another journey?"

He'd sounded incredibly hopeful, and despite the embarrassed flush coloring her cheeks, Piper was forced to laugh. She stretched up and bussed his cheek. "That's as adventurous as I plan to be for the moment."

He put his hand to his chest and fell to his knees. "If this be all I get from ya, love, then I'll die a happy man."

Laughing at his foolishness, she skipped backward down the lane. "Come on, you *eejit*! There are abandoned mansions to explore," she called out. Turning her back to him, she continued on her way, more at ease with his playfulness.

Serial killers weren't such blatant flirts, right?

"You've become Irish in a single day, darlin'. It's my sister's unholy influence, to be sure," he hollered back.

She hadn't expected him to catch her as fast as he did, nor had she expected *not* to hear him charging after her. When he scooped her up in his arms, she let loose a scream, following it up with laughter.

"Jaysus, you pierced my eardrums with that one. Now you'll have to pay a forfeit for deafenin' me for life." His teasing smile begged her to kiss him.

She complied.

When they parted, they shared a look of wide-eyed wonder.

"Damn, you're good at that," she sighed.

"Was you who kissed me, love, so the complimenting should be mine." His lips twisted, and he leaned in to brush his nose to hers. "Damn, you're good at that," he parroted. "Now, climb aboard, the way gets muddy ahead, and I fear you wore the wrong sort of shoes for this excursion."

He shifted her around to carry her piggyback style.

"Onward, good steed!" she ordered with a giggle.

"Oh, Piper, you really should mind that tongue of yours or you'll be in loads of trouble all too soon."

Heat crept up her face when she realized she'd basically called him the Old English version of a stallion. For a moment, she was awash with mortification, but soon enough a reckless energy seized her. Leaning in, she placed her mouth next to his ear. Her lips brushed the shell, whisper soft. "I wouldn't mind if I were to get into trouble with *you*, Cian."

He halted mid pack-mule duty and twisted his neck to look at her. His smile started slow as he realized she was serious, then it blossomed wide. The sight sent butterflies fluttering around in her belly and electricity shooting through her veins. She was seriously in danger of falling for this guy, but maybe it wasn't a bad thing. Perhaps Liz had been correct that Piper needed a spot of fun in her life.

"I'll give you all the trouble you can handle and then some, darlin'," he assured her.

His gaze dropped to her lips, and she leaned forward to meet his seeking mouth. The kiss was a quick hard exclamation point on his promise.

As Cian traipsed the overgrown lane with Piper clinging to his back, he silently questioned how a stranger's shy smile could come to be the thing he craved above all else. And in so short a time! They'd known each other less than twenty-four hours, and yet, the familiarity wrapped around them and made it seem as if they'd known each other forever. Their playful banter made his heart happy, and when she laughed, his spirit felt lighter than it had in all his thirty-five years.

Finally, they rounded the bend, and Cian set Piper on her feet. *And none too soon.* If he had to experience the exquisite torture of her pert breasts against his back any longer, he would lose his mind and tumble her into the high grass, or fall to his knees and beg for her affection—this time for real. "Mind the stone there, love. It's crumbling down and not altogether safe."

They'd not been exploring the estate ten minutes when Cian felt the presence of another. Although his powers were practically nil, he still had small witchy things happen now and again. The sixth sense regarding a threat was one of those. He could also feel intent, and the newcomer had none. Not that he'd let down his guard completely, but he did exhale the building tension.

He caught up with Piper just as she rounded a collapsed half-wall in what Cian knew to be the old pantry. A witty comment was geared to tumble from his lips and he was ready to charm her when he felt another unknown. This time, malicious energy was heavy in the air around them.

The desire to swear up a storm was shoved down deep, and he caught Piper around the waist with one arm. Her surprised gasp was adorable as feck, and he wanted nothing more than to plant his mouth on hers. It wasn't the time.

With one hand, he cupped her nape and drew her gently to him, as sweet as a lover. The other hand was already reaching for the knife he kept concealed at his back. When his lips were level with her ear, he whispered. "Don't give anything away, *cailín*, but we have company. Act as if you're about to make my every fantasy come true."

As he directed, Piper nuzzled his neck, and Cian almost forgot he was supposed to be on high alert. The sensual brush of her plump lips against the hollow of his throat shot straight to his pleasure stick—he refused to call his member a giggle stick, the term his sister was so fond of when mocking her previous hook-ups. When this was all said and done and they were safe once more, he would instruct Piper so as not to distract a poor sod when he was trying to protect her.

"What's going on?" she whispered just before her teeth nipped his ear lobe.

"Jaysus, woman! If you don't stop making my fantasies come true, we'll have a sturdy hat rack on our hands. I promise you, that's no good in a fight."

She sniggered, but removed her lips from his person.

Cian wanted to weep at the loss. "There are two others here, and I find it highly coincidental. One of which is set to cause trouble."

"Cian? Do you know what I am?"

He drew back enough to look down into her wide, troubled eyes. "Yes."

"Hold tight." She mumbled a quick incantation and swirled her hand above their heads, stepping back when she was done.

"What did you just do?"

"Granny Thor—uh, a fool-proof cloaking spell." She played off her blunder with a weak smile. "Those come in handy, don't you think?" Her tone was a little too bright.

Before he could question her slip, she closed her eyes and tilted her head. A deep furrow marred her forehead. "There, in the next room to the right of us. That's our threat."

"You're not trying to keep us from being heard," he murmured softy. "Am I to assume this handy wee spell of yours mutes noise?"

"You assume correctly. Let's get the hell out of here."

"There's another person here. I can sense it."

"Good or bad?"

"No intention to harm, which makes me wonder if the person in the next room is after them, and not me—er, us."

He'd almost given himself away, and cursed how easy it was to be with her. Things tended to flow out of his mouth he'd as soon keep hidden.

She frowned up at him, but stayed quiet and thoughtful. Her gaze darted around as if she could see through the dilapidated walls around them.

"We can't remain here, Piper. We were easy enough to spot not a moment ago."

"Right, come on." She took his hand and tugged him through the corridors of the ruins toward the main exit, pausing when they saw a flash of blond hair. "Stay here, Cian. The cloaking spell will remain in place."

"Nay, love. You'll not go off on your own."

"I'm a witch, and a concealed one at that. No one can see, hear, or smell me. I promise, it's safe."

"We go together, or you don't go at all."

"*Contineo.*" Crinkling her nose, she cast him a sickly look. "Sorry. Be right back."

As she darted away, he reached for her only to discover he was locked in place, with no ability to even lift a hand. *"Piper!"* He growled at her retreating back. *"Cailín,* I'm as serious as—"

Too late. She was gone. As he stood, helpless and fuming, Cian fantasized about all the things he'd do when she returned and freed him. First, would be to wring her long, graceful neck. Second—there was no time to think of a second as a craggy-faced, blond-haired man rounded the corner of the hall. From the fluid, stealthy way the guy moved, Cian knew the hulking brute had been trained in combat.

Bloody hell.

If the man remained on his current trajectory, he'd collide with Cian in less than two minutes. Sweat began to bead along his hairline, and a single drop meandered down his temple. By freezing his movements, Piper had left him a sitting duck.

Just as Cian came to the conclusion a collision was inevitable, Piper rounded the corner. She rushed to his side.

"Exolvo."

Grinning, she grabbed his hand and tugged him forward. Cian was never more relieved to move in his life. As they cleared the door, his cells began to warm to burning. He'd opened his mouth to ask her what bloody brand of magic she intended now, when he was transported to their vehicle in less time than it took to blink.

Swaying from the sudden movement, he grabbed the boot of the car and inhaled deeply. "Jaysus, Mary, and Joseph. Some warnin' would be good."

"Yeah, sorry. I assumed you've teleported before."

"Well, sure and I have, but it's a rare enough occurrence." When his head was clear once more, he dug into his pocket for the keys. "Let's get out of here." He'd rounded his side of the car when he heard Piper swear. "What is it?"

"All our tires are flat. It's not a problem to fix, but if I do, our pursuer will know I'm a witch."

"Or they'll think we changed the tires."

"Unless Ireland is vastly different from America, no one carries four spares, Cian."

"Feckin' hell!" Of course, she was right. He spun this way and that, trying to figure out a solution. Finally, he faced her. "There's nothing for it, we need to get to safety."

"I can teleport us home, and we can return for the car when we know it's safe."

"Oh, sure, and they won't know you're a witch when we disappear without another mode of transportation for ten kilometres."

"Who knew you were such a grumpy ass if cornered?"

When she placed her hands on her hips and glared her annoyance, Cian's internal wiring short circuited. All he could do was stare at her in all her glorious anger with a dumbass grin on his face. "You're a stunner, Piper Kelly."

The sound of her name caused her to jerk. A flash of guilt came and went before she could hide it. It was an effort, but Cian kept his smile in place. Her uncomfortableness spoke of a lie. And though now was not the time for revelations, he'd eat his left shoe if her real name was Piper Kelly.

"Please fix the tires, *cailín,* and let's be on our way."

4

As they sped away from the abandoned house, they each remained locked in their own thoughts. Piper couldn't believe Liz had shown up when and where she did. Her cousin, who had only been spontaneous once in her life, now charged into trouble whenever she got the chance. The blame could be placed squarely at Rafe's door. As a retired sitting-member of the Witches' Council and an occasional spy, he'd added excitement to Liz's normally uneventful life and brought a sparkle to her eyes. But he'd also made her more reckless.

"The other presence we felt, who was it? I take it you knew them." When she squeaked her surprise at Cian's insight, he chuckled. "It's not like I was born yesterday, Piper me love."

"It was just a friend, checking in on me because I forgot to call when I landed."

"And this friend thought to pop in at your exact location without bothering to call you first?"

Piper dug her cell from her purse, and sure enough, there were five missed calls. She flashed the screen in his direction. "Oh, she definitely *did*, but I missed them because I left my phone in the car."

30

Her explanation seemed to satisfy him, because his response was a nod and a wry smile.

"Cian?"

"Hmm?"

"Did you recognize the other guy there with us?"

His mouth tightened, but he shook his head. "No."

The distinct feeling of being lied to settled around Piper's shoulders, and she didn't care for the sensation. Hell, if she were honest, she fucking hated it. Her two-timing ass-fart ex used to lie on a daily basis as if it were an Olympic sport he needed to practice for. Doug had definitely won the gold medal in the scum-sucking, yellow-belly, lying-snake event.

"What have I said wrong?"

She twisted to look at him. "Nothing."

His lips quirked. "Then what have I said that wasn't all-together right?"

Piper snorted a laugh, and the tension was broken. What had she expected? That he'd pour his heart out the second they'd met? They'd known each other less than twenty-four hours. "You're fine, Cian. I'm in my own head at the moment. It has nothing to do with you."

"Do we call it a day, or do we continue our journey?"

Giving it serious consideration, she decided they shouldn't let what might've been a weird coincidence ruin their day. "I've always wanted to see the Cliffs of Moher."

"It's a bit of a drive, but the day's still early yet."

"If you'd rather not, I can come back on my own," she offered.

Wrapping his large, calloused hand over hers, he lightly squeezed. "I've nothing pressing back home. Bridget and Ruairí have everything covered until this evening."

"Ruairí? Wasn't he one of the customers in the bar last night?" She cast him a frowning glance. "It didn't seem as if they got along."

"Not for want of trying on the poor man's part."

"Why does she hate him?"

"No one knows. As children, they were as thick as clover, much to the dismay of our parents. One day, she returned to the house in tears and refused to mention his name again." He grimaced.

"He broke her heart," Piper concluded.

"What makes you say that?"

"Tears and the refusal to mention his name? It's not rocket science, Cian."

He grunted.

"You've never once thought they might've had a romantic relationship?" she asked, curious how men could be oblivious about things of that nature.

"They were practically bairns, *cailín*."

"How old was she when they had their falling out?"

Cian appeared to tally up the number. "Twenty, I suppose."

"Not babies then. Old enough to have fallen in love."

"My sister wouldn't have been fool enough to fall for an O'Connor. Our family has been at war for nigh on two-hundred-fifty years or more. Not that Ruairí isn't a decent guy —for an O'Connor."

Piper smiled because his explanation was *so* male. "Women don't care anything for war games, silly man."

He cast her a searching side glance, and she blatantly admired the wide smile blossoming on his mouth. "And what does a woman care for, love?"

The way his tone dipped when he'd said "love" did funny things to Piper's heart. Nerves caused her belly to tighten and warmth gathered at the apex of her thighs. Or maybe it was the suggestion behind his question. With a quick cough to clear her throat, she said, "Home. Family. Relationships."

"And you have these?"

"Are you asking me if I'm committed to someone, Cian? Isn't it a little late after the kisses we've shared?"

"Sometimes passion rules and you need to follow your heart."

"And sometimes the shit is deep in here and you need muck boots," she countered.

He laughed his response.

"In answer to your oddly phrased question, no. I don't have those." Her voice was sad even to her own ears, and she wanted to smack herself for sounding pathetic.

If Cian noticed, he didn't comment.

Their conversation remained light for their rest of their trip, and they arrived in Liscannor, driving straight to the visitor center across from the cliffs. Excitement brewed inside Piper. As they exited the vehicle, she breathed deeply, ending on a sigh and a happy smile.

Arms resting on the hood of the car, Cian watched her. "It suits you. My homeland."

"I could live here forever," she agreed. "The moment I stepped off the plane, I felt as if I'd come home."

"Perhaps you have," he said softly. "I, for one, wouldn't mind if you stayed for a bit."

They locked gazes.

Looking away was one of the hardest things she'd ever had to do, but she finally managed to break away from his magnetic pull. He didn't even know her true name, and she was determined to keep it that way until satisfied the surname Thorne wouldn't sign her death warrant. Many people, witches and non-witches alike, would see her six feet under for it.

"What do we do first?" she asked with a purposeful change of subject.

"Tickets can be had at the visitor centre. I'll get us a pair if you prefer to wait, or we can tour the centre before our walk."

"Let's walk first and tour the centre second, if that's all the same to you."

"It's your day, darlin'."

She smiled at their easy camaraderie. Who knew this vacation would be such fun, or that being with Cian would be wonderfully drama free? It certainly hadn't been at any other time in her life when she went anywhere with her previous boyfriends. Not that Cian was her boyfriend, but his playful, mellow vibe made her glad he was with her today.

He circled the hood of the car and held out a hand to her. Once hers was firmly ensconced within his warm grip, she fell into step beside him and listened intently as he wove a lively story. Like with his song, he had a way of drawing her in by using the cadence of his skillful voice. She would cheerfully remain mute the entire day if it meant hearing his pleasing monologue. Cian could read her the dictionary, and Piper would be a puddle of goo at his feet.

They obtained their tickets, and he good-naturedly answered the questions she peppered him with. She wanted to know everything from the highest points of the cliffs—214 meters—to the length—about 14 kilometres. He was a fountain of information, and he wasn't lying when he'd said he was a brilliant tour guide. It wouldn't stop her from double checking his answers. For all she knew, he could've made them up on the spot, but she liked his confidence and how ready he was to provide information for her endless questions.

When they got to a particularly scenic area, she reached for her phone to capture nature's beauty. "Oh, crap!"

"What is it?"

She grimaced and admitted, "I forgot and left my phone in the car again. I want to snap some pictures of the view from here."

"I'll get it."

"No, it's too far. I can go, find an out-of-the-way spot, and teleport to the car. You wait here. I'll just be a minute."

As Cian watched Piper jog away, he smiled. She was a bit quirky, but she was proper fun to rile. The longer he was around her, the stronger their connection grew. It worried him, if truth be known. He'd only ever been close to one woman.

Moira.

His smile died away, and he faced the cliffs.

Moira had been beautiful, smart, wickedly funny, and a gas to tease—like Piper. But there, the similarities ended. Moira had been a tiny thing. Barely five-feet, with fiery red hair and a temper to match. She'd burned in bed just as hot as she'd burned out. A part of him had flat-lined the day they put her in the ground. Hell, if he were being honest, it had flat-lined the day she betrayed him. As yet, the spark hadn't been revived. Most days, he still lived a half-life, with his heart frozen.

Piper was a welcome distraction. She was lively and witty. Her intelligence shown from her sparkling dark-honey eyes and tempted Cian to discover the thoughts behind the emotion. Part of him felt guilty. He didn't want to lead her on or invest in another romance doomed to failure. He certainly didn't want his heart to thaw, because the pain was too great. No one could replace Moira. She'd been his everything. Until she wasn't.

A flicker of awareness flared to life.

Danger.

He spun just in time to dodge a knife directed at his kidney. It glanced off his side instead. Cian felt the burn of the blade and the resulting air exposure on the wound. The damned thing stung like a motherfucker.

Throwing out an arm, he knocked away the wrist of his

assailant, then planted a facer to the man's ugly mug with his other hand. The guy recovered faster than Cian cared for, and charged straight for his midsection, wrapping his burly arms around Cian's ribs and grazing his new wound in the process.

The pain—in addition to the unprovoked attack—was infuriating, and Cian saw red. He clasped his hands together to form one giant balled fist and brought it down on the back of his attacker's neck. The vice-like hold eased enough for him to break it.

Cian had learned to fight dirty early in life, and those skills came in handy now. He poked his thumbs in his opponent's eyes and drove him to the ground with a knee to the groin. Had he witnessed the move by anyone else, he'd have given a sympathetic wince, but this fucker didn't deserve his compassion.

"Who sent you?" he demanded, recognizing the bull-like man from the ruins.

"I kill you." The hitman's use of the English language was fragile at best, and for all Cian knew, the heavy accent indicated the guy's homeland was anywhere from Budapest to Moscow. Geography he was decent with, languages not so much.

Cian silently dubbed the man Baran, because it meant ram in Russian, and the guy hit like a fecking battering ram. Also, he smelled like the ass-end of a sheep. Although Cian liked nothing better than a rousing fight, the sheer size of this guy gave him pause. Reason was the better tactic in this situation.

Smiling congenially, he said, "Listen, Baran. It appears we got off on the wrong foot here, man. I'm sure this is a case of mistaken identity."

"No miss-take. I kill."

"If I slept with your woman, I didn't know she was married. I don't—"

"No woman!"

"Ah, so that be your problem, Baran; you need to get laid. Come to me pub, and I'll hook you right up."

Cian's words poured petrol on the fire, and Baran lost what was left of his pea-sized mind. With a strangled cry, he charged again. The impact swept Cian off his feet and brought him down hard on his back about ten feet from his original spot. His ears rang and stars danced before his eyes.

Perhaps Baran would kill him after all.

For sure, the bastard had bruised a few of Cian's ribs and made breathing a wee bit harder than it needed to be.

The next few minutes were spent trading blow for blow and rolling toward the cliff's edge. Just how they'd traveled so far, so fast was beyond him, but Cian had a healthy respect for Moher's cliff face. The drop would be fatal.

Something behind Cian caught Baran's attention, and it was distraction enough for him to get the upper hand. He delivered rapid punches to the burly assassin's pug-like face and drove him toward Moher's rocky rim.

He hadn't expected the meaty hand to grab his throat or hurl him toward the edge, but he should've. Cian brought a fist down on Baran's elbow bend. He, then, let go of the tension in his legs and let gravity pull him down. Baran couldn't hold the dead weight, and as he felt his attacker's hand release him, Cian grabbed Baran's extended arm, dropped onto his back, and tossed him over his head.

One quick, terrified scream rang out, then nothing could be heard but the crash of the waves on the rocks below.

5

Sensing another presence, Cian rolled to his feet and spun.
A quick check of the area showed Piper was the only witness to the fight, and she stood frozen like an antelope sensing danger. Her bright eyes had darkened to a muddy topaz, and a wary expression settled in place.

"This isn't what it looks like, love," he said gently.

"You threw him over the cliff!"

He winced. "Well, yeah, but there were extenuating circumstances."

"You're no pub owner."

"Of course, I am." He visually scanned the area for witnesses. Satisfied they were alone, he advanced toward her. "You were at both my pub and the inn."

Piper stepped backward and raised her hand as if to ward him off.

"Now darlin', stay calm. I mean ya no harm." Cian smiled in what he thought was a reassuring way, thickening his accent to put her at ease.

Obviously, her definition of reassuring was much different from his. Her screech of disbelief hit an octave so high, beasts

38

all over the island were likely howling in protest. Before he could take a step closer, she'd bent and hefted a good-sized rock.

Unable not to, he snorted. "What do you think you can do with that wee thing?"

The widening of her eyes was his only warning before the rock sailed in his direction. Though he twisted, the stone still made contact. The impact to his shoulder caused him to grunt.

"Now why'd you do that? Weren't we having a civilized discussion?" he hollered.

Two more stones were hurled in rapid succession. One grazed his cheek, and he touched where the skin stung.

The damn she-devil had marked him!

"Now look what you've done. You're feckin' mad, you are!" He held out his blood-coated fingers. "You marred me good looks."

Another outraged cry was followed by more rocks. Each impact felt like a brick the closer he got to her. Knocking the final projectile from her hand, he straightened to his full height of six-two and glared down into her wide, frightened eyes. The sight had him softening.

"Piper, darlin', I can—*umphf!*" She kneed him in his boys, bringing him low. She'd just killed the future O'Malley line with one well-aimed shot; he was sure of it. Water streamed from his eyes—he refused to acknowledge them as tears because O'Malleys were made of stronger stuff—and he cupped himself. He'd read somewhere that pressure overrode pain.

It didn't.

At least not in his case.

"I swear to the Almighty that I'd be throwing you over the cliff after that bugger if I was the murderin' bastard you believe me to be. I—*umphf!*"

The metallic taste of blood filled his mouth where Piper kicked him.

Okay, *now* he was damned furious. With a roundhouse kick of *that* nature, the woman wasn't an innocent miss. She had to be here as backup to his earlier assassin; her intent, of course, to finish him off.

Cian dove for her legs, but she danced away and assumed an expert's fighting stance. She was smart to take a stand because she couldn't outrun him. Her single other option was to teleport, but she'd risk greater exposure if she did, and witches knew not to reveal their abilities to mortals.

Left with no choice, he prepared to fight.

Less than five minutes later, Cian rifled through Piper's messenger bag to find her identification. When he opened her passport, he grimaced. Had he been a betting man, he'd have wagered, with her rod-stiffening good looks, she couldn't take a bad picture. He'd have lost a hefty sum.

He frowned down at her still form.

Perhaps she'd pulled the face on purpose in a fool's attempt to trick facial-recognition software? But why go to that length if she could magically travel and avoid detection altogether?

Wasting no more time, he whipped out his smartphone and switched the sim card with another he kept in a hidden compartment of his wallet. When he got a signal, he dialed the number he had memorized.

"Cian! How's it hanging, buddy?"

"Ryker, man, I've had a bit o' an incident here at home, and I need you to run an identity check. Do you think you could help an old friend out?"

"I thought you were retired?"

"True, and so did I, to be sure." He gave Ryker Gillespie a brief rundown of the incident with the assassin before finishing with, "Now, I have another person who may or may not be involved."

"Want me to run facial recognition?"

Cian contemplated the question for all of three seconds. "I thought maybe you could look up her passport in the database, but a full background check wouldn't be remiss."

"Give me the number."

He rattled it off, and within a minute, Ryker was swearing on the other end of their connection.

"Cian, what does the woman look like?"

"Oh, she's a wet dream." He sighed and described her in detail. "But if we're being honest, she screams like a banshee, has a wee vicious temper, and fights better than many o' man I've seen."

"That's because she teaches martial arts at the rec center in her spare time, you damned fool."

"You know her?"

"She's my wife's relation."

"Don't be windin' me up, Ryker. It isn't funny. I'm halfway to falling in love with the woman. I might, too, if I knew she wasn't out to slit my throat as soon as look at me." He reached down and smoothed a lock of hair from the flushed face.

"Shoot me a photo of the woman."

Cian snapped a shot and hit send.

"You knocked her out?"

"She attacked *me!* Drew blood and kneed my bollocks into the next century. What was I supposed to do?" The long stream of colorful words from the other end of the line forced Cian to wince and hold the phone away from his ear. Sure, and he'd stepped in it with his friend. "Knocking her out was an accident, man," he confessed sheepishly.

"Alastair Thorne is going to have your ass," Ryker predicted.

"Why would—*ah, hell no!* Don't tell me Piper is a Thorne. I'll save everyone the trouble and throw myself off the feckin' cliff right now." Cian grabbed the back of his neck and started to pace. He was in deep shite. Everyone who was anyone in the magical community knew of Alastair Thorne. The man was lethal and not to be trifled with. "You have to help me, Ryker. What can I do to fix this mess?"

"First, tell me how badly she's hurt. Should I teleport with my wife to come heal her?"

"I'm worried. She should've woken up by now. And, for sure, she'll have a good-sized egg on her jaw. I'd rather she not sport a bruise around all of Ireland. And there is still the matter of finding out who wants me dead." Cian sighed heavily. "Yeah, I could use the help."

"Take her back to your inn. We'll meet you there. Keep the sitting room clear of people so we can avoid detection."

"Right. I'll see you soon. I'm obliged to you, man."

"Say that if I can keep Alastair or GiGi from detaching your head from your shoulders."

Cian stared at the phone's blank screen for a few heartbeats after Ryker disconnected their call. Gods, he was in trouble. Not only with Alastair Thorne, but with Piper herself. When the woman woke, she was going to be rabid. He toyed with the idea of dumping the whole mess in Bridget's lap and disappearing for the foreseeable future.

A slight moan of pain shook him from his cowardly thoughts. No, he'd take his lumps like a true O'Malley. Bending, he scooped up Piper, and as he straightened, he noticed a petite dishwater blonde staring at him with suspicious eyes. How she'd snuck up on him, he didn't care to know. He was growing soft in his retirement. It would see him dead if he didn't apply his training more.

"Me wife. She tripped and broke her fall on a rock. I need to get her to hospital and make certain her injuries aren't worse than they appear."

"Of course." The woman cautiously approached and

frowned down into at Piper's face. With a trembling hand, she touched a lock of Piper's sweat-damp, black hair. "How badly was she hurt, and what proof can you show me that she's your wife? I don't see a ring."

Damn and blast!

He had to go and stumble across a cautious American.

Bloody O'Malley bad luck.

Pasting on a rueful grin, he ducked his head to meet her concerned gaze. For a moment, he was caught by the overly bright amber irises. "Do I know you?"

Not bothering to answer, she shook her head and probed along Piper's wound with gentle fingers. A barely discernible crackle sounded, and a faint red light arched from her fingertips.

Another witch!

What were the odds?

Not that high.

This woman knew Piper. And likely, with that eye color, they were related.

Cian decided to test her further. "I promise, I'm not abducting her. It's a wee bit hard to produce proof when I'm holding me woman in me arms." He laid the accent on thick, hoping it would work on her as it had with Piper the evening before.

Her expression hardened.

So much for his legendary charm!

"Which hospital are you going to? I'll follow you there," she said sweetly. More than a hint of steel underlay the words.

Yep, definitely a relation of Piper's. Cian was positive, and he wanted nothing more than to bang his head against the boulder behind him.

"Look," he added a hard edge to his tone. "I need to get my darlin' Piper help. Step aside."

The blonde narrowed her eyes as her mouth firmed into a tight, white line. "I'm going with you."

"Fine," he growled. He made it two steps before it occurred to him that as a powerful witch—and she certainly was if she was in any way related to the Thornes—she could teleport them all. Cian turned back, ready to lower himself to ask.

Piper moaned again and curled toward him.

"I've got you, love," he murmured, dropping a kiss on her brow. "Never you worry."

When he glanced up again, it was to see the other woman's eyes had softened. "I think she's in good hands," she said.

With a direct look meant to assure, he nodded. "She'll come to no more harm from me."

"No more?" The frown was back, this time accompanied by a black look.

Gah, he was an eejit.

"Poor choice of words," he corrected. "I'll see her safely back home."

"Or the hospital?"

"Jesus, Mary, and Joseph! Just give over, woman. I know you're related. You have to be with those eyes. Now, use all that blessed magic you were born with and get us to safety before the *gardaí* show up and arrest me." He didn't miss the slight smirk she shot him as she placed a hand on his arm and the other on Piper. "Bloody Thorne witches!"

6

They arrived in Piper's room, and Cian desperately wanted to learn how she'd known where to go without asking. It stood to reason she'd been snooping at some point.

"I'm Liz, and as you guessed, Piper is my cousin."

She failed to mention a last name, but Cian heard what she hadn't said.

"Cian. And thanks for the assist."

"Why can't you teleport?" she asked curiously. "You're like us, if I'm not mistaken?"

He hated to admit he was a warlock without power, but he had no other way of explaining why he couldn't pop home immediately. "A curse. About two hundred and fifty years gone."

"Witches without power... hmm... you must be an O'Malley."

He narrowed his eyes. "What do you know of the O'Malleys?"

"Nothing more than the fact they lost their power to the O'Connors over a feud. Legend has it there's some type of riddle associated with reversing the curse."

Cian stared, dumbfounded.

Of course! He'd forgotten all about it. After spending a lifetime as little more than a regular human, he hadn't paid much attention to the magical side of his family history. *Other than Granny O'Malley's special brew.* Of which, there was none left. He couldn't begin to gnaw on that bone right at the moment, though. He had other problems on his hands, to be sure.

"Right, well, if you don't mind, will you open the door? I have to meet with a healer."

"Healer?"

"If you must know, GiGi Gillespie."

A happy grin spread across Liz's pretty visage. "GiGi is coming here? Awesome!"

"Why do I feel I'm about to be outnumbered by a bunch of wee vicious witches in less time than it takes to blink?" he muttered.

"Because you are?"

Cian just cleared the door to the sitting room when the air around him grew heavy. He paused and shot a look over his shoulder to make sure no mortal strangers were around to witness the magical show about to happen, only breathing a sigh of relief when he saw the place was clear other than Liz.

His old friend, Ryker, materialized with a model-thin blonde. Her blazing blue eyes promised retribution the second they settled on Cian, where he stood holding Piper.

"You knocked her out?" GiGi snarled.

Cian concentrated on keeping his bollocks from shriveling into raisins at her tone. Here was a woman who was confident in her ability to maim. "Not on purpose. *She* attacked *me*. I was merely defending myself."

"What kind of man hits a woman?" She didn't wait for a response, instead she raised her hands, palm up, and called air to assist her in lightening his load.

He grabbed for Piper as she floated out of his grasp, but Liz stepped in front of him and blocked his way. "We've got this now, O'Malley. You can go."

"Go?"

"Yes, *go.*" GiGi shot him a glare. "And the only reason I haven't fried your sorry ass for hurting my cousin, is because you're Bridget's brother, you dumb lug."

Not usually quick to anger, Cian found himself getting salty pretty damned quickly at her unjust behavior. "Listen, I don't care if you are Ryker's wife. You'll no' talk to me in my own home like—" His words ended on a strangled cry. He gripped his throat as his airway was cut off and he dropped to his knees.

Eyes bulging, he stared up at her gloating expression and wondered if this was how it would end for him. All the time spent fighting for the good of the Witches' Council, gathering intel, rounding up the bad guys... and a single, furious female with the power to crush his windpipe would be his executioner. *All over a simple mistake.*

"*GiGi!*" Ryker snapped her name in warning.

The next instant, Cian was on his hands and knees, gulping in heaping lungsful of air and ignoring the discomfort it was causing his abused ribs.

He caught the faintest whiff of expensive perfume as GiGi squatted beside him to whisper, "You'd better never *dream* of hurting her again, no matter how accidental. If I don't kill you, my brother Alastair will."

Alastair Thorne's sister. He should've guessed. Wishing he had a time machine to go back twenty-four hours to avoid meeting Piper, Cian sat back on his heels and nodded his understanding to the sadistic witch in front of him.

GiGi had the bloody gall to pat his cheek. "Good boy."

He barely refrained from snarling, and by the amused gleam in her blue eyes, she knew it.

"Liz, child, please go pack Piper's things. She'll be leaving with us in a few minutes, as soon as she wakes."

"Isn't that for Piper to decide?" Cian slammed his lids closed as soon as the words left his mouth. *Jaysus, he had a death wish.* She'd kill him for sure this time.

The silence lasted an exceedingly long time, and he dared to peek one eye open. Ryker stood behind his wife, grinning like a demented jackal, and Liz ducked her head to hide her amusement, as GiGi watched Cian with a curious look

"Just murder me and be done with it, woman," Cian growled. "Sure, and I'm not one for drawing out torture."

One of her finely groomed brows rose skyward and her lips twitched as if she fought a laugh.

Sweat broke out on his lower back, but he remained stone faced.

A moan from Piper broke the stalemate, and GiGi rushed to her side. She worked efficiently, and the examination was completed before Cian could gain his feet.

In seconds, GiGi had conjured a mortar and pestle.

"Useless boy, go ask your sister for willow bark, chamomile, and lavender oil." He opened his mouth to ask why she couldn't whip those up as well, but she answered before the question left him. "In other words, I want you to go away."

Cian clamped his jaw tight, planted himself next to Piper's side and clasped her delicate hand in his. "I'll stay to see she's healed."

Pausing only a moment, GiGi gave him a brisk nod and conjured the items she needed to go to work.

One minute transitioned to ten, and still, they all stood around waiting for Piper to wake. By the concern on the three other faces, Cian suspected she should've recovered by now. Hell, even a mere mortal should've woken up from that light blow to the jaw. Most knockouts didn't last but a hot minute.

"What's wrong with her?" he finally asked as he rubbed

Piper's cold hand between his two much larger, warmer ones. "The tap to her jaw shouldn't have knocked her out this long."

"I don't know," GiGi admitted. "I agree with your assessment." She touched a stone on her silver charm bracelet and said, "Brother, I need to talk to you."

He felt Piper's hand twitch, and he peered closer at her face.

The ring of GiGi's phone distracted him, as did her quick conversation to relay the circumstances surrounding Piper's injury.

Less than one minute later, the atmosphere crackled, growing heavy then contracting to steal all the oxygen from the room. Seconds later, the air around them settled and another man took up residence in the large salon.

Alastair Thorne, if Cian wasn't mistaken. Of all the warlocks in all the world, *this* one was the guy he didn't care to meet in this situation. Or ever.

The man wasn't as tall as Cian would've thought, no more than six feet one. He had a modest build but completely filled out the shoulders of his navy-blue suit. Bored but alert sapphire-colored eyes summed up the situation in an instant, and Alastair turned his steely gaze from Piper to pin Cian in place. Those same disturbing eyes swept the length of Cian's body and returned to his face to linger for a nerve-wracking heartbeat or two.

What the guy saw was anyone's guess because the elegant warlock was the type who didn't give much away. Not one emotion played out on his remarkably handsome face. He could be a statue for all the life he showed, and yet, his presence was commanding. His look was arrogant, as if he were a supreme ruler and everyone around him was insignificant at best.

"O'Malley, I presume?" The man's voice was as haughty as the rest of him, and Cian bristled at the tone.

"Yeah. And you are?"

Alastair's lips twisted and his eyes lit with cool amusement —the first real emotion since he'd arrived. "Your worst enemy if Piper doesn't wake up soon, son."

Cian swallowed hard and did his best not to soil his pants. He wasn't a coward, but Alastair Thorne was a legend and a deadly adversary. Cian, on the other hand, was known to hold his own in a physical fight, but with no real magic to speak of, he was useless against someone as powerful as this mighty warlock.

Again, Alastair's eyes swept him as if weighing his worth. "You struck her?"

"No!" The word came out as a squeak. Ashamed of his lack of manliness, Cian cleared his throat, lowered his voice, and said, "No. She attacked *me*. I threw up an arm to deflect her punch and she moved into my fist." He inwardly cringed at how implausible it sounded, but it was the truth all the same.

One dark-blond brow shot up, very much like his sister's had earlier. "Aren't you splitting hairs, boy?"

"Perhaps, but it's important you know I'd not strike a woman. Even one who set out to kick my bollocks into the next century." He grimaced in remembered pain. "My darlin' Piper has killed any chance of future O'Malleys from my line."

"Your darling Piper?"

"Oh, leave off torturing him, Al." Ryker clapped Cian on the back. "He didn't harm her on purpose. Piper mistook what she witnessed."

"According to *him*." Alastair's tone switched into dangerous territory.

Left with no choice, Cian recounted the tale, leaving nothing out, but maybe adding a few embellishments because he was Irish, after all, and his people were known for their fabulous story-telling skills.

During the retelling, Alastair examined Piper's head, neck, and jaw. He barely spared Cian a glance when he'd finished.

Finally, Alastair brushed a hand over one of her dark brows. "It's time to wake up, child."

She remained sleeping.

"I'm worried, Al. This isn't normal," GiGi said fretfully.

"No, I agree it isn't normal. If I had to guess, I'd say it's purposeful." He shifted and placed an arm under Piper's legs, moving into position to lift her.

Cian knew he had no right to object, but he found himself doing it anyway. "Just where do you think you're takin' her?"

Everyone in the room froze at his challenge.

Cocking his head to the side, Alastair observed him like he was the rarest of species. "Are you truly going to question *me*, O'Malley?"

Well, no, not if he'd have given it any amount of thought beforehand. But after blustering like a fool, he had no choice. He had to bluff his way through. "Maybe she shouldn't be moved. It might cause more damage."

"More damage than you knocking her out and carrying her here? That type of damage?" Alastair asked dryly, but he eased Piper back down on the table.

Cian didn't know why he argued against the inevitable, but he knew if they took Piper now, he'd never see her again. He positioned himself next to her and stared down into her serene face. With one finger, he trailed her jawline where the knot had been. He felt the slightest movement.

Had she flinched?

"I'm sorry, *cailín*, I didn't mean to hurt you, love," he told her softly. "I'll be prayin' you find it in your heart to forgive me one day."

Leaning in, he kissed her forehead, and as he drew back, her eyes fluttered open.

Relief flooded his heart a second before her fist connected with his nose.

There was no mistaking the laughter in Alastair Thorne's

voice as he said, "Ah, your darling Piper is awake, son. And it looks like she's not ready to forgive quite yet."

7

Piper had been conscious the entire time. Or almost. Cian had repeated the tale correctly, if a little outrageously, and she had indeed connected with his fist on accident. After the initial blackout, she knew she was at a disadvantage. To determine his intent, she'd channeled an opossum and pretended to be out cold.

But Cian had surprised her when he called Ryker, and her curiosity got the better of her, so she remained silent to see how everything played out. Of course, it wasn't to her liking, and having her family arrive en masse was annoying. Not one of them believed she was capable of taking care of herself.

The reason she "woke" now, was to prevent Alastair from turning Cian to dust. Her fake-out had gone on too long, and she figured Alastair had seen through the ruse anyway.

Piper shifted to a sitting position, level with Cian's face. Even with his eyes watering and his nose bleeding, he was attractive, damn him!

"So sorry. I was lifting my arm to defend myself and you ran into my fist."

As she watched, his eyes narrowed but a grudging smile

53

tugged at his lips. Those same all-knowing eyes settled on her mouth for a long moment before they met hers. "No harm was done that can't be undone with one of your spells, darlin'. Now, if you don't mind, you can wave one of your beautiful wee hands and heal my broken nose. I wouldn't be opposed if you removed the cut caused by your rock. If you've a mind to, that is."

"As much as I'd like to, I only use my abilities in emergency situations." She gave a false sympathetic smile.

Cian's brows shot up. "And my life's blood isn't an emergency?"

Reaching a hand out, she grasped his chin and shifted his head one way, then the other. "Looks like you have the flow under control." She couldn't prevent her fingers from lingering in a soft caress of his strong jaw. It was as if they had a mind of their own.

Cian stepped forward and cupped his hand over hers, pressing it to his cheek. His voice was husky as he said, "I was right about you, Piper me love. You're a cruel woman."

Once again, his gaze dropped to her lips and liquid fire seared her insides. With a jerk of her hand, she pulled away. Making eye contact with the room's inhabitants was uncomfortable. She cleared her throat and rotated to throw her legs off the opposite side of the table. Her knees were decidedly weak—and not from the knockout.

The silence dragged on, and she shot a tentative glance Alastair's way. Gentle understanding shone in his sapphire eyes, and Piper had an overwhelming desire to cry. As the Thorne family patriarch, he kept tabs on the comings and goings of the family, and she was in no doubt that he was fully aware of her past relationship failures.

"Thank you for coming all this way, Cuz," she said to him in a low but firm tone. "I..." How did she confess to him she was a faker and had worried them all for nothing?

"No need to apologize, child. Ireland is lovely this time of year." He sent a speculative look Cian's way. "Perhaps Rorie and I should check into this little inn and enjoy the landscape."

Dread filled Piper's heart. She'd picked this place to escape her family's influence, not rain down more trouble on the residents of this small village.

Liz recognized her panic and spoke up, bless her. "Alastair, I think Piper came here to get away from all of us for a while. She won't tell you that because she doesn't want to offend you. She wants to play at being a mortal for a few weeks."

"She plays at being a mortal constantly," GiGi scoffed. "I don't understand why you deny your heritage, child." After giving her an arch look, GiGi relented and patted her hand. "But unfortunately for you, you've landed in the middle of a mess. Ryker and I aren't leaving until we know you're safe."

"GiGi, I can handle anything that comes my way." As protests went, it was lame. Not twenty minutes before, Piper had fought and lost to Cian. Mainly, it was her own fault. Her softer nature wouldn't allow her to hurt him, so she'd left magic off the table and resorted to martial arts.

Who knew he'd be proficient at fighting?

Ryker, it seemed.

"How is it you and Cian know each other, Ryker?" she asked as a distraction.

"We both worked for the Witches' Council." He sent a nod Cian's way. "He would find and procure rare magical artifacts based on my intel."

"I thought that's what Thorne Industries was hired for." The question was legit. Thorne Industries had been acquiring, neutralizing, and storing those artifacts for over a decade in order to keep whatever wasn't stored in the Council vaults safe from those who would use them without conscience.

Ryker grimaced. "There were a few council members who didn't trust your family."

"Harold Beecham," Alastair growled. The air grew thick with his ire, and he immediately drew back his magic. "Thankfully, he's in the Netherworld now."

GiGi shuddered. "And pray to the Goddess he never returns."

Piper had heard the story about how Beecham had murdered Ryker's sister and tried to murder him in the process, all in an effort to wound Alastair. Another reminder that bearing the Thorne name put a huge bullseye on one's back.

But the fact Cian worked for the Witches' Council explained a lot about his behavior and why he had thrown the hulking stranger over the cliff.

Facing him, she said, "I'm sorry I overreacted. I didn't know any of this."

"I tried to tell you all was not as it seemed." He had the nerve to wink. "After giving it some thought, I believe your attack was all in an effort to have my arms around you. You need only ask, love."

An inappropriate snort escaped her, and she rolled her eyes. "Right. That was it."

Alastair surprised her with a seldom-heard bark of laughter. Sobering quickly, he tugged his cuffs down, and said, "Since my sister and Ryker have things under control now, I'll be off. Liz, it was a pleasure to see you, as always. Give my regards to that Maltese playboy you've taken up with."

"Rafe will be happy you thought of him," Liz returned dryly.

"No doubt." Alastair placed a hand on Piper's shoulder and squeezed. "I'll have a tanzanite ring delivered to you within the hour. Wear it at all times, and should you need me, touch the stone. I'll come without hesitation." His expression hardened when he turned to Cian. "Don't put her in danger again or you'll face my wrath, boy."

All signs of joking aside, Cian nodded. "She'll not come to harm under my roof."

"See that she doesn't come to harm anywhere in Ireland." Alastair's tone was icy and commanding.

Piper took umbrage. "He's not my keeper. And he can't be expected to be my bodyguard the entire time I'm here."

"Oh, but he can, and he will. Cian O'Malley will see you safe while you're in his country, or he'll answer directly to me, Piper."

"You realize he has no magical ability, right, Al?" Ryker inserted.

"I'm well aware, but he's wily and, according to you, good in a fight. He'll do."

Piper ground her teeth in frustration. "I'm not a child, Alastair, and I certainly don't need a babysitter."

"You can either allow him to stick to you like glue, or you can come home with me now. Your choice."

Cian's wicked chuckle filled the room. "I'd like nothing better than to stick to you, Piper me love."

"He doesn't mean like that, you tool!" she snapped.

"Who are you to interpret what he means, darlin'? You have your fantasies of what he means, and I'll have mine."

Unable to fully hide his mirth, Alastair chuckled and winked at Piper. "Stay out of trouble, child, and enjoy your vacation."

In a blink, he was gone, leaving her fuming in his wake.

Cian viewed Piper's flushed cheeks with a grin. She was an independent thing, but in all seriousness, Alastair wasn't wrong to demand she have a bodyguard. After learning she was a Thorne, Cian was amazed she'd been allowed to travel on her own at all. That name provoked a powerful hatred within some of the lesser magical families. This much he'd gleaned from

Ryker, who happened to be Alastair's best friend—or so Ryker had informed him once.

Today was the first time Cian had the dubious pleasure of meeting the legendary Alastair Thorne. He couldn't say he'd like a repeat anytime soon. However, if the intimidating-as-feck Thorne patriarch insisted Cian protect Piper while she was in Ireland, then that's what he'd do. It wouldn't be smart to be on the wrong side of a warlock of Alastair's caliber.

"Everybody out!" Piper snapped.

No one looked inclined to comply with her demand.

"I mean it. I need to speak with Cian. *Alone*," she emphasized.

All eyes turned on him, and Cian's grin widened. "We're going to work on the glue part," he assured them with a wink.

"There will be no gluing." Piper's growl tickled his funny bone.

"Now, darlin', don't be hasty. Sure, and there's other things we can do besides 'gluing' but they wouldn't be as much fun."

Red faced and bordering on livid, her entire body trembled.

He struggled not to laugh.

"I'll glue my fist to your face if you don't..." She scowled again, realizing her threat made no sense. "Whatever. You know what I mean."

GiGi's throaty laughter pulled the carpet from under Cian. If asked, he'd have said she didn't have a lick of humor inside that tall, waif-thin body of hers. But she was Ryker's wife, and Cian suspected she had a bawdy-humor to match her husband's.

Leaning in, GiGi kissed Piper's cheek. "We'll go check into our room. How about we meet for dinner in two hours?" She caught Ryker's suggestive look and a secretive smile curled her lips. "Make that *three* hours."

Piper gave her a clipped nod. With her arms crossed and

her toe tapping, she turned her attention on Liz. "I told you at the ruins that I was fine."

"You did. But I needed to see for myself, especially after you mentioned the other guy following you." She'd been caught and didn't try to make excuses for the mischief she'd been up to.

"So you couldn't help but watch the show," Cian concluded, not at all offended by the intrusion of their privacy. After all, he'd been a spy. Turnabout was fair play.

"She's too trusting," Liz told him with an apologetic grimace for her cousin. "I'm sorry, but you know it's true, Piper."

"We all are now and again, to be sure." Trying to cut the tension, Cian walked over to the sideboard and poured two glasses of wine. Falling back into bartender mode came as easy as breathing, and his laid-back manner always worked. These two women needed to mend their small rift. It would give him the necessary time to look into who had sent Baran to assassinate him. "How about you both relax for a wee while? It's been a stressful day. Piper, you can crush me bollocks later, when no one is watching."

She narrowed her eyes, picking up on his sexual innuendo. Anyone else would believe he meant kick him in the balls for what went down, but he knew she was smarter than that. He didn't try to hide his devilish smirk as he handed her the wineglass.

"Oh, there will be ball crushing, *to be sure*," she said nastily, clearly mocking him. "But trust me, it won't be the way you're suggesting."

He laughed all the way out the door.

"He's cute."

Piper dragged her eyes from the laughing Irishman's backside and faced Liz. "And he knows it."

"He might be good for a quick *shag*," Liz said with a waggle of her brows.

"Exactly how long were you scrying, woman?"

"Long enough." Liz showed no remorse, and Piper sighed her irritation at her meddlesome family. "Were you awake the entire time?"

"Pretty much. Thanks for coming to my rescue by the cliff."

Liz waved her hand in dismissal. "I wondered why GiGi couldn't heal you. Between Alastair and her, you should've jumped right up. But I guess he knew that, didn't he? Alastair was too calm to be worried."

"I almost lost it when he threatened Cian," Piper admitted with a laugh. "Did you see him pale? I thought he was going to crap himself."

Liz crowed with laughter. "You were peeking!"

"Of course, I was! I thoroughly enjoy how Alastair can make men wet their pants with a barely implied threat."

"You're pure evil." Liz sipped her wine and shot her a side glance. "But I love you anyway."

"If you love me, you'll help me find a way to ditch my protectors. Cian included."

"Oh no. Not me. I'm not getting on Alastair's bad side."

"As if you ever could." Piper guzzled half her drink. "He adores you because you feed him information on Nash's activities."

Nash was Alastair's son, and for the majority of Nash's life, the two had been at odds. In recent months, they mended their rocky relationship. Nash had taken over the running of Thorne Industries when Alastair stepped down to care for his fiancée, Aurora. She'd been in stasis for close to two decades due to a run-in with Alastair's enemies.

During the interim, Alastair gained his much-deserved reputation. He was a man possessed and he'd set out to destroy those who would hurt his loved ones.

"If Nash ever found out, he'd kill me." Liz, as Nash's right-hand person, was privy to everything that went on at work. "But at least he isn't calling Alastair 'sperm donor' anymore."

Piper nodded. "I'm glad they're no longer at odds."

"Me, too."

"Unfortunately, since all his children and immediate family are matched, it appears Alastair has turned his sights on me." She drained her glass and looked at Liz. "Did you get that impression?"

"I did."

"Wonderful," Piper said flatly. What Alastair Thorne wanted, he got. Usually with very little effort. "I don't want him to play cupid. I want to choose my own mate."

"He doesn't choose them, cuz. He simply facilitates the getting together of said mates by coming up with creative missions to send them on," Liz pointed out with a light laugh.

"Do you think this is one of those times, or was he simply here because GiGi called him?"

"I don't know." Her cousin shrugged—*a standard Thorne response if Piper had ever seen one!*

"And you aren't that concerned?"

"Look, I want to see you happy." Liz reached over and gripped Piper's hand. "If it's with someone like Cian, great. If it's becoming a mother on your own, that's awesome, too."

Turning her palm over, Piper squeezed Liz's hand. "Thank you."

"It's what best friends are for. It's even better that I happen to be your favorite cousin."

"Continue to butt your nose in where it's not wanted, and the title goes to Mack."

"Ouch."

In reality, all three of them were close. Liz, Mackenzie, and Piper had practically grown up together as sisters. Piper couldn't say she wasn't a tiny bit jealous that both Liz and Mack had settled into their happily-ever-after with the amazing guys they'd found, but she was thrilled for them all the same.

"So, about Cian," Liz said with a happy grin. "*Are* you planning to do the dirty with him?"

"I can't say I don't want to. The man turns me on like no one I've ever known. But he's embroiled in a mess, Liz. How do I dismiss the fact he threw a man off the cliff with no remorse?"

"None whatsoever?"

"Not that I could tell." An uncomfortable thought occurred and Piper abruptly straightened, shooting a panicked look at Liz. "Ohmygoddess, I've done it again, haven't I? In the whole of Ireland, I've chosen the one psychotic killer determined to play down throwing a man off a cliff. What is *wrong* with me?"

"He is *not* a psychotic killer. Ryker knows him, and he wouldn't let Cian within ten feet of you if the guy was a murdering bastard with no moral compass." Again, Liz shrugged, but her expression turned downcast. "Sometimes people have to do things they don't want to, but I suspect in Cian's case, it was kill or be killed."

"I'd forgotten about what you went through."

"Right, and had you seen me in the midst of the action, you'd probably have thought I had no remorse either. But I still feel guilt, Piper. The nightmares are the worst."

Not that long ago, Liz had killed a man to defend herself and tortured another to get information relevant to her safety. On the nights Rafe wasn't around, Piper comforted her if she happened to relive the trauma.

Knowing Liz wasn't seeking to dredge up the past, Piper let the comment rest. "So you think maybe Cian is internalizing what happened and showing a cocky attitude to the world?"

"Maybe." With a twinkling side-glance, Liz added, "Or maybe there *is* something wrong with you, and you've chosen the one psychotic killer in all of Ireland determined to play down throwing a man off a cliff."

"Shut it."

***

Two hours after hugging Liz goodbye, Piper was in her room, lounging in the overstuffed chair by the window and ruminating over the day's events. A knock jerked her from her overactive thoughts. Assuming it was GiGi coming to lecture her for some godawful reason or another, she answered the door with a resigned sigh.

Cian filled the doorway and, without trying, sucked all the breath from her lungs. He appeared more serious than she'd ever seen him, and his somber eyes met hers.

"May I come in, Piper?" His tone and the lack of endearment caused her stomach to flip, but she stood back and allowed him entry.

"I owe you an apology." He scrubbed a hand over his face and winced when he came in contact with his nose.

Guilt swamped her. She'd punched him in the face when she woke, and none of them thought to heal his broken nose. Bruising had migrated to his eyes, and the bluish-purple caused those emerald orbs of his to pop.

"Looks like I owe you one first," she said softly. His hand in hers, she led him to the chair by the window and urged him to sit. "Let me repair this for you."

"Based on what you said, I assumed it required a healer like GiGi."

His lack of knowledge in relation to abilities was sad. How was it that a member of one of the Six original families didn't know the basics of witchcraft? She hadn't realized she asked the question aloud until he responded.

"Other than occult items or tools for my job, I've never experienced what a powerful witch could do to the full extent. The last few generations of O'Malleys haven't had true magic in our lives." His shifted his head slightly to stare out the window and locked on a plot of land with a small cottage that adjoined their back yard. "We were cursed a few centuries ago."

"Right. Something about a feud between your family and the O'Connors, if I remember correctly."

"They took what was rightfully ours. An enchanted sword given to my ancestors for a service rendered."

"But you're one of the Six families granted power. How did your magic just disappear?"

"The tale I'd heard was that we were to protect the sword. When it fell into the wrong hands, the god who'd offered it became angry at our ancestors' carelessness. We were no longer worthy in his eyes." Cian shrugged. "It's of no account to me, because I've never had abilities. But Bridget feels the sting of the curse more than the rest of us."

"How so?"

"She lives for the pub. In case you haven't noticed, we reside in an out-of-the-way location. Witches don't care to be the center of attention." He gave her a self-deprecating smile. A moment later, he shrugged matter-of-factly. "We've only managed to keep Lucky's going because of the beer we brew, but the last of Granny O'Malley's potion has run out."

Piper couldn't fathom not having the ability to conjure what she wanted if it was needed. Yes, she shunned magic in favor of mortal pursuits, but in a pinch, she used her gifts.

"How long has the business been in the family?"

"Longer than the curse." His smile didn't reach his eyes.

Did the burden of the business chafe him? She didn't feel she had the right to ask so personal a question on a day's acquaintance. The mystery surrounding the elixir seemed safer somehow.

"How did you have enough of the potion to last this long? Assuming your Granny passed back when your family still had magic and the ability to make more, it should've run out."

"My brother's wife was a powerful witch. She magically multiplied what we had when we needed."

"She can't do it again?"

Sorrow tugged his lips down. "No, love. She died earlier this year. Carrick is still struggling."

"Oh, Cian! I'm so sorry."

He acted like it was no big deal, but Piper could sense it bothered him greatly.

After a light clearing of his throat, he changed the subject back to their original topic. "Too many people have seen my face today. If I heal up in the same day, it'll cause untold interest."

There was logic in what he'd said, but Piper still felt

horrible for causing undue pain. "Let me at least take away any discomfort and cast a spell for your nose to heal properly.

Looking down at her hands, Cian frowned. "Are ya positive you won't be tempted to turn me into a toad for what I'd done to ya today?"

She loved how his accent became thicker when he was disturbed. It wasn't quite as put on as when he flirted, but it wasn't his standard speaking voice either.

Piper raised a hand, displaying three fingers in the air with her thumb tucked over her pinky. "I solemnly swear, I will not turn you into a toad—today."

Throwing back his head, he let loose a hearty laugh.

Her toes curled, and nerves danced a jig in her belly.

Cian seemed to like her piss-and-vinegar attitude, and he wasn't shy about expressing it.

"You're a delight Piper Thorne." He cocked his head slightly. "I'm assuming that's your true last name." His playful grin created havoc inside her.

"Yes. Kelly is my middle name, so it wasn't a total lie."

"Half-truths are still lies, darlin', but I'll not be holdin' it against you, since you didn't know me from ol' drunken Seamus at the time."

Unbidden, she felt a smile form. "That's magnanimous of you. And Seamus didn't look old to me. Drunken, yes. Old, no." In truth, she didn't know how old the ginger-haired pub patron was. He looked to be somewhere in his mid-thirties and possessed of an ageless quality. "He's kind of cute."

"You're not allowed to ogle other men while in me pub." Cian had gone back to what Piper considered his touristy accent.

"I'd have thought after our skirmish today, you wouldn't want anything more to do with me."

Passion flared to life in the depths of his glorious eyes, and any semblance of teasing fled. His gaze slowly swept her face, down her neck and body, then back again before locking with hers. "Our skirmish made our mating dance a little more interesting, don't you think?"

Her breath caught in her throat, and she wanted nothing more than to agree. But Cian was dangerous, in more ways than one. It was doubtful that he was a one-woman kind of guy. He also played games of intrigue and, in the course of those games, he'd thrown a virtual stranger off a cliff without remorse. In the end, she'd wind up alone and potentially regretting their brief encounter if they became lovers.

"Let's fix your nose."

"What did I say wrong?" Cian asked gently.

She shrugged and gave him a rueful smile. "You didn't. I'm just past the skirmishes and games stage of life."

"Without them, life is a lot less fun."

"No doubt for you that's true, but I want a peaceful existence with a man who loves me."

Her words caused him to physically and mentally distance himself. The fun-loving Cian she'd come to know over the last day immediately disappeared. In his place sat a polite stranger.

"I'm not that man, Piper. If you're looking for a fun night or two, I'm more than happy to oblige. Hell, I'd be downright chuffed, but I can't offer up permanence."

"I suspected as much, and there's no hard feelings. Flirting with you was fun while it lasted. But I'm not looking for a fling." As she said it, she realized it was true. No matter how many shagging jokes she referenced, Piper desired permanence. She wanted a man who was in it for the long haul. Not a fly-by-night, love-'em-and-leave-'em pub owner up to his neck in intrigue and danger. "Let's fix your nose."

He leaned forward, and she placed her hands along either side of his face. Closing her eyes, she visualized how he looked when they'd met, the evening before. She pictured the bone and cartilage of his nose returning to normal and the bruising disappearing altogether. Whispering a healing incantation, she swept away his lingering discomfort.

Sitting back, she opened her eyes. Cian's stare was too intense and made her want to take back her statement from a moment before. She fought the urge to relent and tell him she'd take whatever crumbs he offered.

Uncertain where she drew the strength to stand firm, she rose to her feet. "I'm almost positive there is a glamour spell in the Thorne grimoire that will make the scrape and broken nose still appear real to outsiders. The spell will continue for the length of time it would normally take for those things to heal and the bruises to fade."

"But you don't know?"

"I'll call my cousin Spring and ask her. One sec." Piper experienced profound relief when Cian stayed seated and turned his head to look out over the landscape. His presence dominated, and his steady regard had made her question her resolve. Crossing to the bed, she picked up her cellphone and dialed.

Spring answered on the first ring, and within minutes, Piper had the exact thing she needed. She wasted no time casting the spell and sending Cian on his way.

After he was out the door, she leaned back against paneled wood and released a heartfelt sigh. She wouldn't let this bump in the road destroy her dream vacation.

Dinner would've been a quiet affair without the animated conversation of GiGi, Ryker, and Bridget to spice things up. They maintained an upbeat conversation without any acknowledgement of Piper's continued silence.

Cian had chosen to cover his sister's shift as he'd indicated earlier, to allow Bridget to catch up with her coven sister. And Piper found it a challenge to remain at the table when the main subject of her interest was likely next door, slinging drinks to lively pub patrons.

She could use the chaotic distraction of a bar, but if she went there, she'd probably moon over him all night. Self-torture wasn't her gig, and she refused to fawn over a man who was only available for a one-night stand.

The main thing that played on her mind was the problem of Granny O'Malley's elixir—or lack thereof. Bridget hadn't brought it up to GiGi, and Piper suspected she wouldn't for the sake of pride. The woman seemed steeped in it. In all honesty, Piper had been surprised Cian had confessed their issue earlier. However, they'd both been kind and she felt the need to help.

"Bridget, may I ask about Granny O'Malley's special

potion? Cian mentioned you'd used the last of it without any way to recreate it."

Bridget's lips compressed into a tight line, and from the fire in her eyes, she intended to bodily harm her brother for discussing their family business with a total stranger.

Compassion filled GiGi's lovely face, and she touched Bridget's hand. "What's this about?"

"It's true enough. Carrick's wife used to conjure what we needed in the past. Since Roisin's been gone, we've not had a way to create more. We used our last batch yesterday."

"There's no recipe to go by?" Piper asked. She had the fleeting thought that Spring might be able to provide any herbs for the recipe. With her working knowledge of plants, the woman was a miracle worker.

With a grimace, Bridget got to her feet and crossed to an old wooden built-in bookcase. There, she withdrew a leather-bound tome. A distinct thwack echoed in the dining room when she dropped it on the table.

"It's located somewhere within these pages. Damned if I know where, because this bloody book is temperamental and refuses to give up its secrets."

GiGi turned thoughtful. "How did Roisin recreate it before?"

"By doubling our existing supply."

"May I?" Piper rose and skirted the table, stopping in front of the ancient grimoire. "Wow! This might be older than the Thorne's."

"After the first book was gifted by the gods and goddesses to the first witches, this was the next created." Bridget ran a hand lovingly across the embossed Celtic design on the front cover. The tree of life was encircled by smaller, round Celtic knots. In the corners of the book were more Celtic designs, in the shape of triangles. All in all, a beautiful family legacy.

With reverence, Piper traced the design. Her fingers tingled when she came to the tree roots, and they all gasped when the tree lit up. The glow brightened the entire room before fading out.

"What in the world?" GiGi jumped up and repeated Piper's actions, but without the same effect. "Has that ever happened before, Bridget?"

Wide-eyed, her friend shook her head. "Never."

"Touch it again, child," GiGi instructed Piper.

Following the same pattern as she did the first time; Piper outlined the design. The tree lit again, flaring brighter for longer. The grimoire's magical light show held them all enthralled.

"What do you think it means?" Piper asked.

As she drew back, the cover flipped open and the pages fluttered back and forth as if a great wind rustled them. It stopped abruptly, about three quarters of the way toward the end of the book. She eased forward to read the page.

"Think this is your Granny O'Malley's recipe?" she croaked out. She looked at Bridget, who had covered her mouth with her hands and stared at Piper through tear-bright eyes. "We can recreate it, Bridget. It's all right here."

With a squeal of pure joy, Bridget launched herself at Piper and hugged her tight. "You've no idea what this means to my family. No idea at all."

"I'm glad to help. We'll see what we need and gather the ingredients to get started in the morning. We'll have a new batch for you to try in no time."

"Thank you, girl. Your stay is free for as long as you care to remain."

"Nonsense. This is your business, and my money spends as well as the next person's." Piper's tone was firm. "But I won't object to another of your wonderful dinners while I'm here. There's nothing I can conjure that's this tasty."

Bridget hugged her again. "I'll make anything your heart desires."

Can you make Cian love me?

Uncomfortable with the unasked question, Piper glanced down at the recipe in the book. "Let us confer with Spring. There are a few ingredients I'm not familiar with, but it's usually a simple matter to whip up."

"I'll dish up the apple cake while you consult with them."

Ryker spoke for the first time since dinner. "With the vanilla custard sauce?" He sounded hopeful, and Piper was looking forward to another culinary delight.

Bridget's grin was mysterious with a hint of naughty, as was the wink she gave him.

"That's it, GiGi. I'm leaving you for Bridget," he declared.

His wife sashayed to where he sat at the table, dropped into his lap, and pulled his head to hers for a kiss that would set fire to a lesser man's britches. When they pulled apart, the raging desire in Ryker's eyes was enough to scorch all those present. "Bridget who?" he asked in a low, husky voice.

"I've never been able to keep a man with *her* around," Bridget said with a mock sigh.

Piper laughed as their hostess sailed from the room. "I adore her."

"I think the feeling is mutual, child."

She met GiGi's kind, smiling eyes. "I wish all the O'Malleys felt the same." When she realized what had slipped out, she clamped a hand over her mouth. "I... uh... that is... *oh, hell!*"

Their compassion made Piper itchy.

"Give him time, child. It's my understanding he was ill used by a woman in the past. Men are a little thicker in the head than women are about these things."

"Hey! Man right here," Ryker protested.

"I know," GiGi retorted with a sassy smile in his direction.

Piper laughed, as she was meant to.

"I suppose I should pop back to Leiper's Fork and see what Spring might have by way of ingredients." GiGi kissed her husband fully on the mouth. "Keep Piper out of trouble until I return, and save a piece of the apple cake for me. For later." With a wink and a twinkling of lights, she was gone.

"That woman keeps me on my toes. She's the moon to my stars."

Ryker's happiness made Piper envious. She wanted someone as devoted as he was to GiGi. At thirty-three, Piper felt maybe she'd missed the boat. Her Prince Charming was floating off into the sunset on someone else's yacht.

"There is plenty to adore," Piper agreed with a forced laugh.

"Want to talk about it?"

Mortification scorched her cheeks, and she felt exposed to a ginormous degree. "Am I that obvious?"

"No, Piper. I just know how charming Cian is and how susceptible women are to his brand of charm."

"That's what I was afraid of," she said morosely. She plopped down across from him and rested her chin on her palms. "He's freaking adorable and he knows it. How's a woman to resist all that yumminess?"

Ryker chuckled, but otherwise remained silent. That silence seemed like encouragement to confide in him.

"I like him. Probably more than I should after such a short time. But I don't want to fall to the Thorne curse of loving only one man, especially one determined to remain unattached."

"You're talking to a guy who waited over a decade for his wife to forgive him for past mistakes and take him back. I understand unrequited love."

All the moisture in her mouth dried up. "I never said I loved him. That's impossible after only a day."

"I loved GiGi from the moment we met. No one else would do."

"Oh, Ryker. I wish there were more men like you in the

world. Romantic souls willing to wait a lifetime for the one they adore." She toyed with the fork in front of her, debating whether she should ask about Cian or not. Giving into the urge, she met Ryker's kind, patient eyes. "Obviously, you know each other well. Why is he closed off? What happened to make him that way?"

"In our line of work, we saw the worst of people. But Cian still had an open, optimistic view of the world—*until* he met Moira."

Piper immediately hated the woman without ever knowing anything about her. Jealousy she had no right to feel twisted her guts. "What happened?" The question came out as barely a whisper, but Ryker heard.

"We believe she was sent by Zhu Lin of the Désorcelers Society. We surmised she was meant to turn Cian. Later, her motive was confirmed, but she refused to divulge her employer."

"How was she supposed to turn him?"

"Seduce him. Get in his head and make him feel bitter about the loss of magic. Use it to make him a double agent."

Piper's stomach felt queasy. The idea of converting a powerless warlock was ingenious. Had Zhu Lin succeeded, he'd have had access to quite a bit of information to use against those he despised the most: the witch community.

"When did Cian discover the truth?"

"Not until after he was head over heels in love." The words were solemn, indicating Moira had done a number on Cian with her betrayal.

"And he's vowed to never become involved again, I'm assuming?"

"Something like that. Of course, he can be a stubborn bastard at times, but I don't think it's hopeless."

But Piper would beg to differ, because Cian had already told her it was. She didn't bother to say as much to the ever-optimistic Ryker. Let him believe his friend would find love one day.

"I think I'll head up and write tomorrow's must-see schedule. There are a lot of places I'd like to visit before I leave the area." Also, she needed to find another B&B as soon as she could. Obviously, she wouldn't stay here with temptation just a stone's throw away.

For the entirety of the night, Cian had kept a watch on the door. Piper hadn't shown up. Not that he expected her to, but the evening dragged on endlessly with one customer after another annoying the ever-loving bejeezus out of him. He refused to admit he was still peevish by her declaration about wanting a home and family—*or* that he was also a little saddened by it.

Once upon a time, he wanted those exact things, but Moira cured him of his fanciful dreams. He was intelligent enough to know not all women were the same, but his instincts had failed him once, and he daren't risk it again.

"Cian, man, did ya not hear me?"

Seamus had continued to rabbit on about some ridiculous subject or another all night, boring Cian near to tears. He was about to strangle the man just to get some peace and quiet.

"Sure, and I did, Seamus," Cian lied. "Right fun, that."

The ginger-haired man narrowed his eyes but didn't call him out on the obvious falsehood. "So where be yer light-o'-love, Cian?"

He shut off the tap and straightened up tall in his anger,

with a glare for the much smaller Seamus. "Watch yourself. It's not like that. Piper deserves respect."

"For the *buille*?"

"In general," he said, dodging the question about whether she was the one to deliver the blow to his nose.

"Ya sweet on her, Cian?" Seamus's interest was anything but casual.

Cian idly wondered if the other man intended to make a play for Piper. It wouldn't be the first time the man went after his leftovers. Pasting on a smile he didn't feel, Cian resumed pouring the Guinness. "I'm not sweet on anyone, Seamus. You know that. Life is too short to settle for one comely colleen."

He'd just handed off the pint to their part-time server, Sorcha, and was leaning against the bar to take an order from the busty Shelly O'Neal when he felt *her* enter the room. His insides vibrated, and he fought the urge to turn toward Piper like a divining rod seeking water. The last thing he needed was to prove Seamus right.

And although his senses constricted to tune out everything but her, Cian barely spared her a passing glance as he absently flirted with Shelly. If asked, he'd be unable to recall what was said.

No one was more surprised than he when Piper approached Ruairí with her drink request rather than him, and she studiously avoided looking at Cian the entire time the cocktail was being mixed. When she finally had the glass in hand, she turned her back to the bar and surveyed the rowdy crowd before taking a careful sip of her drink.

Surly and out of sorts by her cold shoulder, Cian gestured for Ruairí to take over with Shelly, then proceeded to the other side of the bar. He only stopped when he was blocking Piper's line of sight. Yes, he was being a contrary arse, but her pointed avoidance rankled.

She lifted disinterested eyes to him, and the lack of warmth caused his stomach to flip. He felt an odd sense of nervousness. Firmly tamping down the foreign sensation, he gave her his most endearing grin. "You couldn't stay away?"

"I was bored sitting in my room, and I didn't want to drive the country roads in the dark to find another place to have a drink. I'm afraid Lucky O'Malley's is the only one for miles. Sorry if I'm cramping your style." She flicked her thumb sideways toward the curvy Shelly. "Feel free to carry on as if I'm not here."

As if he could ever fail to notice her!

"Shelly's married to Titan O'Neal. Named because he's roughly the size of a small barn. I'll not be stepping on his toes, to be sure."

Piper's delicious mouth firmed and she shrugged as she looked away, but not before he caught the flash of humor in her eyes. "Well, there must be another poor unsuspecting female for you to seduce."

"None other than you at the present. Care to reconsider your stance on a meaningless fling?"

Color crept up her neck and into her cheeks. The sight made him wonder if she was an all-over body blusher. Oh, what he wouldn't give to find out—other than his heart and a gold ring.

"No. Sorry. It looks like it's just you and your hand tonight, Cian."

He chuckled because she didn't look sorry at all. She appeared downright gleeful. "Once again, ya've proved my point that all women are heartless."

"Oh really? And what does it say about you who refuses to consider anything but a quick 'shag' and a pat on the ass for goodbye?"

"In truth, all I can think about is shagging you and patting your ass," he said in a low voice next to her ear. He yelped when she twisted his nipple. "You have violent tendencies, Piper me love," he growled as he rubbed his abused chest.

"And don't you forget it." With a mock toast, she stalked across the room and found an abandoned table. Immediately, a few brave regulars gathered around her, and Cian had little doubt those plonkers were trying to charm her into their respective beds.

Like a dog on a leash, he followed and was quick to shove aside a few of Piper's admirers to sit down. "What are your plans for tomorrow, darlin'?"

"To explore another town and find a new B&B."

His heart hiccuped. "But you're not done seeing what we have to offer here."

Her black brows shot up, and she insolently raked his body with her seemingly bored gaze. "I believe I have, and I'm not interested in anything else."

"Now you're just being ornery," he charged. A furious look at those lingering to witness their conversation sent the men scurrying. "Bloody vultures! Always trying to score."

Piper snorted into her drink. "Must be something in the water that makes you all a bunch of horny bastards."

Cian leaned halfway across the table to emphasize his point. As expected, she hastily backed away with tell-tale pink tinting her cheeks. "You act like you didn't enjoy the kisses we shared when I know damned well you did."

"I won't lie. You're the best kisser I've ever met to date. But that doesn't mean I intend to drop my panties for you with one come-hither look, Cian."

He went rock hard at the thought of her dropped panties. In his mind, he could clearly imagine every area of the delectable body he'd caressed during their mind-drugging kisses. Shifting in his seat to allow for the tightness in his jeans, he snatched up her drink and took a sip.

"Hey!"

"The next one is on the house," he retorted. "I'm trying to wash away the fantasy of you pantyless, *cailín*."

A GRIM SORT OF PLEASURE FILLED PIPER AT HIS TESTY RESPONSE. Cian wasn't as unaffected as he wished he was. However, she wouldn't push. Chasing a man wasn't her style. If he wanted to have an open, honest, and mutually exclusive relationship, she was game. Hell, she'd probably do backflips. But he'd have to make the first move now. She'd shown her interest and told him what she wanted for the future. Either he was onboard and wanted to work toward the same goals or he didn't. Either way, she wasn't budging. How long her resolve would last was in question. Better to bail sooner than compromise herself.

Liz would've called her a fool for not having hot and sweaty, headboard-banging sex with him, but Piper knew her heart was at stake. She already liked Cian too much and was physically more attracted to him than to all her previous lovers combined. It didn't bode well for her future-husband search, not if she compared all men to the one across from her.

Idly, she let her attention wander over the building crowd. Her gaze swept the bar, stopping short on Seamus. The man watched her from the bar mirror with something close to dislike. *Why?* She'd only met him last night, and he seemed friendly enough at the time.

Leaning forward and lowering her voice for Cian's hearing alone, she asked, "Did you tell anyone who I really am?"

He frowned and shook his head. "No. I know the way of it for your family. I'd not put you in danger, darlin'."

"Thank you."

Cian gave her a brisk nod and scanned the pub with the practiced eye of the secret agent he used to be. "What has your nerves dancing a jig, Piper?"

"Nothing. I'm probably paranoid. My cousin Liz and her

husband cautioned me before I flew to Ireland. I suppose I'm jumpy for no real reason."

His sharp-eyed stare settled on her. "No. There's always a reason, and I suspect you have good instincts."

She scoffed lightly. "There you would be wrong. Take, for example, the worst of the worst man here. Within five minutes, I'd unknowingly have a date with him."

"What does it say that you and I had an excursion today?" he teased.

"That I had to find the most emotionally stunted man here in town?"

He sobered, and she instantly regretted her snarky comeback.

"I'm sorry, Cian. You didn't deserve that." She rested a hand atop his. "Your reasons are your own, and I've no right to be dickish about them."

With a twist of his wrist, he turned his palm face up and wove their fingers together. "I've seen too much, love. I'd not want to break your heart. You're right, I am emotionally stunted and you deserve a man to be whole." His voice was gruff and his eyes regretful.

What he didn't know was that he was *already* breaking her heart. Was she being stubborn by not grasping the bull by the horns? By not spending a few nights basking in the warmth of his beautiful light?

Piper blinked. Then blinked long and slow a second time.
Cian's light!

It burned brighter than it had when she arrived. It had to mean his powers were trying to manifest, right?

"Cian, have you ever *tried* using magic?"

"How did you make the jump from finding the right man to my lack of abilities, darlin'?"

She laughed in the face of his confusion. "Sorry. My brain jumps track now and again. I..." She shrugged, unsure how to explain. "It's just that since I've met you, it seems your magical glow is getting brighter. I wondered if maybe it meant something or if your connection to magic isn't as lacking as you believe."

"Brighter?"

He seemed confused, and she wondered if he'd ever noticed witches had a brighter aura than mortals.

"The aura of a magical being can be blinding, depending on the strength of their power. When I met you, your light immediately attracted me, though it appeared muted." Positive she was making a muddle of it, she crinkled her nose and said, "I'm terrible at explaining these things."

"You're doing grand, love," he said, absently toying with her fingers. "But you believe my 'light' is growing stronger?"

"Yes."

"Will you stick around another day? To discuss magic?"

Because he seemed sincere and his request wasn't heavy with innuendo, she agreed.

"I've got a pub to entertain." He rose to his feet and gave her hand a light squeeze. "Don't give these arseholes the time of day or they'll be falling on you like a starving man on a haunch o' beef. If anyone gets to fall on you, it's me."

She laughed and shook her head. The man was an inveterate flirt. "Does Ruairí need a hand behind the bar while you're on stage? I don't know anything about pouring a proper Guinness, but I can serve what's on tap, bottled beers, and mixed drinks."

His brows shot up in his surprise.

With a grin, she confessed, "I bartended through college."

"Stop it right now, Piper! You're dangerously close to making me go back on my no-involvement rule."

They shared a grin, and he finally nodded. "I can't see as how Bridget would object to your help any more than she objected to her old nemesis, Ruairí, and we could use a hand by the looks of it."

"Anything I should know about tabs or accepting cash?"

"We only run a tab for the night. Everyone pays before they leave." He placed a hand on her lower back and guided her around the end of the bar. "Ruairí can tell you who goes to what bill, and I can spare a few minutes to show you how to pour a proper pint of gat."

Later, when Piper dropped into bed, it was with a smile on her face. Throughout the rest of the night, she'd helped out at the hopping pub. Who knew this tiny village was such a hotbed of fun? Tonight seemed to have an over-abundance of women, and she suspected word got around that the two hottest men in town were manning the bar, with one of them stopping to play lively tunes on occasion.

More than once Piper glanced up to find Cian's admiring gaze focused on her, and she tamped down the urge to preen. With each steamy look he sent her way, she found it difficult to remember her stand on brief flings. It seemed as if every love song he sang was meant for her ears alone, and she tried to remember the man was a practiced seducer of women.

A light tapping brought her head up. She couldn't tell if it was her door or another, and she paused to listen. Again, the tapping sounded, a little louder than the first time. Yep, her door. Curious if her hunch about her visitor was correct, she padded over and turned the knob.

Cian looked fatigued, but still as breathtakingly attractive as always.

"I took the chance you'd still be awake," he said in a low voice. "I didn't get to properly thank you for helping out tonight."

"It was fun," she replied, and found she honestly meant it. She'd chatted with the locals in a friendly, mindless way that was entertaining and carefree as she slung drinks and accepted payment.

"I'd like to repay you for your kindness."

"There's no need. I didn't offer for any reason other than to be helpful, Cian."

"I know, and it's greatly appreciated, to be sure. But I still owe you a debt of gratitude." His tired eyes scanned her face, as if to memorize it, before settling on her lips. "I want nothing more than to kiss you right now, darlin'."

And neither did she. He'd been fueling her fire all night long. Stepping back, heart pounding so hard it was straining the fabric of her shirt, she allowed him access to her room.

He stopped just over the threshold and cupped a hand around her neck even as he stopped her from closing the door with his foot. "If you close that door, it'll be more than a wee kiss I'm delivering."

Her desire to slam the door shut was overwhelming, but she did nothing more than lift her chin to offer her lips.

With a soft groan, he captured her mouth. Fire danced along her veins as he plundered its depths again and again, tasting her like a man starved. For her part, she couldn't get enough of his whiskey-scented breath. The hint of mint made her vaguely wonder if he'd planned this with a peppermint or if he'd come to her directly after brushing his teeth as he prepared for bed. She didn't care either way.

Her naughty fingers found their way under the hem of his shirt to explore the sculpted ridges of his stomach and draw him closer. Reveling at the feel of his hard chest against her unbound, tee-shirt-covered breasts, she moaned.

The kiss lasted forever and still ended way too soon. By the time Cian pulled away, Piper's resolve to hold out for a relationship was a puddle of goo on the floor.

"You can stay," she whispered past her suddenly dry throat.

The corners of his eyes crinkled as he smiled down at her.

After delivering a heart-wrenchingly sweet kiss, he rubbed the tip of his nose against hers. "It's not wise. I'd be too tempted to never leave your bed again."

"I don't see that as a problem." Where she found the daring was in question, but she knew she'd regret it if she didn't try one last time. "I really like you, Cian. Can't you open your heart just a little bit to possibility?"

He traced her furrowed brow and ran his fingertips down her cheek, then dropped his arms to his sides. "You don't see the problem because you *are* open to possibility. And I'd rather cut off my right arm than hurt you, but I can't give you what you want."

She'd tried and failed, and now could only nod, finding words difficult to muster.

"This isn't me playing games. I'm finding it hard to keep away." His serious tone was heavy with regret, and she hated it. "You'll never know how sorry I am that I can't be the man you deserve, Piper."

"I promised your sister I would try to recreate Granny O'Malley's elixir tomorrow. Afterwards, it's better if I head out." She cleared her aching throat. "I guess this is a goodbye of sorts."

He ignored her farewell and only chose to acknowledge her comment about the potion. "Bridget told me you found the recipe. You could've knocked me over with a finch feather."

"Me, too." She rested her hand on the knob of the open door. "It's late, but I'm happy to discuss it more over breakfast."

Taking the hint, he moved the few steps necessary to exit.

On the other side of the opening, he turned back to her. "*Oíche mhaith,* darlin'."

She nodded hesitantly, because she had no idea what he said.

"It means good night," he said with a soft chuckle.

After she closed the door, she leaned her forehead against it and allowed a stray tear to fall. *Why was she so damned unlovable? Why couldn't a man at least attempt a real relationship with her?*

Knowing she'd not find the answers she sought this night, she climbed into bed, positive sleep would elude her.

M ORNING SUNSHINE, FLITTED THROUGH THE CURTAINS AND mocked Piper's foul mood. She could hear the house stirring and knew Bridget would start cooking for the masses soon, if she hadn't already. Still, Piper couldn't find the energy to abandon the bed. She'd only managed a broken three hours of sleep, and she was as grumpy as a bear with a sore paw. If one person said the wrong thing to her today, she might take a swipe at them.

For that reason, she decided to stay abed and conjure her own meal.

As she was warming to the idea, a knock sounded at the door.

After expressing a heartfelt groan and determining that any visitor who was scared witless by her appearance deserved it, she climbed over the mound of covers.

"Spring!" All her ire dissolved in the face of her cousin's sweet disposition. No one could be irritated in her presence. A more naturally stunning woman didn't exist, and Spring always maintained a serene expression, unless it came to the epic clashes with her husband Knox.

Piper hid a jaw-cracking yawn behind her hand. "I wasn't expecting you at the butt-crack of dawn. Isn't it still the middle of the night by you?"

"I couldn't sleep. My excitement got the better of me." With a toss of her tawny curls, Spring swept through the doorway and dropped a canvas bag on the foot of the bed. "I found everything we need for the potion but one item, and I can't wait to get started."

"What about that extra item?"

"I saw Bridget on the way up and she said we could find it at a nearby waterfall." Spring cast a curious glance around the large room. "Cute. Knox and I might have to take a vacation soon." With an impatient wave of her hand, she said, "Hurry and get dressed. Time's a'wastin'."

"Don't take this the wrong way, but I don't like you very much."

Her cousin's musical laughter rang out, and the melodic sound was soothing to Piper's raw nerves. She grinned and bussed a kiss on Spring's petal-soft cheek.

"Where's your husband? He's never far behind."

"Actually, he is this time. I managed to convince him to back off because I'm seriously sick of his overprotectiveness."

Piper paused in pulling on her jeans and stared in open-mouthed wonder. It was well known in their family—hell, throughout the entire witch community—Knox Carlyle *never* left his wife's side if she was going farther than her family home. He'd failed to protect her once with tragic consequences, and—unlike Piper at the moment—he refused to be caught with his pants down again.

"You're joking?"

Her cousin avoided her eye.

"*Where* exactly does he think you are, Spring?"

"Visiting with my sisters."

"He's going to murder us both!"

"He is not."

"He is, too," interrupted an anger-infused voice from over by the doorway.

Piper yelped and scrambled to pull up her pants as Spring sputtered her husband's name. Of course, Piper needn't have worried about her unmentionables since Knox had locked his furious eyes on his guilty-as-sin mate.

"You lied to me." His voice was silky soft with an underlying hurt.

Staring at him now, all six feet two of panty-melting eye candy, Piper wondered why Spring didn't chain herself to the guy. He absolutely adored her cousin and would die for her without a moment's hesitation. How many women were lucky to have a guy like him in her life?

Not many.

Spring opened her mouth but no words came out.

With purposeful strides, he approached his wife, gently tipped her chin up, and gazed down at her with a tenderness so disarming and sincere, it brought Piper's tears to the forefront. She suppressed a girly sigh at how romantic he appeared, struggling between chastising Spring or hugging the ever-loving hell out of her.

He gave a rueful shake of his head and dropped a light, lingering kiss on her pouty mouth. "Please stop taking years off my life."

"It's Ireland, babe. Nothing terrible happens here," Spring countered.

Piper held up a hand. "Not true. Cian threw a big burly Russian off the cliff yesterday."

Both Knox and Spring were nonplussed.

Spring recovered first. "How do you know he was Russian?"

"*That's* your question?" Knox asked dryly. With a shake of his head, he looked back at Piper. "Okay, I'll bite. How do you know he was Russian? Also, who is Cian and why is he throwing big burly men off cliffs?"

After conjuring tea and scones, Piper recounted the entire incident.

"Never a dull moment in this crazy-ass family," Knox muttered.

Because she couldn't argue with his assessment, she nodded. "Truth."

He released a bark of laughter, but before he could say anything more, the door burst open to reveal a harried-looking Cian.

"Who's he and what's he doing in your bloody room?" Cian demanded barely shy of a bellow.

At the first sign of invasion, Knox had lifted his arms and drew electricity from the molecules around him. Blue sparks snapped and crackled between the fingers of his right hand as an energy ball rotated an inch above his palm.

Wanting nothing more than to prevent a bloodbath, Piper inserted herself between the men. "Please stand down, Knox."

"No."

"*Babe.*" Spring's endearment sounded more like a scold. She ducked under her husband's arm, rolled her eyes, and held out a hand. "You must be Cian. I feel like I already know you. I'm Spring Thorne… er, Carlyle." She shot a sheepish grin over her shoulder toward Knox. "You'd think after all this time I'd be used to my married name."

Knox extinguished the weaponized energy ball and postured by folding his arms across his chest, thereby making his sculpted biceps more intimidating—and mouth wateringly delicious. "Especially since you wrote Mrs. Knox Carlyle thousands of times in your diary growing up."

With an outraged cry and an elbow to her husband's stomach, Spring said, "It was an enchanted pen that got carried away."

They all shared a laugh at her blatant lie.

"Yep, this is my family," Piper gave Spring an affectionate smile, then turned her curious gaze to Cian. "Care to explain why you charged in here ready to maim someone?"

Red crept up his neck as he darted a look in Knox's direction. "I don't."

"You don't what?"

"Care to explain, and that's all I'm going to say about it."

His stubbornness was somewhat endearing, as was his obvious jealousy. Piper found it difficult to hold back her grin.

"Was the burly dude Russian?" Spring asked with wide-eyed delight.

Dumbfounded, Cian stared at her. Whether it was her off-the-wall question or because her cousin was jaw-droppingly beautiful, Piper couldn't say. But she tapped a finger under his chin to close his trap. "She's taken," she murmured. "By the guy who would fry you to a crisp and step over your smoldering bones if you look at her sideways."

Cian laughed. "I thought I made it clear to you earlier, I don't play in other men's houses, Piper me love."

Knox held out a hand. "In that case, I'm Knox Carlyle, and it's a pleasure to meet you."

Due to the cramped quarters, they took their tea and scones to the downstairs sitting room to discuss the reason for Spring's visit. Cian couldn't resist taking the spot next to Piper on the loveseat. She'd be gone soon, and the whirlwind of conflicting emotions caused by her imminent departure threatened his peace of mind; a small sense of relief mixed with a larger part of pure regret and a dash of what-if.

With one arm tucked along the back of the sofa, he settled in and stole a scone from Piper's plate, giving her a wink in the process. She returned his cheekiness with a warning look, but said nothing. He caved to the urge to grin as he bit the scone.

Cian didn't miss Knox's watchfulness or Spring's overly curious gaze darting between Piper and him. The husband-and-wife team seemed like an odd couple at first glance. Without a doubt, they were an indescribably beautiful couple. However, Knox remained quiet and on edge, while Spring was bubbly and accepting, seemingly ignorant of the possible dangers surrounding her. Cian had the feeling Knox was always in protector mode around his lively wife.

Spring leaned forward and focused all her attention on

Cian. "Your sister told me about Glencar Waterfall. She was confident the last ingredient we'd need would be in the surrounding woods. Do you know which waterfall she's talking about? Perhaps if you do, we can get an early start."

"Yeah. It's a bit of a drive, and I don't know the ingredient you might be missing, but I'll happily show you the way."

"It's a root, and I'll spell the area so I know it when I see it."

"As soon as we grab breakfast, I'll bring round the Rover."

Knox chuckled as the women exchanged amused glances.

Cian frowned. "What am I missing?"

"We can teleport, Cian," Piper explained with a soft smile. "No need to drive for hours."

"Sure, and you're right. I forgot it was an option." Of course, he didn't think of it since he never teleported without assistance. He felt like a complete arse.

Wordlessly, Piper placed a hand on his knee and squeezed.

His heart stuttered. Here she was, attempting to ease his embarrassment, and she had no reason to offer up anything but anger for the callous way he dismissed her overture last night. Giving in to the urge, he placed his hand over hers and entwined their fingers.

The other couple zeroed in on the gesture.

Suddenly, Cian wanted to squirm. Rarely did he find himself the object of speculative looks, and he didn't care for the attention. Breaking contact with Piper, he leaned forward to grab another scone off the table in front of him.

"How much of the potion do you need?" Piper's tone was subdued and serious.

Cian nearly winced. She hadn't missed him distancing himself from her. "A single batch can last us near to three months, but it stores well. If you could make a half-decade's worth, we wouldn't need to bother you again for a good long while."

. And he wouldn't have a reason to see Piper again.

He should request one batch instead of twenty so she was forced to come back.

Piper rose abruptly with a falsely bright smile. "Five-year's worth, it is." Without looking at him, she said, "Give me fifteen minutes to run up and grab a shower, then we can get going."

After she'd gone, the silence in the room about deafened Cian. Once again, he experienced the urge to squirm under Knox and Spring's scrutiny.

"I'll check with Bridget to see if she needs help with the clean-up. If you want anything heartier to eat than those few scones and tea, come to the table."

He bolted without waiting for a response.

"He doesn't realize he's in love with her," Knox said with a hard laugh.

"He's going to fight it every inch of the way," Spring replied with a sad shake of her head. "I've seen enough hardheaded men to call it."

"I take exception to that." Knox drew her to her feet and into his arms—exactly where she wanted to be.

With a wide grin and a caress of his chiseled jaw, Spring said, "If the shoe fits, babe."

His grunt was his answer. They both knew well his stubbornness and what it had cost them in the early stages of their relationship. However, not a day went by that Knox didn't make a point to show her how much he loved her.

"How do we help them?" she asked.

"We don't." He gave her a firm no-nonsense glare. "We aren't matchmakers, sweetheart. That's Alastair's gig if he chooses to involve himself."

"Piper deserves to be happy, and she's crazy about him."

"You can tell that after a few minutes?"

"An hour, and yes."

"This isn't going to end well if we get involved, Spring. It's for them to work out."

"Please?"

He groaned.

She grinned. "Is that a yes?"

"It's a 'we'll see.'"

"It's a yes," she said with conviction.

"As if I could deny you anything."

She snuggled into his chest and lifted her face, batting her eyelashes flirtatiously. "Because you love me."

"Because I love you," he agreed gruffly.

"Good. Now we need to find a way to get them lost in the woods together and keep them there until they work this shit out."

Knox threw back his head and released a hearty laugh. "I stand corrected. Alastair has stiff competition in the match-making department."

"I learned from the best."

"Mmhmm." He drew her tighter against him and lowered his mouth to hers. "You learned a lot from me, too, if I remember correctly."

"Hmm, speaking of..." She ran a palm over the bulge in his jeans. "We have at least fifteen minutes. We can pop home and return... *after*."

With a wolfish grin, Knox lifted her into his arms. "Hold on tight."

"Always."

As Piper dried off, she thought about Cian and how quick he was to shy away from any intimacy. She should probably tell him he didn't need to go with them to find the root, but if she only had today left to spend in his beguiling company, she'd take it. While in the shower, she'd come to a decision, and she intended to tell him tonight that she was all-in for a one-night stand. If these were all the memories she'd have of the man she was falling for, then she'd be happy for them. Life was too short to throw away the golden opportunities.

And, if the Goddess decided to bless their joining, maybe Piper could have that baby she wanted without the sperm bank. Cian never need know he fathered a child. She ignored the twinge of guilt about excluding him. He was the one who'd said he didn't want commitment or children, and Piper had more than enough money to ensure any offspring of hers would be well taken care of for life. Surrounded by the Thornes, her baby would always know love.

And she could never be underhanded that way.

A child deserved to know his or her *entire* family.

She exhaled a resigned breath as she pulled the shirt over her head. Decision made, she headed downstairs.

"Where did Spring and Knox scurry off to?" she asked GiGi as she sat down to breakfast.

"I didn't realize she was here. But knowing Knox, he's already whisked her back for a morning quickie."

Piper choked in the process of sipping her coffee.

Of course, not a hint of remorse could be found in GiGi's naughty grin.

"You live to shock, don't you?" Piper threw a triangle of dry toast at her, but her cousin magically deflected it with a casual flick of her finger.

"Not at all. I merely call it like I see it. There's no desire to shock."

"Bullshit," Ryker coughed into his hand, causing them all to laugh—too-blunt GiGi included.

"Cian tells me you're off to Glencar." Bridget placed a hand on Piper's shoulder as she refilled her coffee cup. "I can't thank you enough, Piper."

"Whatever it takes to keep your business afloat, I'm happy to do. You've got a great thing going here."

"You're a beautiful soul, and we were blessed the day you walked through our door."

A tight ball of sadness settled in Piper's throat. Why did she feel more at home here than she did anywhere else? Why were her feelings for Bridget close to that of a sibling after two days? It was embarrassing how much she wanted to be part of the O'Malley family, and how much she was going to miss them when she was gone.

Cian chose that moment to join them, and he paused inside the entry, catching Piper's eye. For a long moment, they were motionless, staring at each other. Locked like a tractor beam. The pull between them was surprisingly strong for such a short acquaintance.

Piper was the first to break the invisible hold. She met her cousin's concerned eyes and had to fight the urge to flee. GiGi saw everything. Saw that Piper was more than halfway to falling without it being reciprocated.

Stupid Thorne curse!

Insta-love sucked, especially when the other person wasn't on the same page or even in the same book. Hell, Cian wasn't in the same library.

He was unusually quiet through the meal, but Piper didn't have the energy required to probe into the why of it. Either he'd work through his demons or he wouldn't. She had her own to deal with.

"You don't have to go with us, Cian. We can find the falls with a map." Piper was afraid she'd already scared him off.

He put down his fork and lifted his coffee for a long sip. His brows were knitted together and it was a long time before he set aside his mug and spoke. "You're doing this for the benefit of my entire family. The least I can do is see you to your destination and search the woods alongside you, Piper."

She hated that he'd stopped using endearments, but she understood why. After a tight smile, she concentrated on her barely touched meal.

13

Chapter 13 has been omitted for superstitious purposes. The Unlucky O'Malleys have enough on their plate, don't you think?

14

Cian prayed they found what they were looking for at Glencar Falls. The alternative would be a disaster of epic proportions. Their specific brand of enchanted brew was what drew people back time and time again. They'd take a major financial hit if it was no longer available.

He covertly watched Piper discussing the planned trip with her relatives. She had an easy, carefree way about her. A stillness. Although she was naturally attractive, she had no need to be showy or try to capture the attention of every man present as Moira would've done. Piper exuded calm and appealed to him very much. He'd noticed it at the bar last night. She was friendly and efficient, working in sync with Ruairí and Sorcha with practiced ease. If Cian were being honest with himself, he'd be content to watch her forever.

And because this was an exceedingly bad idea, he turned away to talk to Bridget. "We should be back before the evening shift at the pub. I'll work it with Ruairí tonight if you'd prefer to have another day off."

Bridget studied him, then blew out a breath. "No, you've

been on every night for a month. It's only fair you have a night off to yourself as well. I'll make do with that fecker Ruairí."

She'd said it as if she were walking to the gallows and Cian had to laugh. "Give over, Bridg. He's a gift from the gods at the moment."

"He *thinks* he's a god's gift," she muttered as she scrubbed up the breakfast dishes with more force than necessary. Without glancing up, she said, "We've got more company coming."

Before he could ask her how she knew, Knox and Spring teleported into the courtyard behind the B&B. He stared at his sister in shock and registered the second she realized what she'd done.

"Cian, I *felt* them arrive."

"I felt the air snapping around us, too. This family must be right powerful to put off magic like that."

"I've been around every one of them before, and never have I experienced it." She stared up at him with something akin to wonder. "Is our magic returning, do you think?"

He twisted to view Piper. "She mentioned something last night about my light growing stronger. Asked me if I've ever *tried* to use magic."

"And have you?"

"No. I didn't see the point. I had the tools given to me by the Council. No need to call on abilities that don't exist and knock down our gaff in the process."

"Sure, and with our shite luck you would've," she agreed readily. They both knew how quickly magic could backfire in the hands of a novice. "But perhaps with the muscle in this room, we should try."

The idea made Cian somewhat giddy and disturbed him at the same time.

Magic.

What couldn't they do with the return of the O'Malleys'

power? Wouldn't it be grand to have their ill luck disappear, to be replaced by good fortune? Maybe then he could trust in love again. Yeah, to be lucky in love would fill his heart.

His gaze locked on Piper, and it was as if she sensed his interest, because she glanced over her shoulder. The impact those deep-honey eyes had on his system was immediate and forceful. The desire to sweep her up into his arms and cart her right to bed grew in intensity.

With great deliberation, she turned away.

He shoved aside the sudden wretched melancholy that gripped him, and focused on Ryker, who joined him after Cian caught his eye.

"What's up?"

"I'm no closer to finding out who sent Baran to kill me, and I'll admit to being worried about our excursion today."

"Just stick close to Piper. She'll protect you." Ryker grinned with glee and Cian never wanted to rearrange a face more.

"I'm capable of protecting myself, you scut." He rubbed the back of his neck as his attention tracked to Piper again. "I'm worried, man. I don't want her getting hurt because of my past."

"There will be six of us searching those woods; one of which has the power of a god. Knox is devoted to protecting Spring and, by extension, her family. Piper's as safe as she can be."

Cian kept his own counsel on the dangers the Thornes always seemed to attract because there were times when their luck seemed as faulty as the O'Malleys'.

"Why won't you take a chance on her, Cian? She's not Moira," Ryker said with an oddly gentle tone.

Irritation was instantaneous, and Cian glared at his long-time friend. "I know she's not Moira. She's ten times the woman that she-devil was." When he saw Ryker's compassion, Cian wanted to swear a blue streak. From across the room, the others were staring in their direction. He grimaced once he realized how loud his response must've been to draw their notice.

"I'm after apologizing. Moira's a sore subject."

"I get it, Cian, and I'll say no more."

The words Ryker left unsaid were ringing in Cian's ears.

"When we return from Glencar, I'd appreciate if you could see what you can discover for me about Baran. I'm right worried about my family. Carrick's had enough drama for a lifetime, and Bridget has her hands full with business. The twins are in New York and I doubt they'd be on anyone's radar, but I'll not take chances with their lives as defenseless as they are."

"Consider it done." Ryker's words were clipped with anger, but Cian knew the rough emotion wasn't directed at him. They both understood the vulnerability of having a family to care for.

THE WOODS BY GLENCAR FALLS CREATED A THICK CANOPY, thereby keeping the ground below in deep shadow. Magic haunted the woods and pulsed all around them. Cian could feel it tickling his skin and trying to touch a deeper part of him where the answering magic should reside.

"Here's an image of the root we need." Spring passed the picture around. "It's not a common one, and I intend to enchant the area so it can be found by us while we're in these woods. Once we're done, the spell should preserve the root in case we need more. I also intend to plant this in my garden at home as a backup."

"What are we looking for?" Piper asked as she passed the photo to Cian.

Spring squatted and slowly ran the tips of her fingers over a viny plant by her feet. A faint lime-green light flickered to life. "It will look like this and be located at the base of the trees. Exactly which ones, I don't know."

"Other than me, mortals won't be able to see it, then?" he asked.

Spring smiled and the world seemed like a better place. As certain as the sun rose in the sky each day, that woman had a powerful pure spirit.

"You're not mortal, Cian," she said in her melodic voice. "You're simply without abilities. For now. Breaking your curse is our next order of business."

"Good luck with that, *cailín*. No one's been able to reverse it for over two centuries."

"Because they're not me and they haven't solved the riddle Bridget told us about. But I will."

He grinned in the face of her confidence. "I believe you."

"Good. Now, there are six of us here and I need your help for this to work. Everyone join hands, please."

Cian leaned toward Piper and placed his lips by her ear. "Is she always this bossy?"

"Pfft. They all are. It's hell being part of this family some days."

Drawing back slightly, he studied her face.

She was serious!

She belonged to one of the greatest magical lines in existence and she was discontent?

"They all seem to care for you, darlin'. What's the real problem?"

"Sometimes I despise magic and being part of all this," she confessed, darting a look toward the others. "I want to live my life like a normal person without trouble attached to my name. There's no absence of drama with the Thornes, Cian. So I suppose it's a good thing you don't want any involvement." She gave him a bland smile and twisted slightly to clasp Ryker's hand on her opposite side.

"Cian?"

To his left, Spring waited to join hands. "Sorry."

She sent a barely perceptible chin tilt in Piper's direction. "You couldn't find a better mate if you looked the entire earth over," she murmured to him. "Think about it."

There was no more discussion after her comment. Or at least not for him.

He inhaled sharply as the wave of magic from the others connected and flooded his body. The sensation was heady and stomach churning at the same time. He worried his cells couldn't contain all the amped-up energy and that he'd spontaneously combust.

Piper tightened her fingers with a reassuring squeeze.

Sweat broke out along the length of his upper torso, his stomach cramped, and the loss of his breakfast was a distinct possibility. As the pain was at its worst, he wondered if the curse would kill him rather than allow magic to return to his cells.

The world around him became retina-searingly bright and crisp. All of his senses heightened, and the change made him wonder if all witches walked around with this intense awareness. Cian closed his eyes and only opened them when everyone released hands. He still clung to Piper's, though, and she didn't rush to pull away.

"What did you feel?" she asked.

"Nothing like ever before. The world around me is in sharper contrast. Is it normal?"

"I lost the use of my magic once. When it returned, I had a similar experience as yours. You'll get used to it after a while."

He frowned down at her. "Used to it? This won't go away after the enchantment is over?"

She shrugged. "No way of knowing. Could be your dormant magic woke up forever, or could be that it's all temporary, but I suspect you can do things you couldn't before."

"Like what?"

"The possibilities are endless, but let's try something simple." She called out to the waiting group. "Go ahead. We'll be along shortly."

"We should stick together, Piper," Ryker warned and circled his index finger to indicate the darkened forest around them. "It's not safe to separate."

"You're welcome to wait, but I'd like Cian to try conjuring. We won't be but a minute."

The others exchanged uneasy glances, but eventually wandered off.

"You can show me tonight, darlin', if the magic lasts that long. We should probably stay where it's safe with your family."

"No one knows we're here and five minutes won't hurt anything, Cian. Hold out your hand and visualize an apple forming. You should build it from the core outward. In your mind, picture the seeds, the core, the flesh, then the skin."

He stared at his palm and tried to will an apple into existence. Nothing but a few sparkly lights appeared.

"Again," Piper encouraged. "This time, close your eyes and concentrate on each individual element of the apple until you *feel* it growing."

Cian did as instructed and managed to produce a piece of fruit the size of a large grape. He grunted his dissatisfaction.

"Really, that's not bad," Piper said with a laugh. "For someone who's never done this, it's a good start. Toss that and try again."

Once more, he closed his eyes and focused on the task at hand. Visualizing a larger core with more seeds, he built the fleshy part of the apple in layers, finishing with a shiny ruby-red skin.

Piper's happy laugh prompted him to open his eyes.

He sucked in a breath at what he saw.

There, in the flat of his palm, was a perfect apple.

"Oh, Cian! You've done it! It's better than any fruit *I've* conjured." She flung herself at him, and he caught her with one arm, laughing incredulously along with her.

Over her shoulder, he stared at his creation with awe and a whole lot of pride. "I can't believe I did it. *This* is what true magic feels like?"

"Yes!" She pulled back to kiss him hard and fast. "Yes, you beautiful man! Yes!"

"You sound like I've proposed to ya, darlin'," he teased.

He cursed himself for a fool when her happiness disappeared and pink tinged her cheeks.

"I'm sorry. I guess I was just excited you were able to utilize magic for the first time on your own."

"No, Piper. I'm the one who's sorry. I'm an insensitive prick. 'Tis a fine moment we're sharin', and I thank you and your family for it." He presented the apple to her with a return kiss. His lips lingered, and he brushed his mouth across hers a second time. "You've given me the gift of magic, even if it is fleeting, and it's one I can never repay."

Her smile was so open and honest, his heart beat an irregular tattoo.

"I'm honored to have had a small part, Cian. Truly. Maybe we've broken the O'Malley curse without trying. Wouldn't that be awesome?"

"It would be grand, indeed."

The wind kicked up and whipped long strands of her unbound hair across her cheeks. With gentle fingers, he smoothed it back. Pausing, he held her captive within his grasp and lowered his head to hers. He couldn't stop himself from kissing her more fully. From tasting the unique strawberries and cream flavor that only her lips provided. Nor from shifting forward until the entire length of their torsos were touching.

Their kiss went on for what seemed like forever, but they were interrupted all too soon, and Cian was irate by the intrusion of so perfect a moment.

15

The ground rumbled beneath Piper's feet and she didn't know if it was Spring sending a message or whether an actual earthquake was in progress. Half drugged by Cian's kisses; she was slow to react. The earth shifted, and she clutched at him as her knees buckled. But he offered no stability and fell right alongside her as the ground parted, dumping them beneath layers of dirt. As she landed, her ribs connected with the pointy edge of an underground boulder, and she cried out when Cian's body slammed into hers.

The walls of the cavern where they found themselves entombed echoed his multitude of curses. "Are you hurt, love?"

Other than a garbled groan, she couldn't make a sound. The effort it took to produce that much was excruciating, and she couldn't quite catch her breath.

"Piper!"

The frantic demand required an answer but she couldn't respond with anything more than a small squeak.

"Piper, I need you to tell me you're all right. I can't see a bloody thing." His hands traveled over her head and scalp, feeling for injuries, before moving on to her neck and lower. "Where are you hurt?"

She cried out as his fingers probed her ribs, and he cursed again.

"All right, darlin', I'll go at this a little more gently, okay?"

He felt along her arms and legs, then returned to probe her ribs but with a feather-soft lightness that triggered her tears and gratefulness for his consideration. It hurt to inhale, and she couldn't manage a deep breath, but if she was careful, she could pant in short spurts without causing herself excessive pain.

"Conjure… fire… Cian. Flame… won't… hurt… you."

"Should I conjure a wooden torch just in case?" He sounded wary but determined.

"You… could."

Small flickers of teal light appeared to her left and through those glimpses, she saw the wooden handle of the torch in his fist. She wanted to smile and offer praise, but the sharp stab in her chest prevented anything other than complete stillness. Each attempt at an inhale felt like a hot poker to the chest.

"Fire, dammit!" he shouted.

Ignoring the agony shifting her body caused, she blindly reached in the general direction of his arm. "Try… again." With a quick push of her magic, she leant him what he needed, and the flame sputtered to life.

The light was enough for her to see his face and the wonder associated with creating something from nothing. Cian quickly dismissed his surprise and turned his worried gaze to her.

"Thanks for the assistance. Let's assess the damage, huh?"

With an economy of movement, she snapped her fingers to remove her shirt. The chill was immediate, and she shivered as the cool, damp air permeated her bones. Had she been in full health, she could've warmed herself with her abilities. As it was, she would be freezing in no time.

"Neat trick," he murmured as he propped the torch handle

against the rib-busting boulder. "Want to teach me how to heal you?"

"Can't… novice."

"Fecking hell." He lifted his face toward the opening, roughly two stories above them. "I suppose levitation is out."

She'd have snorted if she was capable, but her pain was too great and now spreading throughout her entire upper body. "Cian," she croaked. "Worse… get-ting… dizzy."

His countenance blanked but from what she could see of his eyes, they looked wild and on the verge of panic.

She closed hers. If he lost it, she might give in to the desire to freak out, too. Struggling to focus, she magically probed the area of her chest. If she had to guess, she'd say she'd broken at least two ribs, one of which had the tip impaled in her right lung. There was no way she had the concentration to move and mend the rib or save herself with a teleport. Even if she could, the landscape where they'd been standing was most likely altered now from the earthquake.

"Cian… go for… help."

He looked at her as if she'd lost her damned mind. "I can't leave you, Piper, even if I could climb out. Can't you zap us out of here?"

"Can't… teleport."

"I don't know how or I would in a hot second." Ragged and raw, his voice told her it was killing him not to be her hero.

Inhaling as deeply as she dared, she said, "Picture the… pathway by… the falls." She gulped air. "Ground beneath… feet." Sucking in another flimsy breath, she finished with, "What it… looked like… when… we arrived."

"I can't leave you alone."

The nagging fatigue got the best of her, and she succumbed with a small shiver and a shallow exhale.

• • •

CIAN KNELT BESIDE PIPER AND FELT FOR A PULSE. HER SKIN HAD quickly lost all color and currently resembled the palest parchment. Whipping off his coat, he covered her in an attempt to keep shock at bay. As clammy as her neck was, he figured he was too late. Waiting for rescue was no longer an option despite his violent objection to abandoning her down here to get help. If he didn't act soon, she'd die.

What had she said about teleporting? He struggled to recall word for word.

"Picture the pathway by the falls. Ground beneath feet. What it looked like when we arrived."

He'd just closed his lids when he heard the horrifying sound of continuous thunder. The ground grumbled and released another shudder. Eyes wide and straining, he searched for the source, but the shadows were too heavy and refused to reveal their secrets.

From above, loose dirt and handfuls of small stones rained down upon them. The knees of his jeans absorbed the first small trickle of frigid water. The second rippling wave soaked the material halfway up his thighs.

Left with no choice, he prayed to the gods that he wouldn't cause Piper more injury as he scooped her up. Right as he geared himself up to attempt a teleport, Knox appeared next to him. Cian wanted to weep like a wee babe, so strong was his relief.

"Keep a firm grip on her. I'm going to get you both out."

Before he could manage a nod, they were back at his home and strong arms were reaching to take Piper from him.

"You are going to get a horrible reputation and likely sign your death warrant with Alastair if you keep showing up with her unconscious like this," Ryker said as he helped lay Piper on the dining room table.

Ignoring him, Cian addressed GiGi. "She's having a rough go of it. If I had to guess, I'd say collapsed or punctured lung. I didn't find any other injuries when I examined her after the drop."

GiGi nodded as she held her hands in the air a few inches above Piper's chest. "Yes. Definitely her lungs." Sparks of purple-hued light traveled from her palms and were absorbed by Piper's body.

"Her lips are blue, sweetheart," Ryker warned with a sharp look at his wife. "Work quickly."

She gave a barely discernible nod.

Spring forcefully shoved Cian aside and took the place across from GiGi. "What do you want me to do, Aunt G?"

"I'm concentrating on her lungs. Do a magical scan of her body and check that we aren't missing anything."

As Cian anxiously observed, Spring used her hands to trace Piper's outline, and like GiGi, she didn't lay a finger on her, instead manipulating energy for a tool. When Spring reached Piper's feet, she gave a small shake of her head. "All clear. Just the ribs and lungs."

"As I thought," GiGi said grimly. "It's odd, though. It's like something or someone is trying to prevent me from healing her. I'm getting major resistance."

"What? Who the bloody hell would do that?" Cian snapped out the questions.

Ryker gripped Cian's shoulder. "Let's do a search of the area. You start upstairs and I'll take the property."

Knox stepped forward. "It'll be faster if I help."

"Want me to check the pub? I can see if Bridget's noticed anything out of the ordinary," Spring volunteered.

Her husband didn't look happy about letting her go off alone, but he gave her a tight smile. "Please be careful, Spring," he said roughly. Leaning in, he closed his eyes and kissed her temple, and in the simple gesture, Knox allowed them all to glimpse the depth of his love for her.

Cian experienced a thickening in his throat and he blinked,

amazed he could be moved to deep emotion by the witness of an innocent kiss. His gaze dropped to Piper, his throat thickened even more, making speech impossible. With a light stroke of his fingers along her midnight locks, he silently begged her not to die.

Wasting no more time, they spread out to search for whomever might be trying to harm her.

16

Twenty minutes later, they were all back in the dining room without any answers and no closer to finding the culprit.

"How is she?" Cian asked gruffly.

"Better," Bridget told him from a chair in the corner. "Carrick is minding the pub. Spring and I set up a protective barrier with Gran's crystals. The wards seem to be holding."

Cian tugged his sister to her feet and gave her a tight hug. He was exceedingly grateful for the affection and support of his family. Whenever the chips were down, they rallied around one another and made the world right again. Perhaps familial love was their true magic. "Thanks, Bridg."

Stepping to the table, Cian gazed down into Piper's pale face. Her color wasn't quite normal, but it was better than the ghostly gray when they'd first been rescued from the cave in. Her lips were no longer blue but the pretty petal pink they normally were.

GiGi had worked tirelessly, it seemed, utilizing her magic to heal Piper.

"I owe you a debt of gratitude I can't repay," he told her.

Her eyes were soft as she looked up from her task. "No. She's family."

"But she was targeted because of me."

"You don't know that, Cian." A deep frown settled between GiGi's perfectly groomed brows. "She's a Thorne, and our family comes with its own baggage."

"If you were being targeted, why would they try to prevent Piper from healing?" Ryker asked with a thoughtful look down at her still face. "You just met her this weekend, and other than Bridget's connection to GiGi through the coven, you have no ties to the Thorne family."

Cian couldn't argue with Ryker's logic, yet in his heart of hearts, he was convinced this was in some way connected to him.

As GiGi soldiered on with the healing, Cian stroked Piper's dirt-encrusted hair back from her forehead. "It's time for you to wake up, Piper me love. You've worried the lot of us, to be sure. With every second you delay; my life remains in peril from Alastair."

Her thick, dark lashes fluttered, but her lids stayed shut.

"I know you hear me, darlin'. Fight to return to us now."

Her eyes flickered back and forth behind her closed lids.

Unable not to, he ran a thumb lightly over her parted lips. "Come back to us, Piper," he commanded in a stern voice.

With a low moan, she opened her eyes. The color was muddied by her pain, and Cian's heart contracted. "There you are, my beautiful *cailín.*"

A tear trickled down to her hairline. "Hurts."

"I know, but GiGi is attemptin' to make it better. You need to work from the inside out to help her." He brushed her lips with his. "Pull strength from me if you need it, darlin', just heal for me now."

A shuddering sigh escaped her lips and her lids closed.

For a second, Cian's heart stopped until he realized she

hadn't passed out or died on him. He pressed his cheek to hers. "Don't be scaring me like that. This old heart can't take it," he murmured.

"Sorry." The whisper was barely audible, but he heard.

"No problem. Let's get you better." He clasped one of her hands in his and touched his nose to hers in a butterfly kiss. "I think it's all about the visualization of healthy lungs and cells, right? Let's do that together."

"Keep talking to her," GiGi ordered urgently. "It's working. I can feel the ribs knitting the way they should."

Relief so great, Cian closed his eyes and compressed his lips as he inhaled deeply. The tension left his body, and optimism replaced it. "Picture pink tissues and open airways, darlin'."

Within ten minutes, Piper was sitting up and breathing normally once again, much to everyone's relief.

"You had us worried, child." GiGi cupped Piper's cheek and kissed her forehead. "Please don't do that again."

"I'll try not to," Piper responded wryly. "Does anyone know what caused the cave in? Spring?"

"No, but I'd bet my favorite rare orchids it wasn't a natural occurrence," she replied.

"It wasn't." All eyes shifted to Knox. "I didn't say it earlier, but I felt malevolence in the air right before the earth shook. No one was in the area, though. If they were, my magical feelers couldn't find them."

"Do you think someone used a cloaking spell?" Spring asked.

"Don't know. It would've had to be unbreakable after what I threw at it. Who has that kind of power?"

"There's a spell in the Thorne grimoire to recall the past. What if we cast it to see if anyone entered the area around the time we did?" she suggested.

"It's worth a try. But first, you and I need to go reinforce that ground above the cavern so this can't happen to unsuspecting mortals."

"Ryker and I can cast." GiGi waved a hand in their direction. "You two go now. I'd feel awful if anyone else was hurt."

"Spring? Did you find the root for the elixir?" Piper asked, clearly concerned about the wrong thing, to Cian's way of thinking.

"Darlin', that doesn't matter right now."

Grim determination was stamped firmly on her face. "It *does*. We promised to recreate the elixir for your family, and a Thorne never goes back on a promise."

With a sigh of frustration, he glanced at Spring.

A small smile played on her lips as she watched the two of them. "We discovered it right before the earthquake. I know exactly where it is."

Bridget touched Cian's arm. "A word."

After they separated from the others, she spoke in a low tone. "Ruairí was sitting at the bar today, asking questions about Piper and who she might be. He recognized her light."

"So?"

"I may have told him you were at Glencar."

"May have or did?"

"Did."

Cian had known Ruairí since they were children, and he'd never detected any ill will from the man. Frustration whenever he looked Bridget's way, yeah, but never the standard spite and loathing between two feuding families. "Was anyone else present?"

"A few regulars, but Ruairí and I spoke outside their hearing."

"I can't see Ruairí hurting her, Bridg. What's the point?"

Her lips tightened and her expression grew stormy. "Maybe we aren't the only ones those conniving O'Connors are at war with."

"I'll speak with the Thornes and have Ryker investigate Ruairí. If we're speaking plain, I'm not convinced it's him, though. He loves you, Bridget. He'd never do anything to hurt you that way."

"But *you* weren't hurt, now, were you? So by association, neither was I."

"Does he know about the elixir? Did you confess to him we need it?"

"What do you take me for? *A brathadóir?*"

"No! But I've a mind not to let anyone know how close we are to losing our home," he retorted.

Her glare softened with understanding. "We won't, Cian. I've a back-up plan if need be."

"Good. Perhaps we won't need it."

As Piper observed the fierce conversation between the siblings from her spot across the room, she thought about the earthquake and Knox's claim it wasn't brought on by natural means. If, as she suspected, Cian blamed himself, he was wrong. This incident felt more like a personal attack on her.

She hadn't mentioned the feeling of her magic being suppressed, nor the pickling sensation along her ribs. Someone had been reversing GiGi's healing in real time. With each knit of the bone, it came undone. With each rejuvenation of a cell, it transitioned back to damaged. Even now, she could feel the attempt on her psyche from an outside source.

"How strong are the wards?" she inquired after Spring left. "Are you two positive no one can get through?"

Ryker's gaze sharpened. "Why? What are you thinking?"

"More like feeling. Am I right, child?" GiGi looked concerned and ready to do battle on Piper's behalf.

She never adored her cousin more.

"It's like a probe inside my brain," Piper confessed. "I'm fighting it, but a headache is forming for all my effort."

"I don't like this." GiGi wrapped a comforting arm around Piper's shoulders. "How do we protect her, babe?"

Ryker shook his head. "I don't know. I think it's time to call Alastair."

"No." Piper held up a hand to forestall the argument. "He's our last resort. The O'Malleys don't need him sweeping in here with his boatload of henchmen unless it's absolutely necessary. It could hurt their business."

"Piper, you are one of ours and someone is targeting you specifically." GiGi believed there was strength in numbers, and she wasn't wrong, but Piper didn't necessarily want to be inundated with family. They were all quick to drop what they were doing and arrive en masse.

"No, Cuz. I'll take care of this my way."

"What about your father?"

Her father was a good option. Formidable, laid back for the most part, and a bit of a pushover when it came to his daughter. Piper would have more freedom with him than with Alastair. Not that she needed to account to anyone, but her relatives could be stubborn fuckers when it came to protecting one another.

With a grimace and a nod, Piper agreed. "I hate to bother him, but maybe he's the best option. You all can't remain around me indefinitely."

"We can and we will if that's what it takes. But we'll find the culprit sooner rather than later," Ryker promised. "In the meantime, call your dad. I know Hoyt. He'll drop everything to be here."

"I don't know what happened to my phone," she said as a way of deflecting.

Cian happened to be returning to their side of the room and detoured to a side table to retrieve it. "Here you are, darlin'.

It took a bath when the cavern flooded, but Knox restored it to new for you."

"Great."

His expression turned questioning.

"I'm being coerced into calling my dad," she explained with a dark scowl. "Just what I want to do—not."

"Why?"

"She needs protection when Ryker and I return home to cast the spell," GiGi informed him. Hands on hips, she faced Piper and said, "It's Hoyt or Alastair. Take your pick."

Cian looked less thrilled than Piper, and she almost laughed. Both men would delight in cock-blocking the hell out of him, but she suspected he was chafing because he would feel the need to be the alpha of their little pack and his desire to protect was likely strong.

"If I've a vote, I'll use it for the magical muscle," Bridget said, then winced when her brother glared at her. "Cian, you're a brave and strong man, to be sure, but you've no magical abilities with which to fight."

Knees still weak, Piper climbed to her feet and placed a hand on his crossed arms. "As much as I hate to admit it, they're all correct. We need my dad here or I need to go home. Not only for my safety, but for your family's, too."

Cian trailed his fingers down her cheek. "Call him."

17

oyt Thorne arrived within the hour.

He was an imposing figure. Standing roughly six feet tall, he was built like an American football linebacker. His black scowl was mirrored by his daughter, and that's where the resemblance ended. Opposite to Piper's coloring, Hoyt was light blond with eyes the color of pale green jade.

"Who's he? Another vermin like the last one?" Hoyt growled. "What's he gotten you into?"

"Dad!" Scarlet with outrage, Piper stepped protectively in front of Cian. "It's not like that. The O'Malleys own this inn."

After a closer look, Cian decided Piper had indeed inherited Hoyt's stubborn jaw, and it was jutting out in her pique. He sidestepped her and held out a hand to her father. "Cian O'Malley, and this is my sister Bridget."

"O'Malley? As in the *Unlucky* O'Malleys?"

"Dad!"

"What? I was just dragged into the middle of a gol-dern mess, girl. You think I don't need to know all the *players*?"

The emphasis was on the last word, and Cian didn't miss

122

Hoyt's meaning. Instead of anger, he was highly amused by the dig. "Yeah. We've been considered unlucky since a thieving O'Connor stole something my family was tasked with protecting."

Hoyt grunted and sized him up before turning back to his daughter. "Gather your things. I'm taking you home."

"No."

"Pip, it's not open for debate. Your ma's worried."

Legs braced shoulder-width apart, Piper crossed her arms and lifted her determined chin a notch higher. "Dad, we have no way of knowing who the enemy is or what they're after. I can't leave Cian and Bridget unprotected."

Cian would swear he saw pride reflected in her father's eyes, but Hoyt quickly shuttered any emotion. "Fine. I'll stay. You go. I won't let anything happen to your friends."

Piper gave away her panicked thoughts the instant her gaze locked on Cian.

He gave a small shake of his head, but Hoyt was too observant.

"Not like that, huh? Crap on a cracker, Pip. An O'Malley? Really?"

Cian's ire rose. "And what's wrong with my family?"

"You're cursed, boy. She'll feel the brunt of it right along with you. She's already got a target on her back because of it, if I'm not mistaken." Hoyt's scathing look rankled.

The blood rushed to Cian's head and rushed back out. He felt lightheaded.

"Dad, stop it. You're being mean."

"No, Pip. I'm being truthful. He's got no magic to protect you the way you need protecting."

Piper's indignation crackled in the air around them, and she balled her fist on her hips as she confronted her father. "It's not his place to protect me. Even if we *were* to form a relationship, which we *aren't* because he doesn't... he..." Her hands dropped to her sides, and she looked like she was about to cry. "It's not his place," she finally managed.

Unable to bear another second of her upset, Cian put an arm around her shoulders and tucked her against his chest. One of her hot tears ran down his neck and into the V of his t-shirt. "I'd protect you with my last breath, darlin'. You need to know that," he told her softly.

She nodded and sniffled at the same time.

He glared at Hoyt, and when Piper's father shot him a sly smile, Cian's jaw became unhinged and about dropped to his chest.

Piper must've felt his sudden startled movement because she shifted to look at him. "What is it?"

He cupped the back of her head and studied every inch of her anxious but still lovely face. "Nothing," he told her softly.

Hoyt shifted closer and placed a hand on Piper's upper back. "I'm sorry, Pip. Your old man can be a bit of a butthole sometimes." He opened his arms and, after a slight hesitation, Piper abandoned Cian for her father's embrace.

He felt bereft.

Once again, Hoyt smiled at him, this time with an air of knowing, followed by a hint of compassion.

"It must be morning on your side of the pond," Bridget said, adding a tight conciliatory smile. "How about I warm up a plate of food and fill your belly to full? I'll provide a pot of coffee to wash it down."

"I reckon I'd like that, ma'am. Thank you."

If Hoyt had had a hat, he would've tipped it. Cian had traveled to America enough to differentiate between regions, and Hoyt Thorne's speech and mannerisms screamed Southern gentleman. Other than knowing the guy was Piper's father and she was somehow a cousin to Alastair, Cian wasn't certain how they were all related. One day soon he'd have Ryker clear it up or provide a cheat sheet since that family tree seemed to have bore a lot of fruit.

After Bridget left, only Cian and Piper remained with Hoyt. Cian was at a loss for words, which had never happened to him since the day he'd started speaking. Uncomfortable under the assessing stare from those eerie jade eyes, he decided Piper was safe enough with her father for the moment.

"I need to see to the pub."

He didn't miss her disbelieving look or Hoyt's wicked glee.

Leaning in, Cian placed his mouth next to the shell of Piper's ear. "The bravest soldier knows when to retreat, darlin'."

She snorted but didn't argue, and he was charmed by her all over again. After depositing an affectionate kiss on her cheek, Cian departed as fast as his legs could carry him.

Piper barely smothered her laugh at Cian's ridiculous comment as she watched his "retreat."

"I like him."

With a long-suffering sigh, she faced her father. "Me, too."

"I suspect your feelings are a lot stronger than mine," Hoyt said with a chuckle.

"Not that I'm ready to admit."

"Has Alastair checked him out yet?"

"The morning Cian played tour guide and then proceeded to throw a man off a cliff."

Her dad's brows shot up, and he cast another look at the empty doorway. "Huh. What was my wily cousin's opinion?"

"Same as yours, I imagine, or I'd have to fight tooth and nail to stay here," she said dryly.

"Not true. We decided long ago to give the next generation free rein." He drew her in for a hug. "But you can't expect us not to worry about you, Pip. And we might put the fear of the gods into the man you've chosen, if only to remind him who and what he's dealing with should he treat you poorly."

She smiled as she wrapped her arms around her father and squeezed. "I love you, Dad." Leaning back to give him a mock glare, she said, "But stay out of my relationships. I'll make my own mistakes, thank you very much."

"And is Cian O'Malley a mistake?"

"Not if he's able to love me." She shrugged. "Maybe even if he's not able. He's charming and makes me laugh. Probably what I need after the last fiasco."

"Unwise to dabble in an affair. You're halfway in love with him, Pip. I can see it in the way you look at him."

"That's my secret to hold and my decision to make, okay?"

"He knows you care," Hoyt said gently, giving her a final squeeze then releasing her.

Her heart contracted. "You've always said I'm an open book. I guess you're right."

He laughed. "I usually am."

"Pfft. Keep telling yourself that, old man."

"I imagine our hostess has finished preparing a meal for me. How about we go into the kitchen and you can fill me in on what's happened so far?"

"I'm a little tired. Do you mind if I take a nap?"

"Actually, I do, Pip." He gave her a regretful look. "You're not going to be out of my sight until we find out who has it in for you."

"Dad, I'll be fine now."

"Just let me grab the plate, and I'll see you safely to your room. Humor your old papa, okay?"

With a tired smile, she nodded.

"Want me to call Liz to sit with you instead?"

"No. You keep guard while I nap. You can conjure your favorite book on farming or something equally as boring."

"There's nothing boring about farming, girl! You take that back," Hoyt scolded with a laugh.

Arm in arm, they strolled into the kitchen. Wordlessly, Bridget removed the plate from the oven and placed it on the counter. With a sharp nod and shooing motion, she sent them on their way.

As Piper snuggled down into the comforter under her father's watchful eye, she smiled sleepily. It was nice having him around. He'd destroy anyone or anything to keep her safe without a second thought, and for this reason, she was able to rest without worry. Knowing she was cared for by family—even if she couldn't seem to find a man willing to risk his heart—made her feel that much more secure and, in some ways, content. Hoyt would be an incredible grandpa to her future child.

As Hoyt perched on the edge of the bed and gazed down at his daughter's peaceful expression, he sighed. He knew she'd never admit it before she was ready, but she'd fallen to the Thorne curse. They were all destined to only have one great love in life, regardless of the type of character their mate turned out to be. Hoyt had seen enough relationship disasters as a result of it.

Piper was in love with the Irishman. The gobsmacked expression was one he was familiar with. He'd witnessed it many times on those related to them. More than most, his big-hearted daughter had a difficult time concealing her feelings from those around her.

"Oh, Pip," he whispered. "I'd have chosen anyone else for you than any of the men you seem to prefer."

As if she'd heard him, Piper frowned.

With his thumb, Hoyt lightly stroked the spot between her

furrowed brows, just as he had when she was a small child. His little Pip had always been an over thinker.

"*Forget the troubles of the day. Let the sun shine on the hay, whenever wild little Pip goes out to play,*" he crooned in a low voice.

Instantly, her forehead smoothed and a soft smile curled her lips. "I love you, Dad," she murmured.

"I thought you were sleeping," he said, equally as quiet.

"Just about."

"Well, doze off already. Your old man is here to kick bad-guy butt if he bothers you."

She giggled as he intended.

"I love you, too, my little Pip."

"Not so little anymore, Dad."

"You'll always be my little girl. No amount of time or growing up will change that."

Her drowsy smile widened, and she peeked up at him. "I hope not. You're the best father a girl could have."

"And don't you forget it."

"It's why I want a baby," she said on a shuddering breath. "I want to shower her with love like you and mom did to me. Snuggle her in my lap and patiently read her favorite book for the hundredth time in a row. Be there to kiss her boo-boos and bandage her scraped knees." Piper toyed with his big, capable hands as she had since she was knee-high to a grasshopper. "Be her compass in a crazy world."

A wave of tenderness washed over Hoyt. A parent always hoped they raise their children right. Seems he did. "And you want your girl's pa to be Cian O'Malley?" he asked gently.

"I think I do," Piper confessed. "But I'm barking up the wrong tree, as you'd say. He doesn't want a relationship, Dad."

"The man I saw downstairs cares, Pip. He may not love you this soon, but he's on his way. Perhaps if you give him time to come to terms with hanging up his roaming ways, he might come around."

"I don't think he will." She looked uncertain, as if she had the urge to say more, but she remained silent.

"Might as well spit out what you're chewing on, girl. I can see it's something right important."

Piper scrunched up her face, then spoke in one rushed breath. "I thought about asking him to father my baby, the Goddess willing."

Because he'd sort of expected she'd say something along those lines, Hoyt didn't react as an outraged father might. "Couldn't hurt to ask, I suppose, but don't be disappointed if he says no. For all his so-called roguish ways, Cian strikes me as an old-fashioned guy. You've only to remove the rose-colored glasses you view him with to see it, Pip."

She frowned her question, and Hoyt was exasperated that the younger generations didn't seem to have the insight into the human mind that his generation did.

"He's the type of man who, once he told you he'd protect you with his last breath, would do just that. Only took me less than a New York minute to sum up that boy. He's all about his family and doing what's right." It pained Hoyt to admit it, but he said, "Cian's one of the good ones, Pip."

"I think my heart already knows that, Dad. It's like the clouds parted and a beam of sunshine lit him up the second I met him."

"Yeah, that's exactly how it was the moment I was introduced to your mother. Prettiest gal I ever did see. Still is, and you look just like her." Leaning down, he kissed Piper's forehead. Although he knew some men's hearts remained frozen against love and Hoyt hated to give her hope where it shouldn't exist, he couldn't resist saying, "Give your young man time, okay? He may surprise you."

Piper woke refreshed and as if she'd shaken the last of their mysterious attacker's spell. Perhaps she had, on some unconscious level. Magic worked wonders during a heavy sleep. Or it could be the wards and her father's continued presence were the real deterrents. Or maybe the guy got tired and moved on. Whatever the case, she was ready to face the remainder of the day.

She sat up and grinned when she noticed the book Hoyt was reading. "Planning to farm in Ireland, Dad?"

Without glancing up, he flipped the page and shrugged. "If you choose to live here, which I highly suspect will be the case moving forward, it would benefit me to learn what crops grow best. Your ma won't want to be too far from you."

"It's only a teleport away. And you have a lot of faith in my ability to change Cian's mind about love."

He peered over the edge of his book. "He'd be a gol-dern fool not to, Pip."

A more supportive father didn't exist. Tears burned the back of her lids. "I want what you and Mom have. Maybe that's why I've been such a failure in the romance department and so desperate to find that perfect person."

"The relationship between your mother and me isn't perfect. Far from it, in fact. But we made a promise to always try to see the other's perspective. We promised to calmly work through any issues as they pop up and never let the sun set on an argument."

"I know unconditional love is reserved for children, Dad. I get couples fight, but you're definitely a role model."

He gave a firm nod. "Just so you know. Life ain't going to be easy, Pip. We've all survived our share of troubles. The witches' wars taught us that. Danger is always lurking right around the corner for us Thornes, and you'd best stay on alert when you're here."

"I thought the wards were strengthened earlier today?"

"They were, and Spring sat with you as Knox and I tested them, but that don't mean you can let your guard down, you hear?"

"I understand."

"And if it takes using your abilities to kick some butt, then you do it, girl. You don't rely on physical strength and learned skills alone."

She couldn't stop her grin. This was her dad. The man whose stern looks and warnings were legendary in their family. The man who everyone believed was a mean old grizzly, when in fact, he was a teddy bear. All his life lessons and caution were from the root of a love so great, family was never in any doubt they were cared for.

"Promise," she said as she placed a hand over her heart.

"Good." He climbed to his feet and snapped his fingers. The book vanished into thin air and a mug of coffee replaced it. "I'm heading downstairs to see if that pretty boy of Spring's found anything worthwhile about the attack in the woods. You drink this coffee and come down when you're ready."

He left her with a quick kiss on the forehead and her favorite flavored latte. As she sat back against the headboard and sipped her drink, she savored the feeling of being well cared for.

Twenty minutes later, she headed downstairs and encountered Cian on the landing. He looked rested and alert. And good enough to eat.

"I see we both had the same idea to nap," she said with a grin.

"Yeah, and you're a sight for these sore eyes. It's happy I am to see you've recovered." He ran a hand through his damp hair. "I confess, you took years off my life, love."

"It may've taken years off my own, and my dad's to boot," she quipped. She touched his arm. "Thank you, Cian."

He appeared befuddled. "For what? I almost got you killed."

"*You* didn't. And I've no doubt you'd have found a way to rescue me from the cavern had Knox not come along."

"You give me too much credit, darlin'. I'd have tried, but I was near to losing my mind when you decided to take a nap back there."

The colorful way he painted her encounter with death caused a bubble of laughter. Leaning close she lowered her voice. "I'll tell you a secret; we Thornes, for all our enemies, are a lucky lot. Maybe it neutralizes your bad luck."

"Your mouth to the gods' ears." His gaze dropped to her mouth and grew heated. "Speaking of mouths..."

She met him halfway and opened to him. The kiss was delicious. A lazy exploration of a potential lover—her favorite kind. His body pressed hers against the wall, and Piper would've stayed where she was to make out with him all afternoon if the sound of a man clearing his throat hadn't penetrated her pleasurable haze.

With a girly sigh, she pushed Cian away much to both of their disappointment if his groan was a good indicator.

"I thought I'd have to throw a bucket of cold water on the two of you," GiGi said from her place beside Ryker. Using her hand, she fanned herself. "Or perhaps take a cold shower myself."

Piper laughed and moved to pass Cian, but he held her back to let Ryker and GiGi go by.

"We'll catch up," he said.

Ryker's lips twitched, but he didn't comment.

Once the others were gone, Cian tilted Piper's chin up and kissed her again. The degree of heat wasn't the inferno of the last one, but it was enough to warm her blood to boiling.

"I can put a meal together and we can head to the park behind the house, if you've a mind," he said huskily.

"Is it wise with the threat?"

"It's my family's land, and we'd be within sight of the house."

"Okay. But let's see what, if anything, Dad discovered first." She couldn't resist running a hand over the hard plane of his chest. "Then I'd be happy to share your meal, Cian O'Malley. You'd better make it good, though, because I'm starving."

"And isn't the question what are you starvin' for?"

She couldn't prevent her sultry smile, and she tweaked his nipple through his shirt. "Brownies make me happy."

He grunted and tucked her arm through his. "Sure, and I was hoping you'd have other appetites for me to satisfy."

As they entered the sitting room, all heads turned their way. Cian wasn't necessarily uncomfortable under all the curious stares, but he didn't exactly enjoy it either. After escorting Piper to a seat, he left to pour her a glass of wine and himself a four-fingered shot of whiskey.

Once he'd handed off her drink, he perched on the arm of her chair. "Please tell me you've uncovered our threat."

Their faces ranged from frustrated to angry and told Cian they hadn't discovered shite.

"Grand," he muttered and chugged his whiskey. "What's our next move?"

"Don't know," Ryker said. "But we can't have whoever this is going around creating earthquakes and making attempts on your life at every opportunity. Others are going to get caught in the crossfire."

"We still aren't positive of the target here," Cian reminded him.

Piper placed a hand on his thigh to gain his attention. "What if it's directed at both of us? Had anything strange happened before I arrived?"

"Other than our standard bad luck? Nah." He smiled down at her. "But to be sure, good fortune blessed me the day you walked into our pub, Piper me love."

She rolled her eyes and jabbed him in the side. "You're laying it on thick again, *Cian me love*. Your put-on accent gives you away every time."

He chuckled at being called out and didn't challenge her comment. "What has you questioning the time before your arrival? Do you think you were followed to Ireland?"

"Maybe." Her expression turned thoughtful, and she rose to her feet. "Be right back."

"Anyone else have a clue what she's talking about?" Ryker asked with a frown.

"I might, but I want to see how this plays out," GiGi replied with a mysterious smile. Her full-fledged grin was smug when Piper returned with the O'Malley grimoire.

The soft glow emanating from the cover increased in strength with each step she took in Cian's direction, and by the time she reached him, it was brighter than the noon-day sun.

Squinting against the glare, he accepted it when she passed it off to him. In his hands, the grimoire resembled a dusty old tome, no light to be seen.

"I don't understand," he confessed, fighting discomfiture at his lack of magical knowledge. "How are you able to turn this on?"

Ryker snorted behind him, then grunted.

Cian could only assume the man's mind took a side trip to naughty-ville and his wife gave him the express train ticket back to reality with an elbow to his ribs.

"Give it to GiGi, please," Piper instructed without acknowledging his question.

He complied and noted that although a slight shimmering appeared in the etchings, GiGi's touch didn't cause the same effect as Piper's.

"Pass the book around to all of you with magic," he urged, growing more curious about how the grimoire would respond to the others. "It's like it's alive," he murmured.

With the exception of Knox, whose god-like powers caused the design to flare bright for an instant then die out, the others only sparked the same response as GiGi.

"It's never woken up that I recall." Cian traced the pattern of the tree's roots on the cover after it was returned to Piper, watching as the heatless fire flared up from the engraved leather. "What is it about you?"

"*Us*, Cian. I believe it's responding to *us*. The first time I traced the pattern, like you're doing now, the response was similar to when I first entered with it. Of course, it lit, but not to this degree. It never flared as brightly, and it becomes more active the closer I am to you." She stared down at the illuminated cover, her expression thoughtful and a little awed.

"If this is like our family's grimoire, you should be able to ask and have it respond," Hoyt informed them.

Spring's head came up and her astonished expression

morphed into delight. "Of course! I'd forgotten about that neat little feature." Bubbling over with excitement, she stood, crossed to Piper, and wrapped an arm around her waist. "Ask it what you want to know. Ask it why it responds to you."

With a deep inhale, Piper met Cian's eyes. "Do you want to do the honors?"

Did he? His heart rate increased with each second he delayed answering. What would he do if the bloody thing portended some cataclysmic event because Piper had arrived and disrupted his world? Knowing he was being ridiculous, yet unable to help himself, he withdrew his hand. "No."

The grimoire went dark.

They all stared in bemusement.

"Think it ran out of battery juice?" GiGi asked dryly.

"I think Cian ran out of hope," Ryker replied in a soft, serious tone.

Cian lifted his head and glared. "Hope for what?"

"The second you shut down, so did the book."

He'd barely heard Ryker for the blood rushing to his head and the pulse pounding in his ears, but he managed.

"Tell me I'm wrong, man. Tell me you didn't back off from fear," Ryker demanded.

Cian's frantic gaze darted between Ryker, Piper, and the grimoire. "I can't."

"It's okay, Cian," Piper said. "We can try another time."

Her gentle understanding shamed him. This wasn't her problem. She could walk away and leave him to whatever enemy decided to darken his door. But there she stood—brave and beautiful—prepared to uncover whatever mischief might be written on the pages, and also ready to yield to his wishes on the matter should they not align with hers.

"This type of magic is new to you, son," Hoyt said, not unkindly. "No one can blame you for being skittish."

Cian wanted to rail at the man for suggesting he might be 'skittish' but couldn't, because Hoyt had spoken true.

With a muttered curse, Cian reached for the heavy tome and Piper's hand. "I'm certain we'll live to regret this, darlin', but if you're willin' so am I." The grimoire seemed happy with his decision and the illumination was more intense this time around. "At least this fecking thing is thrilled."

She laughed. "Do you think you can tone it down a bit before you sear our retinas?"

"I'm not—"

"I wasn't speaking to you."

The glow faded to a mere flicker, but an impatient one at that. If Cian didn't know better, he'd suspect the flashing was the grimoire's way of tapping its fingers.

With a deep breath and a silent prayer to the Goddess Anu, he asked, "What is it you wish to show us?"

The thick, ancient binding whipped back and the pages fluttered at a blinding pace, finally settling on a passage around the center of the book.

"I can't read it." Disappointment was heavy in her voice.

"It's Gaelic," he replied.

"What does it say?" Spring asked eagerly.

"It's the riddle." In the face of all the blank stares, he said, "It has to do with a family prophecy. I'd forgotten about it, because it never mattered to me."

"A riddle." GiGi looked intrigued as she settled into her husband's embrace. "Do tell. Let's see if we can solve it."

Cian silently read the passage three times. With each reading, he grew uneasy until his nerves were a proper mess.

"Cian?" Piper's soft voice held a question, and he knew he needed to answer, but he didn't know how to respond other than to speak the rhyme aloud.

"When the mighty Thorne pricks the heart of the Frozen, the end shall start in motion," he croaked out.

There was a collective gasp.

"The question is which *mighty Thorne*," Hoyt eventually said. "There's a whole heap of us."

"Right, but in dealing with the matters of the heart, I'm going to say the *mighty Thorne* in question is present and accounted for," Knox said with a short laugh and a pointed look at Piper.

Cian stared at her and she stared right back. Neither could break the pull of the other, and the sickening realization they were the ones referred to in the first line of the prophecy smacked them both at the same time.

"You're *the Frozen*, aren't you?" she said achingly, no real question in her tone. Tears shimmered in her horrified eyes. "Am I supposed to *stab* you?"

Ringing started in his ears and it felt as if darkness was clouding his vision.

Jaysus! What if she were?

What if his death was needed to kick-start his family's magic? Was he willing to be a sacrifice for a power they'd all lived without until now?

Hoyt changed positions with Spring and hugged Piper's shoulders. "I think you're taking this too literally, Pip." He lightly rubbed a hand up and down her arm, as if to warm her. "You might touch Cian's heart in another fundamental way."

Her terrified expression dissipated but she didn't appear any less thrilled as she nodded. "Good point, Dad."

"Is that the only line of the riddle?" Spring peered over the edge of the grimoire. "It looks like there's more."

Cian swallowed in an attempt to moisten his desert-dry throat. "There's more."

"Don't keep us waiting. There could be a clue to the first line," GiGi said with her standard impatience.

But Cian knew there wasn't. He dutifully read on. "*When the golden Son sacrifices for the One, only then can the curse be undone.*"

"I wonder who the *golden Son* is?" Spring murmured and gave him a curious glance. "I suspect *you* know, don't you?"

He did, or rather he suspected he did.

Aeden.

He was the only blond babe born to their family in the last two centuries. "I believe I do, but I've no idea who *the One* is."

"Another of your siblings?" Piper had lost her look of abject horror and seemed to be warming to the mystery of it all.

"Perhaps." Cian was aware he sounded cagey, but he suddenly felt his family should be present for this discussion. Talking to virtual strangers about an O'Malley prophecy was wrong.

Perceptive as ever, Piper lowered her voice to ask, "Do you want to stop until you've consulted with Bridget?"

Did he? The book opened for them for a reason where it hadn't before. Maybe these witches and warlocks were the real key to unlocking the O'Malley curse. Despite his inner conflict, he gave her a slight shake of his head and continued. "The final line: *When the Enemy at the Gate is welcomed by the Keeper of the Sword, all that is lost shall be restored.*"

No one had a response. They were all at a loss as to who their current enemy might be.

"Still want to picnic?" Piper asked.

He glanced up from the closed grimoire. All life was gone from it, and the cover locked him out once more. With a grimace and a shrug, he said, "I don't know how much of an appetite I have, but yes. The distraction would be welcome."

"I'll conjure the food if you can produce a basket."

Her expression was watchful, almost reserved, but Cian didn't care to break down her barriers at the moment. He wasn't quite certain how he felt about being considered *the Frozen* in the minds of those around him.

"That'll be grand," he said with a warm smile he didn't feel. "I'm off to put this fecking book away and grab what we need for our afternoon in the sunshine." Maybe the heat of the sun's rays would thaw the part of him that had turned cold and shriveled up when he saw the riddle.

"Cian, the more I think about it, the more I don't believe that—" Piper pointed to the grimoire. "—is meant to hurt you."

"But the truth is we don't know what it means, do we?" His tone was harsh, and she blinked her surprise. Mortified by his surliness, heat crept up his neck. "I'm sorry, darlin'. I suppose this is scrambling my brains a wee bit. It's like mushy eggs up there." He tapped his temple. "And it's got me in a mood."

"Don't stress it."

She touched his arm, and he fought hard not to pull away, but even harder not to tug her close. His conflict was great. "Be right back."

When he returned, he saw Piper had conjured enough food to feed their entire village. "You must think I've a bottomless stomach, love."

"It does look like a lot," she replied with a laugh and a doubtful look at all the dishes. "Okay, I absolutely went over-board. Maybe Bridget would like the leftovers to feed my family."

He grinned and wordlessly packed their meal.

After putting the picnic basket down on the agreed-upon grassy spot, Cian and Piper spread the flannel blanket and sat. They'd barely begun their meal when he asked her the question that had been plaguing him.

"Why has some smart man not put a ring on your finger?"

She paused in taking a bite of her sandwich and sighed. Had Cian not been watching her closely, he'd have missed her quicksilver frown and fleeting sadness.

"I make poor choices," she said simply.

It was his turn to frown. "How so?"

"I either pick emotionally unavailable men or cheating scumbags." She shrugged matter-of-factly and avoided his searching gaze. "I don't know what that says about me."

"It says the male population as a whole is dumber than a box of rocks." Himself included because he fell into the 'emo-tionally unavailable' category. But he doubted he could change. He'd seen the worst of the worst in his line of work, and he didn't have it in him to trust again. Inevitably, he'd be let down, and being disillusioned or abandoned by Piper would crush him.

"I disagree. There are good men in the world. I'm just not lucky enough to find one who wants me," she said softly as she swirled the wine in her glass and gave it her complete concentration.

Cian had no response. He knew all about bad luck, but hers wasn't a matter of that, or so he believed. Had he never met Moira, had he never been a spy, had Piper been the first woman he'd encountered in his life worth loving, he'd have been the first in line to court her. But he was too jaded for her. Too emotionally scarred. But he couldn't speak for the men in her past.

"I want a baby." Piper finally looked up and met his startled gaze. "By you."

Heart pounding and mouth dry, he could only stare.

"You won't have to commit to anything. Just the baby-making process. I'll do the rest. I'll raise and care for him or her," she rushed to add. "I promise they'll want for nothing."

"You intend to deny the child the love of a father?" Why his anger was brewing and why he was so outraged on behalf of a non-existent baby, he couldn't say, but he also couldn't dismiss the sudden image of a devilish little girl with black curls and laughing eyes.

"Well, no. I mean, maybe someday I'll meet a guy I want to spend my life with. I'm open to a relationship. But I..." She trailed off at his outraged sputtering.

"No other fucking man is going to be raising *my* daughter, to be sure!" He swallowed his wine in a single gulp and tossed his glass down on the ground. "It's outrageous to suggest such a thing! As if I'll let some plonker be there when she takes her first steps or cries for her da."

Piper flushed and looked away, but not before he saw her tears forming.

"Forget I asked," she choked out.

His heart was in overdrive and felt as if it intended to come right out through his skin. Although the day was cool, Cian began to sweat. The problem was that he'd never forget the picture-perfect toddler in his mind. Every time he would look at Piper, he'd imagine her belly swollen with his seed or a child's tiny arms reaching for him.

"I'll do it," he heard himself say. "But you'll marry me."

Her head whipped in his direction and he winced at the sound of the crack. She did, too, right before rubbing her neck. He repositioned himself so her back was to his front and worked the neck muscles with his thumbs in an effort to ease her discomfort—*and maybe so he could hide from her.*

"You don't love me, Cian, and I won't marry a man who won't give his complete heart to me."

Her voice had an achingly tired quality, as if it cost her to say no.

"I can't give it to any woman, Piper," he said in a low voice as he drew her back to rest against his chest. "But you have my admiration and respect. I promise to be a good husband to you."

"And our child? Will you not be able to love him or her?"

"What kind of question is that? Of course, I will."

"So you can offer love to our offspring but not me?"

His arms tightened around her. "Children don't set out to destroy a man."

He felt her sharp inhale, and he shifted, uncomfortable with what he revealed. Why he'd admitted such a thing was beyond his comprehension, and he wished the words back.

Seconds later, she relaxed within the circle of his embrace and rested her hands on his forearms. She stayed unusually silent, and together they listened to the stream gurgle and the wildlife around them go about their daily lives.

It seemed like hours later when she said, "I could never hurt you, Cian. I love you."

For the second time since they'd sat down, she'd stolen his wits. "Moira swore the same," he blurted.

"And because of one woman, you can't ever trust again?"

Piper's question was straight to the point and designed to make him question his long-held belief that love was a heartbreak waiting to happen.

"I don't know," he admitted. "She damaged a fundamental part of me." Until that moment, he couldn't admit it. But saying the words aloud sounded ridiculous. Had someone come to him whinging about their poor crushed heart, he'd have counseled them to move on and find another. He'd been unable to do the same. Perhaps he'd had one too many disappointments in life, or maybe he feared he wasn't strong enough to do it all again. Remaining carefree worked for him, and he wasn't ready to abandon a tried-and-true practice.

"I've always likened myself to a tree," Piper said as she continued absently stroking the hair on his forearm. "I bend with the wind. Become dormant for a while as I gather strength to start again. Allow my environment to shape me to a degree. But in the end, I'm determined to stand tall."

"You make a fine tree, darlin'." He drew her tighter to him and kissed her temple. "A fine tree, indeed." Chin on her shoulder and cheek tucked against hers, he said, "I wish I had half your strength."

"Maybe your dormant stage is a little longer than most," she suggested.

He couldn't miss the hopeful note in her voice.

"Don't pin your dreams on me, Piper. I've warned you once, I'm not a man to commit."

She pulled away and twisted to face him. "And yet you want me to marry you to give our child a father. What is that if not commitment?"

He stared at her, helplessly hopeless.

. . .

It wasn't difficult for Piper to see she'd disconcerted Cian. The blatant bewilderment on his face said as much. There was some, as yet, undefined emotion in his eyes as he thought over what she'd said, and she couldn't dismiss it. He *wanted* to believe, to love her, but he was terrified for reasons he refused to voice to either of them.

As she waited, the shutters fell into place and he lost his hopeful light. For one brief second, he seemed open to possibility. And just as quickly, it was gone.

She wanted to weep.

Turning away to hide her dismay, she said, "We should go back. The day turned overcast." She didn't admit the clouds were mostly influenced by her. That the dark mass rolling in represented her bitter disappointment and her regret for confessing her true feelings. Soon, the torrential rain would start and would probably continue until she found a way to shut off the pain of his rejection.

"If I could love anyone, it would be you, Piper Kelly Thorne."

His words were barely audible, but she heard them. They were another harsh blow despite the fact he was trying to ease her suffering.

"Thank you for that, I suppose," she replied, equally as low.

"What will you do now?"

With a surprising swiftness, rage consumed her. "What does it matter to you?" she snapped. "Do you want me to tell you I'll pine away? That I'll peruse sperm bank websites, looking for the perfect specimen to fertilize my eggs because you—" She choked off the rest of her accusation.

He didn't deserve her anger simply because he didn't want what she was offering. Any expectations were her own. She'd been the foolish one to blurt out her desire for a baby.

Piper hung her head. "I'm sorry. That was unfair."

His strong arms drew her against his solid, warm chest, and she fought the building sobs. "It's all right."

"I have to go," she choked out. "I have to go."

With no clear mind as to where to go but knowing she had to leave immediately or humiliate herself further, Piper teleported away. Strangely, she found herself in the field by the ruins Cian had taken her to on her first day in Ireland. She'd been reckless to use magic without first probing the area, but the chances of anyone knowing she'd come to this crumbling estate were small.

As she strolled through the dilapidated shell of a structure, she allowed her mind to imagine the lives of the people who'd lived here. She pictured a happy family, with children chasing each other through the hallways, as their parents looked on with indulgent smiles and warned of imminent disaster should they not slow down. In her mind, she and Cian were those parents and the children were rambunctious twins who spoke their own private language.

As soon as the little ones were out of sight, her lusty husband would press her to the wall as she laughed at his naughtiness. He'd steal kiss after kiss, and he'd cop a feel in all the right places that made her hot and bothered.

Drawing on her magic, she swirled her hands and painstakingly recreated each room as she envisioned it. All the years of suppressing her power, trying to be the normal one, was ignored as she reconstructed the exterior of the building, placing stone by stone and reinforcing them. She aged the rock walls with only a thought and the match was spot on.

Within a half hour, the place was as resplendent as she assumed it once might've been. Probably better, since she added modern touches, including indoor plumbing, electric, and stylish bathrooms fit for a princess.

She intended to buy this place. If she had to use an enchantment spell to influence the property owners, so be it.

This grand mansion would be her sanctuary when she needed to escape. Her test-tube babies would be raised here, and they'd run these fields in their bare feet with a puppy or three nipping at their heels. Love and joy would overflow their hearts as it overflowed hers whenever she watched them.

Piper might even ask her father for farming tips. Or maybe she'd raise a few horses. Her kids would go nuts for horses.

She stood in the middle of the lane and admired her handiwork with a smile of satisfaction for a job well done.

"Impressive."

A scream was ripped from her very soul, and she spun around with a hand on her heart. "Cian! What are you doing here?"

"I could ask you the same, darlin', but I can see what you've been up to." He nodded at the restored building with an expression of wonderment. "I'd no idea witches did things like this. I guess I assumed they hired out the work. Like I said, it's impressive."

"I'll return it to ruins before I leave."

"'Twould be a shame if you did." He approached and smiled down at her. "I'm betting the old girl has never been so grand."

She turned away from the admiration in his gaze, knowing it was only that, and would never be anything more.

"I couldn't help it," she confessed. "It was like all the magic I'd shunned all these years ganged up and possessed me. If I didn't do it, I'd probably have imploded." She shrugged. "What can I say? I adore this place."

"Talk to Bridget. She might sell it off since she's got no plans to restore it."

"Wait, *what?* This is O'Malley land?" She couldn't believe her ears. He'd taken her to his family's estate the first day without ever telling her the truth?

"Yeah. We were interrupted before I could give you the full

history." He grinned and urged her toward the front door. "Now *you* can give *me* the tour."

Her heart ached every single time she witnessed that wicked smile of his. He employed it so effortlessly with such devastating effect, all the while he was oblivious to the ravages his careless charm caused her.

"You go ahead. I…" What could she say? That she couldn't stand to be around him and not beg him to love her? How pathetic could one woman be?

Once again, she had the urge to run, but he caught her arm and drew her close. "It's all right, Piper. It's all going to be all right."

"I don't want your pity, Cian," she snapped as she struggled to pull free.

His arms tightened, and he heaved an exasperated sigh. "And you won't get it from me." He tilted up her chin and forced her to meet his steady stare. "I care about you and your wee battered feelings, Piper. I *do*," he insisted when she would've objected. "I'll do whatever is necessary to protect you, like I promised your da. That means against my own cold heart. And I'll give you your baby, if that's what you need. But I want you to think more on it. I want you to be okay with only that small part of me and nothing more before the point of no return."

She couldn't believe her ears. Cian had just offered her heart's deepest desire—minus his love. All without the insistence she marry him and remain in a one-sided relationship. To clarify, she asked, "With no stipulations? No marriage?"

His expression turned sour, but he nodded all the same. "No marriage. And should you meet the guy you want to spend your life with, I only ask that you introduce us. I'll need to judge the character of the man who'll be father to my child."

He sounded like he'd rather eat razor blades than meet any

future husband of hers, but she'd agree, because she needed a baby more than she needed her next breath of air.

"Now, show me your future home, darlin'. I can't wait to see what you did with the old place."

She pulled him back as he started to move away, and flung her arms around his neck. "Thank you, Cian."

"Well, like I said, you need to be sure. Talk to your da or to Liz. Weigh the pros and cons. O'Malleys are stubborn feckers with a powerful desire to fight the world. You'll be signing up for a headache of epic proportions with any child of mine."

She laughed, happier than she'd been in days. "Duly noted."

That night in the pub, as Cian played each of the songs in his set, his heart wasn't in it. His attention continued to stray to the door, but he doubted Piper would show after the emotionally charged conversations they'd shared that day.

Tonight, for the first time, dissatisfaction made him restless. Nothing had changed but the meeting of one sexy witch and a handful of her family. He told himself he was the same man he'd been a week ago. But essential parts of him had changed.

Knowing what he did of the O'Malley riddle, he wondered if he was resisting the inevitable. Had Piper already pricked the heart of *the Frozen*? Or did the line indicate and require more than any of them imagined?

During the first break, he headed to the bar. A few adventurous females worked hard to grab his notice, but he paid them no mind. His thoughts were consumed with Piper and the first part of the prophecy. More and more, he felt like he was fighting a losing battle.

"Why are ye in the dumps, Cian?" Seamus asked then took a long guzzle of his brew.

"I'm not," he snapped. "Mind your business."

"Got to be a woman," Ruairí said. As Bridget passed by, his morose gaze trailed her and he lifted his glass in a silent toast. "Only a woman can bring a man so low."

"What woman? The American?" Seamus grimaced. "Heard they were all evil and always out to break a poor man's heart. Most likely they want to bust his bollocks in the process."

"It's not the American," Cian growled the lie as he stomped around the end of the bar and poured himself a drink. Odd, how Seamus had pretty much quoted him without being privy to the conversation Cian had exchanged with Piper, her first morning at the inn.

"Sure, and you're going to be a surly sod and kick us out if we call you a fecking liar. But you are, Cian," Ruairí said with a snort.

"Leave off, Ruairí O'Connor." Bridget smacked him upside his head. "Or I'll throw you out myself."

"Bridg, I've a right to be powerful angry about the blow to my head, but since the blow you gave to my heart hurts more, I'll let this one go." He spun in his seat to face her. "But don't interfere with one broken man counselin' another. I've a mind to help Cian so he don't make the mistakes I did and suffer a lifetime for it."

As Cian watched in amazed horror, Bridget's eyes filled with tears.

"You're a fucking arse!" she shouted in Ruairí's face. "A complete and utter arse!"

The pub was silent for a full ten seconds after her departure, before finally returning to the normal roar of a crowd. Ruairí remained staring at the door long after Bridget's jaw-dropping exit.

"What did you do to her, man?" Cian asked him cautiously, not wanting to provoke another outburst from anyone.

After spinning back to face the bar, Ruairí shrugged. "I

asked Bridget to marry me sixteen years ago. Then I kissed another woman after she said no."

"That makes no sense. She can't be angry at you for moving on," Seamus sputtered. "She's touched in the head, to be sure."

"Seamus, get the fuck out of my pub."

The ginger-haired fool realized he'd stepped over the line with his comment the instant he got a good look at Cian's livid face. Seamus began to stammer. "I-I dinnit m-mean it the w-way it sounded… I… he… she… j-just commiserating, I am."

"Get out or I'll pound your face until not even your own mother recognizes you," Cian warned. He'd had enough of Seamus's toxic fun at everyone else's expense. "And don't return until you can keep a civil tongue in your head, you arse."

Seamus dug for his wallet, but Cian pointed toward the door. "Just go. You can settle up with Bridget, if she's willing to let you back in. Mind, you'd better have an apology to serve up when you *do* return."

With a brisk nod and a resentful glare, Seamus weaved toward the door. When he'd reached the exit, he cast one last long look at them.

Cian flipped him off.

"I suppose you want me to leave, too?" Ruairí asked then drained his drink.

"Nah. You need to don an apron and take over Bridget's shift. I imagine it'll be a while to cool that fiery temper of hers." Cian dumped Seamus's abandoned beer mug into the sink and wiped the counter.

"I'm sorry."

"It's all good, O'Connor. I suspect I don't know the half of it. You confirmed what I'd long since wondered."

"I still love her, but to Bridget, I'm the enemy at the gate."

Cian fumbled the glass he'd been in the process of picking up. "*What?*"

"I said I still love her."

"No, the *other* part."

"To her, I'm the enemy at the gate?" Rauirí repeated uncertainly and seemingly confused. "What's that to do with anything?"

"You brilliant bastard!" Cian sandwiched his friend's head between his hands and kissed him hard, full on the lips. "You bloody, bloody brilliant bastard!"

With a scowl and a hard swipe of his mouth, Rauirí glared. "The entire village is going to think I threw over Bridget to toss you, you prick."

Cian grinned. "Want another smack on the lips to drive it home?"

Rauirí laughed and shoved him. "Feck off. And you can tell me why I'm so smart after you go take care of what's making you dance." He shot a look around and gave a nod in the direction of Sorcha, who was hanging with her friends. "It's slowed down enough for one bartender, and I can have Sorcha man the tables and the wash up. Go on with you."

"You're a good friend to our family, Ruairí. Even if Bridget can't see it and I forget to tell you when it merits."

"Yeah, yeah, yeah. Get. I have to convince the pub we didn't just escape the closet we were hiding in."

Cian laughed and bolted for the door.

From the shadows outside the window, the real enemy watched. He noted the second Cian's attitude changed as whatever Ruairí O'Connor said hit home. Cian jogged toward the exit, and his laughing mouth settled into a wide smile. An air of hope and expectation hung around him.

Fear clawed the enemy's guts.

If the O'Malleys fulfilled the prophecy, then he was buggered.

Resolve firmed his spine.

He'd had no trouble hiding his dastardly deeds until now, and he'd no reason to believe he wouldn't get away with it for good. No one suspected the mastermind behind the horrific incidents surrounding the O'Malleys in the past, and they never would. *He* knew how to play a part and wouldn't let them figure it out. All he needed was to tweak his latest plan from chasing away the B&B residents to permanently doing away with them—or rather, *one* in particular.

It was time for Cian and his family to suffer another stroke of bad luck.

Piper Thorne needed to disappear. And soon.

Then he could report back to Ronan with news of his success.

"What are ya doing out here?" came a low, hoarse voice from behind her.

Piper wasn't too surprised by the fact someone had discovered her outside under the moonlight, her entire family was on high alert. But she was disconcerted by the age of her visitor. He turned out to be a small blond-haired boy who looked far too thin for any child. Even though he was fair in color, he had the look of an O'Malley. Maybe it was the stubborn chin and suspicious forest-green eyes.

"Recharging my batteries," she replied in a voice as quiet as his had been. "What about you?"

"Rechargin' me bat'ries." He barely managed to get the words out, but she understood him.

She smiled at him and patted the wet grass beside her. She didn't mind having a damp seat for a bit, not when she could snap her fingers and dry her clothes. The occasional indulgence in magic wasn't wrong. It was like having a cheat meal on a diet. And since coming to Ireland, she felt more comfortable with her abilities.

"Do you recharge under the full moon often?" she asked curiously as he sat down.

He shook his head.

She wasn't an empath like her cousin Alastair, but she didn't need to be to read how wounded this young boy was. It hurt her heart to think he was struggling. No kid should have to deal with trauma so young in life. And he had. It was the only reason the child wasn't in his bed dreaming of toys and treats instead of out here, wearing a haggard look of someone ten times his age.

Turning her face up to the light of the moon, she inhaled the cool night air.

He mimicked her action, and Piper fought a smile.

"It's healing, isn't it?"

"What?" he asked. His little voice sounded rusty to her ears.

"Mother Earth. Mr. Moon."

"Yeah."

But he hadn't sounded certain, and her heart ached for him. Because he didn't know her, she didn't have the right to question why he was truly out here and awake this time of night. She simply allowed him his own space.

"Why do ya need t' heal?"

She looked down at him to find him watching her with wide, haunted eyes. Her heart melted on the spot and she instantly tumbled headlong for another O'Malley male. *This* one she wanted to bundle up and keep forever so she could protect him from all the world's evils.

"I'm in love with the wrong man." She shrugged a shoulder matter-of-factly.

"Who?"

"Doesn't matter."

"Does if he beats ya. Does he beat ya?" He sounded angry on her behalf, and again, Piper fought a smile.

"No. As far as I know, he's a great guy."

"No' so grand if he don't love ya back. He's a bloody eejit."

Ah, out of the mouths of babes.

"Hmm. You may be right. He must be an eejit."

The boy gave one decisive nod, then reached out his tiny hand to nestle into hers.

Piper's heart stuttered, and the sudden urge to cry overwhelmed her. She gave his hand a light squeeze. "Thank you."

"Yeah."

Her lips twitched again but only after he turned his face up to the moon and closed his eyes.

A deep voice cut through the night. "Aeden?"

The boy jerked his hand away from hers as if burned, and folded in on himself, causing Piper's mama-bear instinct to surge to the forefront. She wrapped an arm around his shoulders and twisted to face Cian.

"What are you doing out here with my nephew?" He didn't sound accusatory, merely curious. His look was somewhat awed.

"Nephew?" She'd assumed he was an O'Malley, but she hadn't quite figured out who he belonged to. She hadn't gotten far enough in her acquaintances with Cian or Bridget to delve into their personal lives. "He's Bridget's son?"

"No. Carrick's."

He plopped down on the other side of Aeden and gazed up at the moon. He inhaled deeply. "It's healing, isn't it?"

She smiled until it occurred to her, he'd heard her conversation with his nephew. Now, mortification swept through her, lighting her face on fire.

Thank the Goddess for the darkness.

"Yes," she replied tightly.

Within her embrace, she felt Aeden shift to look up at her. The clear question in his eyes made her nod. Leaning close enough for only him to hear, she whispered, "Yes, Cian's the eejit."

The tiny hint of a smile was her reward. Although he didn't return her hug, Aeden shifted closer and rested his cheek against her breast.

She caught Cian's amused look. "Lucky kid. He might be breaking the O'Malleys' unlucky spell."

"Pervert," she mouthed over the small blond head.

Cian looked oddly happy when he winked, closed his lids, and turned his face back up to the moon.

Aeden shifted to stare at his uncle.

"We all need healing on the rare night," Cian said without opening his eyes.

The boy drew back slightly and checked Piper's reaction. She smiled as she leaned back on her hands and repeated Cian's pose.

Aeden seemed to grasp no one was going to demand answers as to why he was outside rather than in his bed. From the corner of her eye, Piper witnessed him mimic her. Her smile widened.

The three of them sat in silence for about five minutes. Then, without warning, Aeden rose to his feet and flung his arms around her neck.

She hugged him tightly and rubbed his back, barely managing to avoid a wince at the initial feel of his ribs and knobby spine. He hurried away, and she stood to watch as he ran through the gate opening and rushed into his home next door.

"Thank you," Cian said gruffly from beside her.

She tore her gaze from the closed side-door and turned it to him. "Whatever for?"

"For being kind to Aeden when he needs it the most. For not sending him away after he disturbed your peace."

"He's adorable. Why doesn't he speak to you?"

"Noticed that, did you?"

"Yes. It was as if he was trying to hide. Why does he fear you?"

"Not me. The world."

She stayed silent for him to elaborate.

He proceeded to tell her the tale. "My brother's wife died in an accident. Aeden happened to be trapped with her dead body and that of his near-fatally wounded aunt for nigh on two hours. He stopped speaking to anyone but his da, and he suffers night terrors."

Piper sucked in a pained breath. "Poor tyke."

"Yeah."

"Is this the incident that happened eight months ago?" At his nod, she asked, "How old is Aeden?"

"Just turned seven."

"Do you want me to discuss his case with GiGi? She might be able to help him."

"That's Carrick's call, but I'll pass on the offer to him."

She nodded and turned her face toward the moon a final time.

CIAN WATCHED PIPER. HE'D HEARD HER TELL AEDEN HER reasons for the healing, and his heart had swelled with the glory of it. He was getting used to the idea of them as a couple, and he didn't dislike it.

The moon's rays caressed her face like that of a lover, and he'd never seen a more incredible sight.

"Gods you're beautiful," he said in a thick, husky voice, unable to help himself.

Her tone was dry when she said, "Everyone's attractive in the moonlight, Cian."

"Not as attractive as you, love."

She stilled. Two feet separated them, but it might as well have been two kilometres. Piper would remain on guard against him because she wasn't the type to dally, despite what she'd offered.

"Thank you," she finally replied. After sitting and drawing her knees up to her chest, she acknowledged him with a look when he sat down beside her. "What brought you out here tonight?"

"Couldn't sleep. The woman I'm craving isn't in my bed."

"We have the rest of tonight," she said in a voice so quiet, he almost didn't hear.

His lungs seized and desire shot to his groin. He wanted her as he'd never wanted another. Not even Moira. Maybe it was Piper's kindness toward Aeden. Maybe it was his new ability to discern how different she truly was, but he finally recognized the truth: he loved her.

Although his stomach was a bundle of knots, he drummed up the courage to tell her. "Piper—"

His confession was aborted by the sight of a shadowy figure lurking along the fence line between the inn and Carrick's house. "Stay here."

Jumping up, Cian hugged the darkness under the trees and crept toward the gate. He was happy his brother kept the hinges well-oiled as he soundlessly moved through the opening. Two feet away from the intruder, recognition struck.

"Meghan?" Cian was flummoxed as to why Carrick's sister-in-law would be skulking around his place. "What are you doing here at this hour?"

She let out a meep and spun to fully face him with a hand on her heart. "Cian! You near caused my heart to fail."

"I asked you a question, Meg. What are you doing here?" His tone was steely, but then again, he'd never cared for the woman. She was as sneaky and underhanded as they came, and he'd seen her lust when she looked at her sister's husband, not caring who noticed.

She squared her shoulders. "I was checking on Aeden. I know he wanders at night."

"And just how do you know that?" Cian demanded. "Have you been spying on him?"

"No… yes… but not the way it seems." She sounded tentative and not at all like the crafty woman he knew her to be.

"Why don't you explain to me how it is?"

She cast a nervous glance at Carrick's house, as if she hoped for rescue, but Cian knew his brother would never serve up the help Meghan desired. Carrick detested the woman as much as the rest of them.

"Since the accident, since the loss of his mother, Aeden has been getting worse."

"Tell me something I don't already know, why don't ya," he snapped.

"Shh. You'll wake Carrick," she scolded with a dark frown.

She winced and touched her scarred cheek as if the change in expression hurt. Perhaps it did. The angry mark had been a devastating blow to her legendary beauty; blinding one eye to the point the iris was leeched of color and her pupil was cloudy. The scar dragged down the entire right side of her face.

"And you don't want him to realize you're stalking his family?"

"Yes… *no!* I'm not stalking…" She trailed off, and she must've realized she had no effective way to convince Cian differently. He'd caught her in the act. "All isn't as it appears, Cian," she said. The pain in her voice almost convinced him of her sincerity, but he'd dealt with lying women in the past.

"Get you gone, Meghan, and don't let me find you here again."

"Cian—"

"No!" He said harshly. "I'll not accept excuses and lies. Stay away from Aeden. He doesn't need your toxicity."

"What's going on out here?"

Cian and Meghan hadn't heard Carrick open the door, and as a result, he startled them both. Cian was the first to recover and shot Meghan a furious glare. "I found her skulking about."

"R—uh, Meg?" Carrick didn't sound as mad as Cian would've expected, nor did he look as angry. Instead, his brother's eyes darkened with confusion, hunger, and something that appeared remarkably like love.

Cian's heart beat faster. It would be difficult to dig out Meg's claws once she got them into Carrick.

"Carrick, I..." She shrugged and looked at him with mute appeal.

The unspoken apology in Meghan's voice surprised Cian, and he didn't quite know how to react to this softer side of her. He'd only ever seen the gorgeous but spiteful woman who'd gotten what she deserved; a savage, ugly mark on the outside to mirror what was in her nasty heart.

As Carrick and Meghan stared at one another, their unspoken communication bothered Cian. When he had his brother alone again, he intended to beat some sense into him. No way would he allow Carrick to fall under this evil hag's spell.

"Go away, Meg," Cian ordered with a warning edge.

Carrick glared at him. "Stay out of it, Cian. It's none of your concern."

Shock caused Cian to take a step back. The fury radiating from his brother disconcerted him. "Carrick—"

"I mean it. You don't have a clue what's going on, and I'll thank you to stay out of my personal life."

"You'd let this minger into your life—into Aeden's life—knowing she's the reason Roisin is dead?" Cian's voice shook with his disbelief and rage. Like the rest of the family, Roisin's death had hit him hard. The polar opposite of Meghan, Roisin brought light and laughter with her wherever she went. "Are you mad, man?"

Carrick surged forward, fists at the ready.

Meghan stepped between them and placed a hand on Carrick's chest over the area of his heart. "Don't. He doesn't know, Carrick."

"Know what?" Cian demanded, mindful of the fact Piper had joined them. "Tell me, Meghan, what don't I know? Have you been carrying on an affair? How long has this been going on? Before Roisin's death?"

Pain and frustration crowded Carrick's visage and his lips tightened as he met Meghan's wary gaze.

"You made me promise," Cian heard Meghan whisper. "You'd best be sticking to it, too."

"Promised what?" Cian snapped. "What is going on?"

With a choked sob, Meghan turned on her heel and fled into the darkness.

Carrick's tortured gaze strained to see her even as the black night shielded her from view. Finally, he released a shuddering sigh and faced Cian, casting Piper only a cursory glance. "Stay out of my business, brother, and go home."

"I can't do that, Brother. I'll not let you make the same mistake I made with Moira."

Cian heard Piper's sharp intake of air and his heart beat extra hard. Whatever they'd started, whatever he'd been about to confess to her earlier would have to wait. The moment was ruined by ugliness and bitter memories.

"What was that about, Cian?" Piper asked quietly as they walked toward the back of the inn. It had hurt her to hear his nastiness in respect to Meghan and Moira, and Piper wondered if he held a poor opinion of all women in general.

"It's not for you to worry about," he replied in a low, angry voice.

Her disappointment was keen. Part of her had hoped he trusted her enough to let her in, but he'd confirmed he didn't. Nor would he ever. "Fine. I'll leave you to it. Good night."

As she picked up her pace, he ran to catch up, grabbing her arm to swing her back around.

"I'm sorry, Piper. It's not you that has me salty." The apology was heavy in his tone, and his expression held regret. "That woman is poison to everyone and everything she comes in contact with. I'd not have her taint your world in addition to ours."

Understanding for his bad behavior came. Piper wouldn't completely excuse it, but she could forgive. Feeling the need to warn him, she touched the hand still holding her arm. "She's a powerful witch, Cian. Be careful of her. If she's truly as awful as you suggest, you'll be defenseless against her magic."

"You think she's enchanted my brother?" he asked, as if the thought just occurred to him. He shot a worried glance toward Carrick's house.

"It's possible. He appeared taken with her—and very much in love."

A sickly expression passed over Cian's face. "How do we break her hold on him? Can you help me? I'll not have that foul bitch dig her claws into him."

"Of course, I'll help." She pressed her palm to his worried face and drew his attention back to her. "We'll protect your brother and Aeden from her. I promise."

His relief was palpable, and he enfolded her in a crushing embrace. "Thank you."

She rubbed his back in soothing circles, noting the slight tremble of his muscles. Whatever and whoever Meghan was, she scared Cian, and Piper would kill the woman herself before she allowed her to hurt him or his family. Especially Aeden.

"Will you tell me the story?" Piper didn't want to be pushy, but she needed background on the situation if she intended to help.

"Come. It's getting chilly, and this requires a drink and the comfort of a fire."

She followed him into the house, shooting one last look over her shoulder. She couldn't shake the feeling someone was watching from the shadows. After Cian had left her to confront Meghan, the sensation of another presence struck her, and it hadn't abated.

Was Meghan's evil reach all-consuming? Did it stretch like tentacles, able to wrap around everyone and everything, to spread poison, like Cian suggested?

"Do you think she's *the Enemy at the Gate*, like in the prophecy?" Piper asked, as she accepted the glass of wine he handed her.

"Nah. I think that's Ruairí, based on something he said tonight. I'd not had a chance to talk about it before now, but he said it plain while we were tending bar."

"What was it?"

"He was waxing on about his feelings for my sister. His exact words were, 'I still love her, but to Bridget, I'm the enemy at the gate.'" Cian shook his head in wonder. "I don't know how I didn't figure it out before. Bridget should be the rightful *Keeper of the Sword*, as she's the eldest O'Malley."

"Right! *When the Enemy at the Gate is welcomed by the Keeper of the Sword, all that is lost shall be restored.*" Piper's excitement made her squeal and she flung her free arm around his neck. "You brilliant, brilliant man!"

Cian laughed and pressed a light kiss to her mouth. "I said much the same to Ruairí."

"Bridget needs to accept and forgive him."

Some of Cian's joy fled from his face. "It will be snowing in hell when that happens. I suppose we'll never be blessed with our rightful magic."

"Miracles happen every day. Don't give up hope, Cian."

"Oh, I'll never give up hope, love."

The twinkle in his eye and the devilish smile on his tempting mouth sent a rush of warmth through her. She fought the urge to fan herself.

With his gaze locked on her mouth, Cian stepped closer, took her glass, and placed it on a nearby table without looking away from her. "We should start on that baby," he said huskily.

A thrill electrified her nerve endings and she shivered. Now that the moment was at hand for them to make love, Piper experienced misgivings. Oh, not because she didn't want him —*she absolutely did!*—but because his hunger was raw, bold, and it caused her stomach to summersault. She'd never felt a desire so fierce, and it frightened her.

"Cian—"

He didn't give her time to think. He captured her mouth. Any objections she had melted under the heat of his touch. She moaned and pressed closer as she wrapped her arms around his neck and tangled her fingers into his thick mane of hair.

His kiss made her burn, but not as much as his touch when his hands skimmed her naked skin under her sweater and cupped her breasts through her lace bra. Or as much as the length of the erection pressed against her belly. She dropped her head back with a breathy sigh, and he rained little bites along the column of her exposed throat. Piper moaned his name when he tasted the V between her neck and shoulder.

An arctic blast of cold hit them, and she sucked in a breath so sharply, she coughed.

"What the hell?" he cried out, releasing her to face the direction of the attack.

Piper's father lounged in the doorway, blatantly unapologetic.

"It was getting hot in here," he remarked as he straightened. "I thought you wouldn't want a witness to your... *activities.*"

Piper wished for another shock of cold air as her face flamed.

Cian surprised her when he laughed. "I'm grateful for the interruption. I'd hate to be found bare assed and immersed in *activity* here in the public room. It might embarrass my darling Piper, to be sure."

If her face could get any redder, Piper was positive it did, although she must be as scarlet as a tomato. "I hate you both so much right now," she muttered and shoved Cian's back.

He laughed again as he wrapped an arm around her waist and pulled her against him for a quick kiss. His sparkling eyes gleamed in the low light as he said, "No, you don't. Not even a little bit. You adore me as much as I adore you."

She stared; not quite certain she'd heard him properly.

"We'll have a conversation to that end soon enough, Piper me love. But in the meantime, we need to get back to the subject of Meghan and protecting my brother's family." Cian's hot gaze dropped to Piper's mouth and he exhaled a frustrated sigh. "You have the power to make me forget my own name, darlin'."

She didn't confess he'd done the same to her.

And he thought he held no magic!

Pfft! The dampness and ache between her thighs begged to differ.

"Right," she replied, albeit a little breathlessly. "We need to guard against that wench."

"What wench?" Hoyt asked as he strode farther into the room. "What did I miss tonight?"

"Carrick's sister-in-law isn't a very nice person, Dad. Cian believes she's out to cause trouble, and I wonder if she isn't the one who has kept us distracted with the cave in and other things so she could work her wiles on Cian's brother."

Cian wore a dumbfounded expression. "How did I not think she might be the one behind our troubles?"

"Perspective. You might be too close to the situation." Piper shrugged. "You've known your townspeople forever. I figured it might not occur to you to believe they could be at the root of the bad luck we've been having lately."

"She might've hired Baran."

"Baran?"

"The Russian who tried to crush my spine on the cliffs," Cian explained absently.

Piper could see his mind was racing a mile a minute as he tried to make all the pieces of the puzzle fit.

"Well, someone did," Hoyt agreed. "It's doubtful your past

would come knocking when you've been out of the field as long as you have."

Cian's brows shot up and a wry smile curled his lip. "You've been talking to Ryker."

"There've been attacks on my daughter's life. Did you really believe I would sit back and do nothing?"

"No. You're a right fine father, and I'd expect you'll not rest until you find the source," Cian said, his tone heavy with respect and admiration.

"Thank you, son."

As she watched, Piper saw the two most important men in her life bond over a common goal: her safety. Her heart was full in a way it had never been.

Understanding passed between Hoyt and Cian, and he was happy for it. Piper's father wouldn't stand in his way when it came time to eliminate the threat against their beloved girl and would, in fact, assist him in the process.

He suspected Hoyt saw what it had taken Cian too long to recognize; that the woman had captured his heart from the start and wouldn't let it go anytime soon. Surprisingly, Cian was thrilled and not at all reticent anymore.

He lifted her wine glass from the table and handed it to her. "Have a seat, love, and let's discuss what needs to be done about Meghan."

After they were all comfortable, with Piper tucked against his side, Cian told them both about the story. "We don't know much about the accident that took Roisin's life other than Meghan survived in place of Ro, and Aeden is suffering for it." He sipped his whiskey before continuing. "Every day, Aeden becomes more withdrawn and has constant night terrors, in the daytime, too. He believes an evil monster is trying to destroy us all."

"He may be right." Hoyt's countenance was grim, and he frowned down into the amber liquid in his tumbler. "If this Meghan is as bad as you say, he may sense her intent."

"I agree," Piper said and sat straighter to meet Cian's concerned look. "Perhaps he senses the darkness under whatever false pretense she shows him. It's also possible he fears her for a different reason—her scars. They make the side of her damaged face absolutely grotesque. It might be horrifying to a child his age."

"I'll talk to Carrick and see if Aeden's been in contact with her." Cian shook his head at the idea his brother would let that monster within a foot of his son. They all knew how wicked Meghan was; even Roisin had understood her sister wasn't a good person. "Meg tried to seduce Carrick a number of times in the past, despite the fact he was happily married to Ro. Until tonight, I'd never believed he would fall for her," he said in disgust.

"Maybe he hasn't. Don't judge what you don't know, boy," Hoyt warned with a pointed look. "If she has strong magic, she might be influencing him, where she couldn't before."

"Why now and not when Roisin was alive?" All this talk of magic made Cian's head hurt. He wasn't naive to what might be possible. Hell, in his ex-line of work, he'd learned all about trickery. He'd also learned a long time ago that love spells and potions weren't effective and, more often than not, backfired.

"If their relationship was true, nothing could've broken them up." Hoyt shrugged and sipped his drink.

A trickle of suspicion ran down Cian's spine. "You've been the victim of another's treachery?"

The other man snorted. "You're perceptive, boy. I'll give you that."

"Dad? What's this about?" Piper leaned forward. Concern tightened her mouth and a frown drew her brows together. "Did someone try to steal you from Mom?"

"Not me. Your mother from us, and it doesn't amount to a hill of beans anymore. It's past history, Pip." Hoyt gave her a self-assured smile. "Don't you worry about your old dad none. That good-for-nothing failed miserably. He didn't stand a chance against the Thorne's charm."

"As a recipient of that unholy charm, I can vouch for the truth of your words," Cian said with a laugh.

Piper elbowed him lightly in the ribs. "Shut it, you!" She addressed her father. "How did I never hear that story? Mom's fond of reminiscing."

Hoyt's expression turned dark and a hard light came to his eyes. "We don't mention his name. There's power in a name."

"Sounds like Voldemort," Piper muttered with a snort. "'He who must not be named.'"

Cian recognized the Harry Potter reference, although he'd never read the books or saw the movies. When they'd come out, it was all anyone could talk about. Even Bridget had fallen under the spell of those books for a time. But he understood Hoyt's desire to keep quiet about the past. A name *did* hold power, and it could be wielded to hurt.

"So it is possible for Meg to sway him with an enchantment while he's suffering Roisin's loss?" Cian asked, wanting to clarify.

"Possible, yes. Probable, no, unless she's utilizing black magic. Most witches shun the dark arts."

"We all know how unstable that power is and what it could ultimately lead to, Cian. A witch would need to be desperate to resort to it," Piper explained.

"Yeah, that I know. I'm just trying to find a reason for my brother's actions tonight. He's never defended Meghan in the past unless it was Roisin's request. He'd not do it if he felt she was the reason for Ro's death."

Nothing made sense to him, but he intended to delve deeper into the who and what of it all. Cian would be damned if that she-devil seduced his little brother under his watch. Bridget would need to be alerted to the newest development, too. She'd need to keep a keen eye on what was happening should Cian not be around.

"Is there a spell to drive her away?"

"Maybe not drive her away, per se, but we can easily erect wards to keep her off the property." Piper jerked as if a thought suddenly occurred to her. "Dad, wouldn't the wards you and Spring put in place have kept evil intenders away? How far would that extend from the property?"

"We only spelled this here inn. It doesn't extend to the pub or Carrick's place, but we could easily do that now." Hoyt gave a firm nod, as if he liked the idea.

"I'd be grateful if you did." Cian finished off his drink and stood up. "But I think morning is soon enough. I can't see Meghan returning tonight."

Father and daughter grimaced, and it lit Cian's nerves afire. It was no secret they'd been through things like this before. Perhaps he should take heed of their warnings.

"You can go to bed, Cian," Hoyt said. "Pip and I will take care of what needs to be done. We've found it's best not to delay."

Cian gave them a tired smile. "Then I'll stay and help, or at least see what I should do if the gods decide to grace us with abilities in the future."

"The first rule of casting is to protect yourself and others. We do this by creating a protective circle and setting enchanted candles around the perimeter on five points of the drawn pentacle," Piper instructed.

"Drawn, as in chalk or paint?" Cian asked.

She laughed lightly. "You *can*, but we don't. In our attic, we have it routed into the wooden floorboards. But if you're in the open or in a non-designated spell-casting area, you can just use your hand and create one using elemental magic."

"There's a room here at the inn. I've been in it once or twice, but never explored it to see all it offers." Cian shrugged. "Never saw the point without the abilities."

Piper shot a quick look at her father and when he gave a small nod, she asked, "Will you show us the room, Cian?"

"This way." He led them to the built-in shelving unit that held the O'Malley grimoire, and he instinctively grabbed it. His hands began to tingle and he almost dropped the book in his surprise. A quick glance at the cover showed it had woken at his touch.

"It seems to like you, son," Hoyt said with a deep chuckle.

"It's similar to a woman and easily charmed by the holder. Shutting down when it doesn't get what it wants, and flirting with possibility when it does."

Piper swatted his arm. "That's a piss-poor view you have of women."

She didn't appear to be truly offended.

He grinned and couldn't resist stealing a kiss from her beguiling lips. "Of course, I didn't mean you, love. You're the exception to the rule."

With a snort and an eye roll, she said, "Right, player."

"The room?" Hoyt reminded them, breaking the flirty, seductive spell around Cian and Piper.

Wordlessly, Cian ran the flat of his hand under the lowest shelf until he felt the lever. After pressing it into the wall, he heard the lock disengage, and the shelf parted about an inch. The secret entrance was designed to part only enough to allow a finger hold, and let a person swing the door outward. Another latch on the opposite side would allow them to exit.

As soon as Cian crossed the threshold, he started down the stairs. There was no electricity, but the lights flared to life illuminating the way.

"Interesting," Piper murmured. "Are they on a motion sensor?"

He shook his head. "It's always been this way. It's the only magic, along with the grimoire, that still exists for my family." He held out a hand to her. "Mind the steps. The way gets narrower through here."

Her delicate hand felt right in his, so he kept hold of it even after they reached the bottom of the stairs. As they entered the cavernous chamber under the inn, the wall sconces flared to life and the dancing flame revealed a ten-foot-wide pentacle on the stone floor. In the center stood a wooden altar with runes burned into its surrounding panels.

The moment Piper stepped into the circle, those runes

woke and pulsed with a low light. "This is incredible," she breathed. Her awe-filled gaze swept the entire space. "It makes me want to perform ceremonies. Can you believe it?"

Cian had always felt uncomfortable here, as if it didn't quite belong to him. Maybe it was because he didn't have magic and the room intimidated him, or perhaps he felt a greater power here and it made him feel small. But he'd avoided the place whenever possible in the past.

Seeing it through Piper's eyes gave him a new appreciation. "Should I join you?"

Her wide, welcoming smile was all the answer he needed. With a deep breath and a silent prayer to the gods he wouldn't blow up the inn with his novice attempts, he stepped into the circle.

An electrical current ran the length of his body, much stronger than when he'd first picked up the grimoire. "I feel strange," he confessed. "Like my cells are waking up and a charge is chasing through me."

"It's the magic of the place," Hoyt informed him. "Unless I miss my guess, your home was built on a ley line."

"As in one of the mythical ancient sites that channels the earth's energy?"

"Yes. And not so mythical." Hoyt crossed to a tapestry hanging prominently on the rock wall at the far side of the room. "Look here. It's a map of Ireland, and there's a network of lines." He snapped his fingers and produced a small flame. Holding it close to the tapestry, but far enough away not to set it on fire, he examined the map. Using a finger on his other hand, he tapped a spot. "If I'm not mistaken, this is your home. All the lines intersect here."

Piper's face lit with wonder. "Are you saying this is the most powerful spot in Ireland, Dad?"

"No. Come here and I'll show you."

Cian placed a hand on Piper's low back and guided her across the room.

Hoyt gestured to another place on the tapestry. "This is the Hill of Tara. The ley lines all connect here as well as these points here, here, and here."

"It's a pentagram and it encompasses the entire center of the country!" Piper exclaimed with a laugh.

"Exactly." Hoyt gave her an approving look. "We're standing on the western-most point of the pentagram."

Cian squinted at the map. "That's Sullivan land there, and Ruairí O'Connor once told me his family owned land to the North." He gestured to the top of the pentagram. "I've a mind to believe that's theirs. But I don't know these other two."

"Well, no one owns the Hill of Tara now, right? I mean, isn't that national trust or something?" Piper asked.

"Yeah, close enough. It belongs to the Irish government and they operate through the Office of Public Works."

"I wonder who owned the land prior?"

"It's changed hands many times over the years. It was rumored to be the main hold of the *Tuatha Dé Danann,* and later became the place where the High Kings of Ireland were crowned." Cian shrugged. "It makes much more sense now, as to why the land was chosen for the ceremonies."

"It's where the *Lia Fáil* rests. The Stone of Destiny," Piper said.

"Ah, you've done your research. Perhaps one day soon, I'll take you there," he said with a warm smile.

"I'd like that." But her excitement over the discovery had dimmed and she wouldn't make eye contact. She quickly crossed back to the altar, leaving Cian out of sorts.

A deeper understanding of her reticence occurred to him, and Cian realized he needed to talk with her soon. He had to confess his feelings and lay his heart in her hands to do with what she would, and preferably before she left his home.

The grimoire flared blindingly bright then died down to a pulsing glow.

"I believe the heart of *the Frozen* has been effectively pricked," Hoyt said in a low voice with a speculative look at Cian. "Am I wrong?"

He met the older man's cunning, all-seeing eyes. "No. You're not wrong."

A smile of satisfaction curled Hoyt's mouth. "Good."

"You don't have any objections to the two of us?" Cian asked curiously.

"Not a one, as long as you intend to treat her well." Hoyt's brows raised in challenge. "You *do* intend to treat her well, right, boy?"

His grin came unbidden, and Cian cast his gaze toward Piper, who had squatted to study the ruins on the altar. "I intend to treat her like a queen, if she'll have me, Mr. Thorne. You've nothin' to fear from me."

"Excellent. Now let's get the gol-dern show on the road so I can get some shut-eye."

PIPER DIDN'T LIKE HER FATHER AND CIAN CONSPIRING ON THE far-side of the room. It certainly made her edgy and unsettled. When they joined her in the pentacle, she noticed Cian seemed lighter of spirit and the grimoire he held flickered happily. Even her father had a gratified air.

"Do I want to know what you two were talking about over there?" she asked dryly.

"Never you mind, Pip. These old bones are tired, and I'd like to get sleep before the sun rises. How about we strengthen the wards?"

She couldn't tamp down the mild irritation when she saw Cian grin. "Neither of you are going to tell me, are you?"

"In due time, Piper me love." Cian placed the book on the

altar. "Show us a fool-proof spell to ward this old inn, if you don't mind," he commanded softly.

The cover flipped open and shuffled a handful of the thick pages.

"Gaelic again?" Piper asked, in frustration.

Hoyt peeked over her shoulder and shook his head. "I don't reckon it is. Cian?"

"Not Gaelic. Not Latin." He scrunched up his face and scratched the back of his head. "I'm at a loss."

"You might want to ask it to translate the passage," Hoyt suggested mildly.

Piper and Cian shared a rueful look. It appeared he hadn't thought of it either.

After he made his request of the book, the lines transitioned to English. A single read through showed her it was a straight-forward spell, similar to the one they'd originally planned to use from their own family grimoire.

"Okay, so the next step is for us to light the candles." She glanced around, not seeing any. "I suppose I could conjure some."

"Everything you'll need is in the box under the altar." The three of them spun toward the stairwell to see the newcomer. Carrick had his hands tucked in the pockets of his jeans and his shoulders were lifted, as if uncomfortable. "My wife used this place to cast on occasion."

"Carrick—"

He held up his hand to cut off whatever Cian was about to say. "I came over to explain what you saw earlier. I saw you'd left the bookshelf ajar and assumed you'd be in here."

Carrick was roughly the same height and build as his brother, topping him by maybe an inch. Other than possessing the O'Malley green eyes, a resemblance to his older sibling was minor. Where Cian's hair was sandy brown, Carrick's was black. And though they both sported facial hair; it was easy to see Carrick spent money on professional grooming. He also chose a sports jacket and button-down shirt, where Cian favored Henleys.

Piper would be hard pressed to say who was better looking, but Cian's rougher, down-to-earth appeal was hard to ignore. On the other hand, Carrick appeared more world-weary and sad; broken in a way that made Piper's heart ache for him.

"We wanted to strengthen the wards for your home and the pub," Piper explained. Her skin felt tight, like they'd been caught doing something they shouldn't. She couldn't explain away the sensation, but it deepened when a frustrated scowl darkened Carrick's boyishly handsome face.

"Leave Meg out of whatever you have planned," he growled. "It's not for you to force her away."

Piper was stunned by his insight. "How did you know what we intended?"

He joined them at the altar and used his thumb to indicate his brother. "Because I know how much my family likes to put their nose into my personal business."

"You're confusing me with Bridget," Cian snapped tightly. "But know I'll protect my own, and that includes your stubborn arse."

"Meg is no longer a threat." Turning to Piper, Carrick sent her what seemed like a beseeching look. "Don't add her to your spell… *please.*"

Instinct told her to listen to Carrick, but Piper could clearly see Cian's unhappiness with his brother's request.

"How about we simply ward out evil and ill-intent on all your family properties? Then, if Meg truly has your best interests at heart, she'll have no problem returning." Her gaze darted between the brothers, and she held her breath, hoping her compromise would do the trick and lessen the tension.

Carrick relented first, and he gave her a wide, warm smile.

"That works for me." He held out a hand. "We weren't properly introduced. I'm Carrick O'Malley."

Piper shook his hand and returned his smile with one of her own. "Where do you fall in the order of all five siblings?"

"Middle. The twins were born a few years after I arrived to disrupt things."

"Where do they live?" She sent a questioning glance Cian's way. "Should we protect their homes too?"

"Thanks for thinking to include them." He rubbed her back. "They're in the States, love. I've not heard word of them for a wee bit, but if there was trouble abound, Bridget's contacts would've informed us. She's got a wide network of friends."

"Fair enough. Carrick, do you wish to join us?"

He frowned and knelt to touch the ground. "It feels strange here. I've never experienced the pulse before."

"The Thornes tell me the inn is set upon a ley line." Cian pointed to the tapestry. "There's a grid woven into those old threads."

Carrick nodded thoughtfully. "Roisin once spoke about the energy of our home. I'd no real idea what she was talkin' about, if I'm honest. But I've been here before and not felt what is flowing through me. I don't know how to describe it."

"You don't need to. It's happening to me as well. I think this woke when Piper arrived." Cian showed him the grimoire. "Did you know the fecking thing lights up?"

"What?" The shock on Carrick's face was comical, and his mouth sagged open even as he fought to close it. The result resembled a trout.

Although she tended to shun magic, Piper had learned all the basics when she was a babe at her father's knee. The Thornes were all well-versed in all things magical for their own safety. Watching newbie warlocks react to things she took for granted was enlightening and humorous at the same time.

"Piper, come show Carrick what this can do." Cian held out

his hand to her, and she moved closer to take it. He shut the cover and touched the grimoire's etchings with his free hand. As expected, it lit like a Christmas tree.

"Feck!" Carrick exclaimed as he stepped back. "Is that normal?"

Hoyt laughed. "For some. Your family's grimoire is as old as I've ever seen, son. I'm betting it has all sorts of tricks we've never heard of before."

A meow caught Piper's notice. A second later, the resident black cat strutted into the chamber. The book hummed and settled on a muted glow.

They all stared, stupefied.

The sound increased as the cat drew closer.

Hoyt was the first to react. "I'll be a gol-derned monkey's uncle. That's the first time I've heard one make a noise."

"At least it's a happy sound," Piper added in a shaky voice. "I suppose it could've growled at us if it wasn't."

The brothers exchanged a wary look.

"It won't bite, fellas. Never you worry. It does, after all, belong to your family. You're safe." Hoyt slapped Cian on the back and shot Carrick an amused grin.

Cian exhaled a ragged breath. "Right."

In the end, Carrick watched them perform the enchantment from a bench by the room's entrance, and the contented cat purred within the cradle of his arms. Melancholy came off Cian's brother in waves, and Piper assumed he was remembering times that he'd watched his wife cast down here. She was sad for him. How horrible it must've been to lose his wife in such a tragic accident and have his poor son emotionally scarred for life!

After they closed the circle, she approached him. "Your son is the sweetest thing, Carrick. I'd like to take him for ice cream before I head to the next stop on my trip."

He looked beyond her shoulder to Cian then back to her,

brows drawn together, showing his confusion. "Aeden spoke to you?"

"Yes. Right before you came outside."

"He *spoke* to you?"

Not understanding why he was so incredulous, she half turned toward Cian, wishing he'd join their conversation. She wasn't certain what she was missing here.

Picking up on her uncertainty, Cian came to her rescue. "I told you Aeden doesn't speak to us, darlin', and he never speaks to strangers." He placed an arm around her waist and addressed his brother. "Aeden was thoroughly taken with our Piper tonight. Cuddled right up to her breast and held an entire conversation, he did."

Wind could've knocked Carrick over at that point and he stared at Piper as if she had three heads.

"Was it wrong to talk to him?" she asked nervously. She hated to think she'd upset Carrick by encouraging his son to sit with her after his curfew. She'd only meant to comfort the boy and ease the haunted look in his eyes.

"No," Carrick choked out. "No. I thank you for your kindness to my son. I have to go."

"I'm sorry if I upset him, Cian," Piper said as they traversed the stairs to her room.

"You didn't. Not in the way you believe." Cian sighed tiredly and ran a hand through his hair. "As I told ya before, Aeden's been suffering since his mother died. He's shutting down and is lost in his head more days than not. But with you, he was normal for a time. And for that, I thank you." He paused outside her door and with an achingly sweet smile, tucked her hair behind her ear. "Carrick would've thanked you, too, had he not been so taken aback. Your kindness to Aeden was a good thing."

She couldn't help but worry what would happen to the child after she left. And with that thought, she once again felt like crap at the idea this wasn't her home, and she would be moving on soon. "Tomorrow, we'll make your Granny's elixir, and if we haven't discovered who's causing our mischief by the day's end, I should probably get going."

Alarm flared on Cian's face, and he shook his head. "Don't go before I've had a chance to talk with you, Piper. Promise me."

"Oh-kay," she drew the word out in her confusion. His intensity was odd in the face of everything.

"I've things to say. Things that need a better setting than a darkened hallway and my poor knackered brain attemptin' to form the right words."

She imagined he wanted to drive home the point he wasn't couple material, and her heart ached at the thought. Her urge to hide was stronger than her desire to be with him right then, and she turned her back to open the door. "I'll see you tomorrow."

His hands came down on her shoulders and he drew her back against his chest. He held her tight, and she allowed it, absorbing some of his strength. She only had to get through tomorrow without making a complete cake of herself by throwing herself at him and begging him to love her. Then she'd be able to go off and lick her wounds.

"Good night, Cian," she choked out.

He groaned low and long. "I can see this can't wait."

He swept her up into his arms, and she released a meep as she grabbed his shoulders for support.

"What are you doing?"

"You'll see soon enough." He kicked her door closed with his heel and carried her to her bed. He didn't dump her in the middle of the mattress like she half expected, but set her down on the edge as if she were made of the finest porcelain. Squatting in front of her, he caressed her lips with the pad of his thumb.

"I made a discovery tonight, Piper." His voice was tender and caused her heart to flip in her chest. "Right before I saw Meg, I'd intended to lay myself bare to you. To tell you that you've wormed your way into my heart. To tell you that *you* are *the Mighty Thorne* who pierced this old frozen heart of mine."

The pounding pulse in her ears almost drowned him out,

and she needed to clarify what he'd said. "You're trying to say you c-care about me?"

"Nah. Not just care." He grinned, and her whole world seemed right. "I love you, Piper Kelly Thorne."

An explosion rocked the room.

Cian dove for her and they both tumbled onto the mattress, his body over hers to protect her from whatever the latest unknown threat was. When nothing more happened, he lifted his head and frantically looked around the room. His attention was caught by a flicker out the window, and he ran for the door.

"Stay here!" he called over his shoulder.

Piper scrambled up and over to the window. The whole landscape seemed to be on fire, and a two-story wall of flame blocked her view of Carrick's house. Her desire to ensure Cian's family was safe overruled any concern for her own safety, and she teleported into the side yard. She arrived mere seconds before him, and he swore under his breath when he saw her.

"I told you to stay behind, Piper!" he hollered, giving her a small shake. "I'll not risk your life."

"You aren't risking it, I am. And we don't have time to waste arguing. We're under attack," she snapped.

A single thought as she touched the ring Alastair had designed for her, alerted him of the newest strike. Within seconds, he was there and had summed up the situation. "Who's in the house next door?"

"Carrick," she said. "Please stop him—" she gestured to Cian. "—he's trying to find a break in the fire wall and he'll get hurt."

For all intents and purposes, Cian was still a mortal, and Piper knew without a doubt that if he tried to fight those roaring flames, he'd be injured.

Alastair spared a single glance for the people approaching

behind her, then gave her a short nod and ran to where Cian was preparing to jump through the blaze.

"Never a dull moment in this family," Hoyt said grimly. "I see Alastair has this taken care of." He addressed GiGi and Ryker. "From what I can tell, the fire is surrounding all the buildings belonging to the O'Malleys'. You two take Bridget and secure the pub. Piper and I will check this area."

"On it," Ryker said. "Be careful. This strikes me as another thought-out attack."

"Me, too."

Ryker's words froze the blood in Piper's veins. She sought out Cian and was relieved to see Alastair had used his power to create a break in the wall for Cian to run through. However, when he used his water elemental to pull water from the atmosphere and douse the flames, they flared higher and spread toward him at a blinding speed.

"*Greek fire!*" she screamed. "Alastair, get out of there!"

He must've realized what he was dealing with at the exact second she'd shouted, and he teleported, barely managing to save himself from becoming a human torch.

Horror choked off Piper's ability to reason, and as she stared at Carrick's house, panic set in. "They won't know what this is! They'll try to fight it on their own and get incinerated!"

"No. That won't happen. Look." Alastair gripped her face between his hands and forced her to turn toward the inn. "The building is untouched. The fire can't get to it."

"The wards are too strong," Hoyt agreed with a nod. "This is a distraction, with an added bonus of destroying a witch, should any try to put it out with water."

"Another attempt on the only one who might be around to use her power against it," Alastair said grimly with a nod to Piper. "This was meant to hurt her."

"Whoever is out to get me, is doing a mighty fine job," she choked out. "But why? I've never done anything to anyone."

"You don't have to, child. You're a Thorne, and someone in this godforsaken country recognized you right away." Alastair ran a practiced eye around the estate. "We're sitting ducks out here in the dark. Let's—"

Piper felt a hard punch to her chest and cried out. Instinctively, she lifted her hands to the place where the pain was beginning to worsen. Thick, sticky fluid seeped through her fingers and oozed down her arms. She pulled her hands away to see what it could be, when her father's shout penetrated.

She'd been shot.

Hoyt caught Piper before she dropped. The movement saved his life. A second bullet missed him and hit the wall behind his head.

"Get to the house!" Alastair shouted the order.

Hoyt wasted no time and envisioned the dining room of the inn. He arrived alone, and realized he hadn't given Alastair time to grab his arm to join the teleport to safety.

He laid Piper on the table and went to work, praying to the Goddess, Alastair could take care of himself.

"You hang in there, Pip. You hear me, girl? You hang in there for your old dad." He cut away her shirt and saw the bullet's entry point. Turning her on her side, he checked for an exit wound. There wasn't one. "Pip, you're going to need surgery, but I've got you covered. Your job is to stay with me, you got it?"

Hoyt applied pressure to the wound with one hand as he frantically fumbled for his phone with the other. "Rebecca? I need you to prep a room for surgery. Pip's been shot."

"Piper?" his wife gasped. "Piper's been shot?"

"I don't have time to talk. It's bad, honey. Chest wound and the bullet's still inside."

"Get here. I'll be ready."

A commotion at the door drew Hoyt's notice, and he dropped the phone in preparation to fight.

Cian entered, white-faced and frantic. "Piper?"

"She's been shot, son. I'm taking her to my wife. She's a surgeon. She'll know what to do." Hoyt promptly went back to saving his daughter's life. Visualizing what he needed, he conjured a weighted compress and placed it on her chest with a quickly worded chant to maintain constant pressure, then he hefted her into his arms.

"My family... I... Piper..."

It wasn't hard to see Cian was torn.

"Stay. I'll be back for you when she's out of the woods, Cian."

Wasting no more time, he transported Piper to his wife's surgery center.

Rebecca had already prepared the operating room and was there to greet him. Her dark hair was tucked under a cap, and she wore a pair of scrubs with dancing unicorns.

Hoyt almost smiled. Those damned unicorns were for Piper's benefit. They were the only magical thing their daughter had ever embraced.

"Bec?" His met his wife's worried mocha eyes. "Save her," he said in a choked voice. "Don't let our baby die."

She gave him a brisk nod, already in competent-surgeon mode, and went to work.

Cian was losing his mind. He had no idea what was happening with Piper and no way of contacting Hoyt to find out.

The second Piper was gone from the premises, the flames disappeared as if they'd never existed. Only the scorched property lines told the tale.

His exhausted family had all been bundled into the main living room of the inn, and there they stayed under Alastair Thorne's watchful eye. The warlock was once again pristine in a blue suit and gleaming white shirt. The only indication he'd been involved tonight was his tight expression and grim mouth. Every so often, he'd sip his scotch, but he never glanced up from the book he was reading.

"What do you hope to find there?" Cian finally ground out. "What's that fecking book going to tell you that we don't already know?"

One of Alastair's dark-blond brows shot up, and he shut down Cian's rant with a look.

After a long moment, Alastair sighed, placed a finger between the pages, and closed the cover. He finished his drink, set the tumbler down on the table, then addressed Cian's question.

"This is an accounting of all the bloodlines in the witch community, boy. So far, you've been unable to identify the threat to Piper. I'm searching for someone who has something to gain by her death."

"Like an inheritance or something?" Carrick asked.

"Or something," Alastair replied dryly.

"Out with it, man." Cian ran a hand through his sooty hair and belatedly thought about a shower. "What's the 'something' you're chewin' over?"

Respect for Cian's deduction caused Alastair's nod of acknowledgment. "You're smarter than I gave you credit for, O'Malley." With an all-encompassing glance at the room's occupants, Alastair rose to his feet. "I believe our villain wants to stop a Thorne/O'Malley union."

Cian's soul shriveled and his stomach twisted into one solid knot. "Have you narrowed it down?"

"Not yet, but I will."

"Why do you believe that, brother?" GiGi's worry marred her forehead.

"All the attacks on Piper and Cian came when they were together." He ticked off the incidents on his fingers. "If I'm not mistaken, you were together on the Cliffs of Moher, the first time." At Cian's nod, Alastair continued. "The second was when you were both in the woods of Glencar." Again, Cian nodded. "This time, you were both in Piper's room, when the fire started."

"*Jaysus!* So it's not necessarily an attack on her, but on us as a couple," Cian concluded.

"That's my belief, yes."

He felt as if Alastair had pulled the rug out from under him. With no way to narrow down their assailant, the only way to keep Piper safe was to stay away from her. She'd continue to be a target here in his home.

"We'll find who's doing this, Cian." Ryker placed a comforting hand on his shoulder. "I promise, we will."

"You can't make a promise of that magnitude. And I can't take the risk to Piper's life." His heart was crushed under the blow of this discovery. "She'll be safe in America, though."

"Cian—"

"No, Bridget. We'll put it out that she died tonight." He swallowed, praying it wasn't true. "Her father will agree to the plan to keep her hidden. And whoever's striving to keep us apart will get his wish. For now."

As Cian stalked from the room, Alastair sighed.

Young love. They were always so quick to make snap decisions without weighing all the options.

He met his best friend's steady stare and almost smiled. Ryker knew him too well to believe Alastair would simply let this end here. He'd find the threat and eliminate it without compunction.

"Until now, our villain has kept you on the run, reacting to each attack without giving you much time to think." He hardened his tone and said, "That ends now."

Carrick and Bridget exchanged a worried look.

"Do you have anything to add, O'Malley?" Alastair asked as casually as he was able. In reality, he was boiling mad inside. But who and what he was forced him to contain his anger or he'd destroy them all with its power.

"We're worried about Cian, if we're honest," Bridget said in her brother's stead. "He's already had his heart ripped out once. He'll not be able to survive this should anything happen to someone else he cares about."

"I think your brother is far stronger than you give him

credit for," Alastair replied, not unkindly. "But your worry brings me to my first question. Is there a jilted lover who might want to hurt Cian?"

"None that we know about." Carrick shot a questioning look his sister's way and answered Alastair when Bridget shook her head. "Moira was the only woman who ever held his heart, but she's dead."

"Ryker, make sure of that, won't you?" Alastair directed. When his friend nodded, he posed his next question. "Knowing what I now do of your family's prophecy, and knowing the first line refers to Cian—and possibly Piper—I have to ask: who stands to gain if your magic doesn't return to you?"

"The O'Connors," Bridget spat.

Alastair almost laughed at her vehemence. "That's the obvious answer, yes. But who else?"

"Aren't those thieving bastards enough?" Her outraged question echoed off the walls around them.

Alastair did laugh then. "They've had over two hundred years to make your life miserable, Ms. O'Malley. And from what I've gleaned, they are more likely to cause mischief in other ways." He met her furious gaze head on. "Like seducing and abandoning a young woman?" he ventured to suggest. Tears filled her wide, angry eyes, but he hardened his resolve. "I've met Ruairí O'Connor, and I know him to be a decent man. If I had to guess, I'd say he's not behind this attack." He softened his tone. "I don't believe you think he is either."

As if to add weight to his comment, the front door burst open and a harried Ruairí ran into the room. All his focus was on Bridget as he crossed to her and ignored everyone else.

"Bridg!" He tugged her to her feet and hugged her, purposefully disregarding the little fact that she shoved roughly against his chest. "Don't be fightin' me on this, woman! I've had years scared off me life."

Alastair grinned. "That's one suspect we can rule out."

"Get off me, you fecking eejit," Bridget growled with a swift kick to Ruairí's shin.

"*Ouch!* You're a she-devil, to be sure, *mo ghrá,* but I'll allow that you've had a scare tonight." He cupped her cheeks, and she bit at his hand. "Well, at least I know you're not hurt," he muttered as he jumped backwards to avoid another injury. He surveyed the room, and a concerned expression crossed his face. "Where are Cian and Piper?"

"Piper is… gone, and Cian needed alone time." Alastair tugged his sleeves. He didn't believe this particular O'Connor was behind tonight's events, but it was always wise to be cautious. It was never good to reveal all one's cards in a game of chance.

"Gone?" Alarm coated his response.

It was Bridget who eased his worry. "Back in America."

Alastair sighed his frustration. *Why did the Irish have to be so disgustingly forthright?*

Ruairí nodded absently. "If I'm not mistaken, this isn't the first attack on your family recently," he said to the O'Malley siblings. "I want to help. Tell me what I can do."

"Get back to your side of the fence," Bridget snapped. "You're well aware, you are, that O'Connors aren't welcome here."

Ruairí narrowed his eyes and compressed his mouth in a tight line. After a long moment, he growled his irritation. "I'll go, but know this, Bridget O'Malley; you're going to have to deal with what's between us sooner rather than later. I'm done with your anger over ancient history."

In an instant, her hand was wrapped around Alastair's empty tumbler and the glass was sailing for Ruairí's head. "I'll give you ancient history, you prick! You're thick as shite."

Ruairí had the reflexes of a cat, or he'd anticipated her rage, because he ducked and the glass shattered on the wall behind him. For the longest time, he stared at the shattered particles on the floor without comment. However much he'd tried to hide his feelings, a wave of sadness rippled out from him and washed over Alastair.

As an empath, Alastair had the ability to read another's deeper feelings, and O'Connor's indicated he was suffering over Bridget's continued rejection. Was it motive for the man to undermine the O'Malleys' future happiness and potential return of magic? Alastair didn't believe so, but he'd been blind-sided by another's resentment in the past.

The snap of GiGi's fingers pulled him from his musing. The tumbler was restored to its original state and rested back on the table where Alastair had initially placed it.

Ruairí headed for the door without a backward glance. "If you need me, Carrick, just ask. For sure, your stubborn-arsed sister won't," he said as he exited.

"One day, you're going to tell me what went down between you and Ruairí, Bridg, and don't say nothing, because we'll all know you for a liar." Carrick rose to his feet. "I've a need to check on Aeden and Cian. But I'll be mulling over who might want to harm the family."

THE BEEPING OF A MACHINE PRECEDED THE SQUEEZE OF A blood-pressure cuff on Piper's arm. The muted overhead light was still bright enough to make her wince, and she squinted against the glare.

"She's waking up," her mother said in a low voice as she tore away the Velcro holding the cuff in place.

"Mom?" How she came to be here she could only guess, but the previous night's events were sketchy to Piper's groggy mind.

"Yes, sweetheart." Her mother gripped her hand. "Take it easy, you're recovering from surgery."

Already, Piper could feel the knitting of her flesh underneath the bandage. "Good old magic."

"And good old medical know-how," her father added with a raspy chuckle. "You're lucky your mother is a talented surgeon, Pip."

She shifted her head to see her father rise from a bedside chair. "Dad."

"This is starting to be a habit: you getting hurt, and me keeping vigil by your bed."

A laugh bubbled up, but it wasn't at all humorous. "What happened?"

"In the midst of all the commotion, you were shot in the chest." He struggled not to show his rage, but Piper couldn't miss it, along with his frustration. "Once again, you were targeted."

"I still don't understand why someone wants to hurt me."

Rebecca put her arm around Hoyt and rested her head on his shoulder. "It's not you personally, sweetheart," she said. "Or at least Alastair doesn't believe so. He holds a theory that someone wants to prevent you from forming a relationship with Cian."

"Too late," Piper said with a half-smile. "We've already started one."

Hoyt winced. "About that, Pip…"

Trepidation caused Piper's stomach to flip-flop.

Her mother patted Hoyt's chest. "This can wait until she's completely well."

"We both know that's only a matter of a few hours, Mom. Tell me." Piper sat up and reached for the glass of water on the tray table next to her. After taking a few sips, she braced herself. "Okay, out with it."

"Cian asked that you not return."

Piper sucked in a sharp breath. She found it difficult to handle her mother's compassion. Her father's anger on the other hand, well, that she could manage because it matched what was brewing in her own chest. "Those were his exact words? Am I not to return to his home, or was it to Ireland in general?"

"Does it matter?" her father asked gruffly.

"I believe it does," she replied, moderating her voice not to reveal her inner turmoil. She didn't want to set her father off. If he thought she was hurting, he'd rip Cian apart limb by limb for abandoning her after she was shot. "Not returning to his home indicates he has no desire to continue what we began. Not returning to Ireland, on the other hand, would suggest he's concerned for my safety."

"You're splitting hairs, Pip." Hoyt surged up from the chair and stormed to the window. There was a barely leashed fury inside him, and Piper would hate for Cian to get anywhere close to her dad in the coming hours.

"You weren't there when he told me he loved me." She fought to keep her anguish at bay. The reality might be that Cian didn't love her enough to fight.

Hoyt turned abruptly. "When? When did he say it, Pip?"

"Right before the explosion of fire."

His mouth tightened.

She didn't want to sound woefully pathetic, but she had to ask. "Dad? Do you think he's trying to keep me away for my own safety?"

"I think he's trying to save his own ass, if you want the truth."

Deflated, Piper blew out a breath and leaned back against the pillows. Perhaps Cian *was* trying to save himself, but he also had his family to consider. The image of Aeden rose up in her mind and she knew without a doubt, she'd have done the same as Cian to protect that sweet child. "Don't judge him too harshly, Dad. He's got a lot of people relying on him. A lot of family who might be hurt."

"And what about you?" Hoyt demanded.

Her temper erupted. "What about me? Huh? Do I think this is sucky? Abso-fucking-lutely! Am I hurt?" She bit off a sob. "Yeah. I'm hurt. Do I understand that he has four other siblings and a nephew who might get caught in the crossfire? I do."

Her father's face softened with compassion.

"I get it, Dad. I get why he… he… I get it, okay?"

"Oh, Pip. You have a world of love in that heart of yours."

And no one wanted it.

She sat up and started the process of removing the leads from her chest. "If you don't mind, I want to go home."

"I'd prefer you were where we can monitor your recovery," Rebecca said gently.

"Mom, we both know I'm already back to one-hundred percent. Between your skill and magic, I'm recovered." Piper tried to smile and failed. "Besides, I'm sure you have other patients scheduled today."

Rebecca Walsh-Thorne was a gifted surgeon and in high demand for her talent. Piper couldn't remember a time when she wasn't. Today would be no different since her mother rarely slowed down other than on weekends. She'd always insisted Saturdays and Sundays were family time, and she wouldn't budge or allow anyone to intrude.

"If you don't think I would cancel my schedule to care for you, you've lost your mind, my sweet girl." Her mother cupped her cheek and placed a tender kiss on her forehead. "You come first, above and beyond anyone else."

"I appreciate that you care, Mom, but I promise I'm physically well."

"Don't think I didn't notice you avoided *emotionally* and *mentally* well," Rebecca countered dryly. "However, I know a woman needs downtime to heal. You're free to go, but you must promise to rest. And your dad will escort you home." She held up a hand. "Don't argue. It's the equivalent of a nurse's aide wheeling you to the car."

"The great Dr. Walsh's unbending rules, Pip. Just give in. I do." Her dad offered up a half-hearted grin, though worried lines on his face indicated he was still troubled.

"Fair enough." Piper swung her legs over the edge of the bed. "Am I allowed to use magic for a change of clothes or am I expected to wear this hospital gown home?"

Rebecca laughed and sailed toward the door. "Well, you certainly don't want your father dressing you. He'd cover you with a burlap sack and overalls."

Surprised she could laugh with the fresh crack in her heart, Piper shot her dad a grin. "She's not wrong."

"You're a gol-derned stubborn mule, is what you are!"

"Dad, I'm not arguing with you. I'm going back."

"I blame *you*, Alastair. You've got it in your fool head that she needs to be bait." Spitting-nails furious, Hoyt paced Piper's airy living room. "She barely survived the last attack."

Alastair straightened his tie and tugged on his shirt cuffs, perfecting his already pristine appearance. "I am only here to make suggestions. What Piper chooses to do is entirely up to her."

"And you *suggested* she hightail it on back to that god-forsaken inn to flush out some crazy person."

Ire flashed in Alastair's sapphire eyes. "Hoyt, she's no safer here than there."

"Now that's a dammed lie! She's a hundred times safer, and you derned well know it."

Lifting two fingers to his brow, Alastair scrubbed back and forth, as if Hoyt's rant was giving him a tension headache. It probably was if the throbbing of Piper's own skull was any indication. They'd been going round and round on this topic for the better part of an hour. Hoyt had mellowed from livid to hot under the collar since the subject of Piper's return to Ireland came up. But he became fired up again at a moment's notice.

"Dad, *enough*. I'm a grown-ass woman and I'm tired of hiding out here."

"It's only been two days, Pip! It's not like it's been two years," Hoyt pointed out with no little sarcasm. "It's doubtful that underhanded rat is going to suddenly crawl out from whatever hole he's burrowed in and expose himself. He'd rather take potshots at you in the dark."

"So tell me, what is the appropriate amount of time to twiddle my thumbs and wait? One year? Two? When will he get bored and go away?" She flopped down on her double-wide loveseat and dropped her head back to glare at the innocent ceiling. "We've scryed, we've cast spells, we've created wards— all the magical things I'd rather not have to do—but *nothing* has worked." She lifted her head and sent him a beseeching look. "I can't run forever, Dad. I deserve a life, however short it may or may not be."

Hoyt perched on the ottoman at her feet and rested a hand on her knee. "I love you too much to risk your life, Pip. Don't ask me to stand back and do nothing."

"Oh, Dad." She couldn't relay the myriad of feelings building inside—adoration, frustration, exasperation, under-standing. All she knew was that she couldn't hide out here in her home when the only man she'd ever truly loved was an ocean away and dealing with the fallout of their magical connection. Initially, when she'd heard he didn't want her to return, she'd taken it to heart. But it wasn't long before her fighting spirit emerged. "I promised Cian I'd create his Granny's potion. I'm not going to bail on him or his family when they need it for their financial survival."

"If that's the only reason you're returning, I can make the elixir." Alastair shrugged casually, but Piper sensed he'd said it to get a rise out of her, to make her confess to another, more profound reason for wanting to go back. "A potion isn't worth putting yourself in a killer's crosshairs."

"Whose side are you on?" she snapped.

"Yours, dear girl. Always yours."

Somewhat mollified, she turned to her father. "I love Cian. And I'm returning to Ireland, because I'm a Thorne and I don't run from trouble."

Pure triumph curled Alastair's lips upward in the same way crushing disappointment pulled Hoyt's downward.

"Excellent!" Alastair slapped Hoyt on the back—none too gently—and willfully ignored his cousin's glare. "Do you need to pack, or should we pop back immediately?"

If Piper didn't know better, she'd believe old Cousin Alastair had a horse in this race. She was certain of it when her dad dug a hundred-dollar bill out of his wallet and held it up. Alastair swiped it and tucked it into the breast pocket of his suit coat with a shit-eating grin.

Piper had to laugh.

"We're both going back with you, Pip."

"Poor Cian is going to feel cock blocked with the two of you there." She rubbed her temples. "And that doesn't bode well for my love life."

"You're worth the wait, child. I suspect your young man knows this." With a smile and a wink, Alastair strode out of the room.

Silence reigned for a full two minutes as Piper waited for her father to speak. Hoyt wasn't one to *not* insert his two cents into a situation such as this. But as the seconds ticked by and as he said nothing, she began to feel perhaps she'd misjudged him.

"No lecture, Dad?" she asked gently. "No 'You're a gol-dern hard-headed mule, Pip'?"

"No lecture. Your mother and I have raised you to be an intelligent, free-spirited woman. There isn't anything more we could say or do that'll make a difference." When he looked at her, there was a sheen of moisture coating his eyes. "I'm proud of you, Pip. So very proud. And I don't want you to ever doubt how much we love you."

"If I had any doubts, I think you both assuaged them when you saved my life after I'd been shot."

Hoyt winced. "Don't remind me, or I'm liable to lock you up and throw away the key to keep you safe."

"That's the thing, Dad. You *can't* keep me safe. Life is full of risks. But you and Mom have prepared me, and I'm ready to live my life to the fullest."

"With Cian?"

"If that's what he wants."

"I've never seen another man look at you the way he does. I'm glad he realized he cared before it was too late."

"Me too. Now, it's going to be a matter of convincing him that he's not the one putting me in jeopardy and that sending me away isn't the best course of action."

"If anyone can do it, Pip, it's you."

She dove for his embrace when he spread his arms wide. "Thank you for your faith in me, Dad. I love you so much."

"Always." His arms tightened right before he released her and tilted up her chin. "And I love you more," he assured her with an affectionate smile.

"You always say that but it's not possible."

"I love you infinity," they said in unison then laughed. They'd played their little game from the time she was a small child. Each proclaiming to love the other more. It always ended with "I love you infinity."

"Gather what you need. I'll let your mother know we're leaving soon."

"Do you think we'll ever find the person who wants to hurt me?" Piper asked in a small voice.

"I don't know, Pip, but we'll dern well try."

CIAN RUBBED HIS EYES AND BLINKED TO CHECK HIS VISION AS Piper strolled into his living room. Although a huge part of him wanted to send her right back to America, an even larger part wanted her to stay with him forever. One glimpse of her uncertainty was all it took to have him rush forward and wrap her in a tight embrace.

"Piper." He expelled a heartfelt sigh. "You're a foolish, foolish woman to return here."

"I couldn't stay away, Cian."

He hugged her tighter. She didn't give one peep of protest over his fierce embrace, and for that, he was happy because he had the burning desire to crush her against him. He had to convince himself she was really alive and well.

"I'm powerful angry with you for returning. But my heart… it felt like it had taken a battering with you gone." Finally remembering her injury, he drew back and frantically unbuttoned her shirt to search for the wound. "Are you alright? Does it still hurt? Should you be restin'?"

She prevented his clumsy attempt by clasping his hands between hers. "Cian, stop. I'm fine. I promise. Not even a mark remains."

He simply stared at her, all the things he was unable to say bottled up in the back of his throat.

Piper placed her palm against his jaw. "I promise I'm okay."

He jerked her back into a hug and rested his cheek atop her head. His gaze connected with Hoyt's. "You're too trusting, Mr. Thorne. She's not safe here, and you know it."

"You try arguing with her." Underlying the other man's resignation was a fondness for his daughter's stubborn ways.

"We've plenty of that in our future, to be sure," Cian said with a grin. "Now, if you would step out of the room, I've a mind to kiss my woman all proper like."

Hoyt chuckled but exited all the same.

"What's considered 'proper like?'" Piper asked. Her face was alight with curiosity, hunger, and no small amount of anticipation.

"I think you fecking know," he growled.

He claimed her mouth—mainly because he had to. Her kisses drugged his mind, heated his body, and had him clinging to her like a drowning man to a life raft.

This was all he'd ever dreamed about; a woman who loved and desired him beyond reason—and she did. Even had she never admitted her feelings, Cian felt it in Piper's desperate response and her inability to let him go.

When they paused to gulp ragged breaths, he pressed his forehead to hers and breathed her in. "I love you, Piper. I think I have from the moment you spit your drink in my face. And when you threw rocks at me on the cliff, I knew you were a warrior woman. *My* warrior woman." He paused to kiss her again. "I won't lie and say all this doesn't terrify me or that I didn't pretend it was only physical between us, but I'll trust you not to break my poor wee heart the way Moira did."

"One day, you can tell me the circumstances surrounding her betrayal, but whatever it was, I promise I won't do the same thing. I love you, Cian." Her tender reverence as she traced his jawline caused his heart to hiccup. "I'm willing to give us our all, if you are." Her eyes widened at his prolonged silence. "Please say you are," she whispered.

"Yeah," he replied gruffly, right before he gripped her hair in his fist, gave it a light tug, and lowered his mouth to within a mere inch of hers. He pressed his arousal against her and grinned "I'm as willing as a man can be, darlin'."

Her fingers outlined his erection through his jeans. "I can feel your willingness," she quipped.

"Don't be fondling me lucky charms!"

"Why?" A sinful smile curled her lips and the last dregs of

Cian's blood surged into his dick. He couldn't answer her if he wanted to, because all his concentration was now below the belt. When she unzipped his pants and gave him a rub, he groaned. "I think sex with you is going to be *magically delicious*, Cian O'Malley."

He barked out a laugh at her sauciness. "Am I going to see green clovers, pink hearts, orange stars, and those yellow moons?" he countered.

She paused in her ministrations to frown up at him. "How long has it been since you've eaten Lucky Charms?"

"Never?" He hissed out a breath when she abruptly released him and stepped back.

"*What?* This relationship is doomed. I just can't talk to you."

"Don't ya be torturing me, woman! In this house, we finish what we start." Cian reached for her hand and shoved it back down the front of his jeans. "I'll eat those fecking things once a day and twice on Sunday if you don't stop."

She broke down in a fit of giggles, and Cian laughed, helpless against her amusement.

"Your face was priceless," she crowed.

He cupped her breast through her shirt. "I imagine it was. Now wiggle your fingers and lock the door, why don't ya? I'm craving *your* lucky charms."

Piper impatiently brushed his hands aside and lifted her top over her head.

Despite Cian's skill at removing female underclothes, his hands shook as he unfastened her bra.

Her blazing-hot skin reacted to the cool air, and her nipples hardened in response.

He paused to take in the entrancing sight and breathed in at the beauty before him. "Hello, lovelies. I've waited a lifetime to see you."

Piper's trill of laughter triggered his grin.

"A week, Cian. You've waited a *week*."

"We can discuss why time runs differently for you and me… *after.*" He curled his hands around her breasts, weighing and relishing the feel of them. The brush of his thumbs across the tight buds elicited her soft moan. Ducking his head, he captured one tip in his mouth.

Her fingers curled against the back of his head and she tugged him back with a fistful of his hair. "Does that mean you're jackrabbit fast in bed?"

Too fascinated by the way the low light caught and highlighted the glistening tip of her left breast, he didn't immediately process what she'd said. When he did, he glared up at her.

"I'm highly offended you'd believe something so foul of me. Just for that, you're getting three orgasms before I get me lucky charms off."

She giggled as he toppled her onto the sofa, and he smothered his own laughter against the silky-smooth skin of her throat.

The friction their laughter caused, registered mightily with his dick, and his eyes practically rolled back to greet his brain from pleasure of chest on chest. She opened her thighs wider, arched her hips, and rubbed the length of his erection.

"Oh, please no! Not three orgasms," she cried with blatant insincerity; the back of one hand pressed to her forehead.

He didn't bother to hide his laughter the second time. "You've got a wicked mouth on you."

"I'm known for my wicked mouth." Her grin was pure deviltry and the sultry smile would've brought him to his knees had he been standing. With a pointed look at his crotch, she said, "Very wicked mouth."

"Stop it right now, or you'll not get the first orgasm I promised. I'll spend like a pubescent boy and be the laughing stock of me pub."

Her husky laughter sent more blood surging to his dick.

With a rough groan, he crushed his lips to hers and sought entry with his tongue.

Her hands were everywhere: touching his skin, cupping his ass, shoving down his jeans. And he'd never felt so desperate to sink into a woman. The musky scent of her arousal filled the air and almost sent him over the edge of madness because he'd never get enough of her addictive fragrance.

Their teasing took a backseat to their lovemaking, and within the embrace of his arms, Piper became a wanton goddess. He, the mere mortal willing, ready, and able to worship at her feet. Every thrust brought him closer to being burned by her sun. Every panting breath she released was a command for him to work harder and bring her to completion.

After every single drop had been milked out of him, and after her second rapturous cry rang out; Cian rested his brow against hers and inhaled huge, gulping breaths of air into over-worked lungs. She did the same, and the push of her breasts into his chest made him wonder how fast he could recover to do this all over again.

He grinned as his mind circled around to her jackrabbit comment from earlier. "Perhaps time doesn't run differently for us, after all, Piper my love."

"Mmm. I'd say you have the timing down pat."

Cian chuckled and shifted his weight to roll them over. Flat on his back, he tucked her head against his pounding heart. "Sure, and there's always room for improvement."

He felt the movement of her lips as they curled into a smile.

"I've no complaints, and if you want to use my body for practice—you know, for that improvement—I'm game."

"That's what I like best about you, darlin'. Your willingness to be a team player." Her golden laughter filled his heart to full. "Piper?"

"Hmm?"

"I have no objection if you want to fondle me lucky charms."

"Any day of the week and twice on Sundays?" she asked in a drowsy murmur.

A laugh burst out of him, and he tightened his arms around her. "To be sure."

"I won't hide out."

"And I won't have you hanging about in public for all the world to see while there's still a target on your back."

Piper threw up her hands in her anger. "Cian, this is ridiculous. We might never find who's behind this. The best we can do is live life normally but remain alert."

"There you're wrong, love. I'm more determined than ever to find them. We've too much to lose."

"I won't hide," she repeated firmly.

"Don't look at it as hiding. Look at it as keeping my bed warm." He was sprawled in a comfy chair with one leg draped over the arm. The crackling fire in the hearth backlit him and made him look like temptation personified, but Piper was too irritated to act on her desire to climb onto his lap.

He tried to cover his knowing grin with a mug of coffee, but he failed miserably. They'd been burning up the sheets for the better part of a week, and she still didn't feel as if she could get enough. The man was a sex god in bed. Piper craved his touch morning, noon, and night. She was an addict, and Cian was her drug of choice. The problem was that he knew and exploited it.

Still, she wasn't a pushover. *Much.* "I'm not kidding, Cian. I might as well have stayed back home. I'm tired of being cooped up and I want out."

"I'd be happy for you to go back home if it will save your life." His tone had turned hard and there was a coldness in his expression. It gave her a moment's pause. The other time he'd seemed so distant was when they spoke of commitment. Was this his way of getting rid of her after he'd gotten what he wanted? Had she misread the signs?

Frustrated tears threatened, and she'd rather punch his annoying face than shed them.

Cian sighed heavily and climbed to his feet. After placing his coffee cup on a side table, he crossed to her and tilted up her chin. "Piper me love, I can't help Bridget run the pub and guard your delectable body at the same time." He kissed the tip of her nose. "You either go home or you don't step foot outside these walls. Those are your two options. Make your choice."

A loud pop from the logs in the fireplace punctuated his statement, annoying her further. "You're not the boss of me."

She might as well stomp her feet and stick out her tongue like a child. And yeah, her tone was petulant, but so what? His bossiness grated on her last nerve. Piper almost told him as much, but his booming laughter rang out and made her smile—reluctantly, at that!

Her inconvenience was nothing compared to theirs. Bridget had called all the visitors booked for the next month and either rescheduled or refunded their deposits. All for Piper's safety, and with minimal complaint. Hoyt had written a check for double the amount of what they'd lost, but it still didn't make up for the inconvenience or the potential loss of return customers.

Piper snuggled into Cian's embrace. "Fine, I'll stay inside."

"Even if another incident like the fire happens."

She thunked her forehead on his rock-hard pec. "Even if

another incident like the fire happens," she dutifully replied with her crossed fingers hidden behind his back.

"Let me see your hands, darlin'."

Aghast, she drew back and stared at him, open-mouthed. "Why... what... how... *you don't believe me?*" Her voice shot up an octave with each word, clearly giving her away.

A single arched brow was his answer, and as he stared down at her with all-knowing eyes, his lips twitched as if he fought a laugh or struggled to hold back the words that would label her a liar.

Piper wasn't one for lying, but she understood the only way to remotely pull it off was to stand firm and not back down. In a battle of wills, the person who blinked first conceded the field.

He'd just reached for her hands when the door slammed open. In walked a petite redhead with a peaches and cream complexion, a form-hugging black dress equipped with plunging neckline—Gucci, if Piper wasn't mistaken, and an attitude that screamed she was owed the world.

The woman's calculating gaze summed up the scene in a second, and she adjusted her expression accordingly. Her countenance took on a shocked, heartbroken look and she batted wide, wounded eyes at Cian. "Darling? What is this?"

Darling?

Acid burned the back of Piper's throat and she wanted to hurl. She dropped her arms from around him and moved back a few steps. Dear Goddess, please don't say she'd hooked up with another cheater.

Based on Cian's reaction, he was positively shell-shocked. He hadn't taken his stunned gaze from their visitor.

"Cian?" Piper didn't want to sound like an outraged wife, but she certainly needed an explanation as to why another woman was calling him "darling" and acting as if *she'd* been betrayed because she found them hugging.

"Cian." There was an over-infusion of warmth in the newcomer's tone as she sauntered forward, wrapped her arms around his neck, and drew his open mouth down to meld with hers.

"*What. The. Actual. Fuck?*" Piper wasn't aware she'd snarled the question until Red shot her a triumphant smile.

"Who's the outraged maiden, darling? Another one of your playthings?"

Without any other thought other than to maim a bitch, Piper charged. Cian was faster and wrapped an arm around her waist as the redhead sidestepped to safety.

"I'll give you a plaything, skank!" Piper shouted as she struggled within the circle of Cian's firm hold. She kicked out but missed Red's shiny, waxed shins.

"Oh, Cian! She's *delightful*. I can see why she might hold your attention—for a short while."

Her tittering laughter almost caused Piper to stroke out. The sensation of her blood freezing and her heart hardening was visceral. She went cold inside and ceased her struggle.

"Let me go, Cian. *Now,*" she demanded when he didn't immediately comply.

Cian ignored her and focused back on Red. "Moira."

Moira?

Piper knew she'd lost the second Cian spoke his ex-girlfriend's name. Her chest felt the same as it had after the cave in —*crushed*—and she wanted to bolt. But she wouldn't. She needed to see how this would play out and discover how the hell that bitch had returned from the dead.

"I've missed you dreadfully, darling." Moira had the nerve to wipe away a crocodile tear and place her hands over her heart. "You don't know what I've been through. Then to come home and find this..." She released a choked sob and pressed her knuckles to her mouth. "You know I've never minded your meaningless flings in the past, but can you send her away so we could have quiet time?"

Piper wished they were *her* knuckles, and she wanted to use a ton more force as she applied them to Moira's face.

"I… we all thought you were dead, Moira." Cian's voice held wonder and what sounded like a touch of fear.

"You've moved on? I had no reason to believe you wouldn't, but…" A consummate actress, Moira perched on the chair's edge and buried her distraught face in her hands. *"Oh, Cian."*

Not for one second did Piper think this farce was real. If Moira had truly loved Cian, she'd have been shocked, hurt, angry, and possibly run for the door. But she hadn't. And Piper hadn't failed to see Moira's crafty gleam, right before the hysterics started.

"Piper…"

Her face went numb, and she couldn't drag her gaze away from Moira, who peered through parted fingers at them. The woman was shrewd enough to recognize the dismissal in Cian's tone.

He blocked Piper's view and set his hands atop her shoulders before pulling them back as if burned. He balled his fists and held them rigid by his sides as if he didn't want to betray Moira by touching Piper again.

Her eyes locked with his and she could see the uncomfortable apology he wanted to say but couldn't seem to voice.

"Don't do this," Piper whispered. "Don't welcome her back in."

"She was my fiancée."

"Precisely. She *was* your fiancée."

"Is," he corrected. "She *is* my fiancée. I…" Cian shrugged in a helpless manner.

He'd chosen.

No more words were needed.

Piper held up a hand to forestall anything else he might say. "I got it."

Four long strides took her out the door and into the hallway. She hadn't realized Cian was on her heels until Moira said, "Oh, let her go, darling. We both know she's nobody."

Unable to hear anything else through the ringing in her ears, Piper rushed up the stairs to her room.

CIAN'S STOMACH REBELLED AS HE STARED AT THE EMPTY doorway with the disturbing feeling he'd just royally screwed the pooch. Piper couldn't get away fast enough, and he couldn't blame her. What the devil made him say Moira was his fiancée? The treacherous hellcat had been gone from his life for over two years, and didn't deserve his loyalty. But they hadn't formally broken up. He'd fully intended to rectify the situation back then, but he'd gotten the not-so tragic news of her death. And until she'd strolled into his home today, he'd believed he'd never have the chance to find closure.

Sure, and it wasn't gladness in his heart when he'd first seen her tonight. If he'd felt even a smidgeon of happiness, he'd have hied it straight to the doctor to have his head examined without delay.

"Cian? Darling?"

Furious with himself, with her, and with Ryker for not uncovering her whereabouts before now, he whirled on her. He could feel the heat of his rage climbing his neck, and that seething fury was bubbling up inside his mouth, ready to spew ugliness like a volcano. Like lava flowing unimpeded toward the sea, the harsh words were gaining momentum and ready to decimate everything in their path—namely the triumphant bitch before him.

Had she really thought she could walk in here and flutter

her lashes with a butter-wouldn't-melt-in-her-mouth smile? Did she think to have him eating out of her hand?

Apparently, she did.

"I'm not your darlin', Moira. You lost any claim you had when you betrayed me and humiliated me in front of the Witches' Council." He strode back across the room. "You faked your death to boot. Who does that?" With his hands on his hips and a black scowl on his face, he said, "I'll tell you. A right horrible minger who doesn't care for another person but her fucking self."

"What is this about, Cian? That little slapper who ran away? She's not woman enough for you."

He reeled back as if she'd struck him, shocked she'd had the bollocks to insult Piper, yet again. "Piper is worth a thousand of you, Moira. Make that one hundred thousand. And I'll not have you insult her in my house. It'll take me a week of Sundays to fix the mischief you've whipped up this night."

"Mischief," Moira murmured. "Yes, I suppose you'd see it that way, wouldn't you?"

She rose to her feet and sashayed to him. Each movement a rolling step designed to add sway to her ample hips. If Cian didn't despise her to the lengths he did, he might appreciate the effort she was putting forth to seduce him. As it was, she made his skin crawl.

She touched his arm, and he felt a sharp stab.

"What the bloody hell was that?" He jerked his arm away, but not before her ring pierced his skin a second time.

Moira touched her hand to her mouth as if she were surprised, then made a production of appearing contrite. "There's a burr on the bottom side of this ring. I'm terribly sorry. Until it tears my clothing or scratches me, I forget it's there." She gave him an innocent smile, but he recognized her game. "I'll drop it by the jeweler this week. I'd hate for anyone else to get hurt."

"Yeah, you do that. Better yet, why don't you go right now? You're not welcome here anymore, Moira. If I see you again, you'll wish I hadn't."

Her cat-like blue eyes turned a dark and stormy gray. A corresponding clap of thunder sounded outside and the resulting rumble shook the walls of the inn. "Careful, Cian. There's no telling what I'd do if I thought you didn't love me anymore."

With a contemptuous scoff, he gripped her elbow and escorted her none-too-gently out of the room, down the hallway, and out the front door. "Don't come back, Moira. You're not to set foot in this house again. Nor the pub." He leaned forward until they were practically nose to nose. "And you may not fear me, but I've right powerful friends in Alastair Thorne, Hoyt Thorne, and Ryker Gillespie. They'll happily see your arse take a one-way trip to hell for hurting Piper's feelings the way you have."

Her fury was palpable, and a small part of Cian worried about her retaliation. She wasn't a novice witch, nor was she afraid to use her abilities to cause havoc. In fact, it wasn't hard to imagine she was behind many of his family's misfortunes as well as his and Piper's more recent bad luck.

It begged the question: how did she get past the wards? Thorne magic wasn't impossible to break, but Cian suspected it would take multiple witches working together to do it.

Lucky, Bridget's beloved black cat, chose that moment to cross Moira's path. The feline hissed as he danced sideways, ready to attack her given the slightest provocation. Animals had an innate sense if a person was good or bad, and Cian would trust Lucky's instincts every time.

With a guttural growl that rose to a screech, Lucky launched himself Moira's ankle and clawed for all he was worth. The fiendish glee Cian felt when he saw her face pale was sure to score him points with the devil.

"Get this fucking cat off me!" she screamed.

Fear for Lucky's safety had Cian scooping up the cat. He doubted Moira was above hurting the little beast. "Goodbye and good riddance to you, Moira."

"Watch your back, Cian," she warned.

He heard the promise in her voice, and knew to take heed. It was doubtful she'd try anything with everyone on guard. Moira was nothing if not deliberate. She'd take the time to regroup.

Cian eyed the staircase. A large part of him wanted to have it out right now, but Piper wouldn't hear him. She'd been too distraught for reason when she'd fled. Later, after he'd washed away the evilness still clinging to his skin from that she-devil Moira, he'd tell Piper the truth of his feelings and pray she'd forgive him for being too slow to react. He'd confess he'd been stunned stupid by Moira's arrival.

A quick text informed Piper they needed to talk in the morning. In it, he asked her not to leave until they had. With his second, he notified Bridget and Ryker of his plans to head to the bar and asked they check the strength of the wards when they got back. If he switched jobs with Bridget tonight, he could bartend, drink his fill, and not worry their houseguests would be left unprotected. But his first priority would be to wash the taste of Moira out of his mouth.

Piper was leaving. And Cian was a total ass because he hadn't come after her, which meant he fully intended to let her go. Her chest ached and it legit felt like her heart was literally breaking in two.

Engaged!

After all this time, he claimed to still be engaged to Moira. One would think death—or a faked death in that horrid bitch's case—would void any promises made. And had that not been enough, the fact she'd double crossed him and ruined his career should've put a damper on his things.

"Dick!" She threw her stuff on the bed, then dug her suitcase out from underneath with an aborted sob.

Why had she expected better from a man who, a mere ten days ago, was a self-proclaimed player and who refused to open up to real love? Did he seriously only want affection that came from that lying skank Moira? Anyone could see her aura was peppered with ugly and she had no true emotion to give.

But who was Piper to question the tastes of men? Chalk it up to her fucked-up radar.

She didn't bother folding her clothes as she dumped one

item after the other into her suitcase. And when she got to the Lucky Charms t-shirt Cian had given her just yesterday as a memento of their first time together, she balled it against her mouth to muffle a rage-induced scream.

All Cian had asked was that Piper not do to him what Moira had. Yet the second the other woman had returned from the dead, Cian had abandoned Piper like yesterday's news. Whatever the two of them had begun to build couldn't stand up against whatever it was he'd desired from Moira. His heart *still* remained frozen to all others. Piper included.

She momentarily paused what she was doing and looked around her wrecked room. It was as if a cyclone had struck when she wasn't paying attention. A small shiver of unease struck. Her rage had created this destruction. Another reason she avoided magic; in the wrong hands, without mindfulness, it was lethal.

Wasting no more time, she used Liz's sure-fire packing enchantment to finish the chore as she went to retrieve her toiletries from the bathroom. She caught her tear-ravaged reflection in the mirror.

How ridiculous was she to let someone turn her world upside down with lies and half-truths again?

No more.

She was done with romantic love.

Her gaze dropped to her flat stomach. Pressing a hand to her abdomen, she promised herself that she'd only ever bend over backwards for her little munchkin from here on out.

She'd gotten pregnant the first time they'd had sex. The instant his sperm connected with her eggs, a sensation of rightness hit her, and she'd known. She supposed she could urinate on a stick, but she didn't need to. The additional magic coursing through her was too strong to discredit.

The Goddess had finally seen fit to entrust another's life into Piper's keeping. She wouldn't let either the baby or Isis down. She'd stop trying to be mortal. The Goddess had granted her abilities for a reason and to deny the gift felt sacrilegious. She wouldn't continue to disrespect her gifts any longer.

Bathing her face in cold water, she mumbled a quick glamour spell to eliminate the evidence of her breakdown. She didn't feel any less tired or worn down, but her entire countenance glowed with vitality and beauty.

Piper grunted at her reflection. "Today starts a new day, Piper Thorne. Don't you waste another second on stupid men, do you hear me? From here on out, it's you and the baby." She caressed the flat area above her womb. "We'll make our own family circle, munch," she told it. "Mom and Dad—or rather, your Gran and Grandpa—are going to spoil you rotten. So are your cousins Liz and Mack. You're going to adore them, munch. They're my best friends in the entire world."

Piper firmed her stance. With a twitch of her fingers, all her toiletries flew into the other room. Did she imagine her magic was stronger than before?

"Pfft. *The Mighty Thorne,* my ass." She paused on her way back into the bedroom. "Maybe my dad is *the Mighty Thorne* and he'll shove an ice pick into the heart of *the Frozen,*" she said aloud to her baby. "It's no more than he deserves, I'll tell you that. Yeah, I get that he's your father, but Cian's a fucking jerk. You'll be better for not having him in your life. The fickle shit."

A pang struck her heart, but she firmly shoved aside the hurt.

He'd done this. *Not* her.

Piper zipped her suitcase, verbalized the words to restore the destroyed room, and made one last visual inspection. Not a single trace of her remained.

"Good. Cian should be happy," she muttered.

The feeling to get out of this house ASAP was clawing at her brain. It caused her skin to prickle and the hair on her neck to rise. She intended to forego a flight and simply teleport, but she couldn't leave without thanking Bridget for her hospitality. The main problem was that she didn't want to leave her room and run into either Moira or Cian. If she did, she didn't know what she'd do.

"You're a Thorne, dammit!" she scolded. "Stop acting like a chickenshit and woman up."

Gathering the last of her courage, Piper stepped into the hallway, but came up short. "Seamus? What are you doing here?"

Ugliness shifted in his expression, flitting away so swiftly, she wasn't positive she'd witnessed it.

"Cian asked that I shuttle you to the airport. Are you ready to go?"

Had he anticipated her desire to flee? Perhaps hoped for it?

"Not quite yet. I want to say goodbye first."

"He doesn't want to see you, girl. Don't know how much plainer he has to make it."

The snappish words were a knife to her heart, but she refused to show their effect on her. "It's not Cian I intend to speak to, Seamus. I owe Bridget a courtesy."

His eyes narrowed and irritation flared in their charcoal depths.

Piper stared at him in confusion. When she'd first met Seamus, he'd been mellow, his eyes a dull, pale blue. There had been no sign he was a witch. Today, his irises were startlingly different—*a witch's tell.*

"She's not available." His tone was terse and bordered on hostile.

"I'll see for myself, thanks. Please step aside, Seamus." She hoped he didn't hear the tremble in her voice.

"Ye Thornes always have to make things difficult, don't ye?"

Fear formed a tight knot in the pit of her stomach. It never ended well when someone referred to her family as a whole. That type of malice always indicated trouble.

"We do." She shifted onto the balls of her feet. "Why don't you tell me what this is about?"

A grudging respect lit his face and he smiled. "Cool as a cucumber even facin' your own death."

Fuck!

Suddenly it all became crystal clear: the attacks, the accidents, the assassins—they'd been sent by Seamus.

AT THE END OF THE BAR, CIAN GUZZLED THE LAST OF HIS Guinness, slammed his glass down, and gestured for a refill.

Ruairí picked up the glass and wiped the condensation from the bar's surface. "Why don't you stop this nonsense and follow your true heart, Cian?"

"Why don't you mind your own fecking business?"

Ruairí continued as if Cian hadn't spoken, picking up empties and scrubbing down the counter. "Love is the most precious gift in life, man."

"Right, and you're one to lecture me. Bridg—"

"This isn't about Bridget. It's about you and the colossal mistake you intend to make by letting that girl go back to America. And for what? That *hoor* Moira? Because she's returned to twist you in knots?" Disgust was heavy in Ruairí's voice, and he threw down the towel with a furious glare at Cian. "Bridget's right. You're a fecking eejit!" He spun to go but turned back with a stormy frown. "Did Seamus find you?"

"No. Why?" Cian didn't have the bandwidth to deal with Seamus right then. Piper was certain to be upset, and Cian hadn't found the words for when he crawled back to beg her forgiveness. He'd never felt more miserable in his life.

Yeah, he'd found the courage to break things off with Moira. He'd faced those heartbreakingly blue eyes and seen her for what she was. Those peepers had always been able to shred him in the past, but not anymore.

"Beautiful Moira," he whispered. Underneath all that gorgeous was nothing worth loving.

"Beautiful Moira, my arse," Ruairí retorted, misunderstanding Cian's meaning. "Where has that betraying bitch been these last years, Cian? Scarlet for your ma for havin' ya! I can't believe you've been taken in by Moira's continued lies." He stalked off to serve another customer.

After Ruairí's words sunk in, Cian experienced a burning need to get to Piper. His friend was right. Moira was a betrayer, and she'd come back for a reason. Cian had overlooked the real reason she was back. Sure, and it wasn't to kiss up to him.

"*Fuck!*" Cian surged to his feet. Or attempted to. He used the bar as a crutch as he swayed and tried to focus on the wall clock. Something was wrong. He shouldn't be this pissed after a single pint.

"O'Connor..."

Ruairí paused in putting the money in the drawer and glanced over his shoulder. "I'm not refilling your glass, Cian. I'll not help you drink away your woes."

"*Ruairí.*"

His urgency must've registered, because Ruairí became a man alert.

"What's going on?"

"The room shouldn't be spinnin' this—" Cian swallowed down the nausea in the back of his throat. "—fast."

"Not after one pint of plain or you're the worst sort of Irishman, to be sure."

"The room is spinnin'," Cian stated again, more emphatically. Mere seconds later, his legs quit supporting him.

He heard a shout as he crashed to the floor.

"SEAMUS MCCLEARY, WHAT THE DEVIL DO YOU THINK YOU'RE doing?" Bridget's strident tones rang out.

His eyes locked onto Piper, promising a reckoning, and she felt the chill down to the marrow of her bones.

"Run, Bridget!" She flung her bag at Seamus's head. *"Run!"*

As he batted away Piper's suitcase, Seamus swore long and loud.

Piper didn't give him time to act and quickly twisted to deliver a back kick to his stomach. Ill-prepared, he crashed into the wall behind him with a solid thud.

Wasting no time, Piper sprinted toward a stunned Bridget and grabbed her hand. "We've got to *go!*"

They made it to the stairs in record time, but so did Seamus.

Piper practically shoved Bridget down the steps then spun back to face her would-be attacker.

Use your magic.

The phrase whispered through her brain, reminding her she had a powerful arsenal at her disposal. Calling her elemental magic with a mere thought, she blasted Seamus with arctic air. Ice crystals formed on his skin, and his lips turned blue.

"*Contineo,*" she cried out.

Her shouted command locked him in place.

"Take that you, asshat," she muttered.

Piper made it to the second landing when she heard Seamus thundering down the stairs. Terror kicked her heart rate into high gear. Her enchantment should've lasted until she released him.

How the hell had he broken free?

The only plausible explanations were that he was prepared for her spell *or* he had an accomplice, who was scrying and waiting to reverse whatever she threw at him. Neither possibility thrilled her.

Piper and Bridget rounded the last landing and plowed into

Moira. They all went down in a heap of arms, legs, and creative swear words—the last on Piper's part as the edge of the half wall connected with the soft tissue between her ribs. The air escaped her lungs in a rush, but inhaling more was a labor.

What was it with these asshats abusing her ribs?

She spared a worried thought for her little peanut, but the other women had broken her fall for the most part.

"Piper!" Bridget attempted to drag her to her feet as she cast a frantic look toward the stairs. "You've got to move, woman!"

"Can't… breathe…" Piper dredged up enough brainpower to touch her tanzanite ring and send Alastair a telepathic cry for help.

As Moira rose to her feet, an evil smile curled her lips. "Convenient. Two of you in one place. This should be easy." She backhanded Bridget, then drew back and kicked Piper in the same place that she'd connected with the half wall.

Piper's agonized scream echoed around the foyer. The unfolding events were hazy for her as blackness dotted her peripheral vision and her focus narrowed to sucking in labored breath after labored breath.

The atmosphere around them crackled, and she was aware of a blinding white light. In the back of her conscious mind, she heard Seamus beg for mercy and a man's derisive bark of laughter. A triumphant smile curled her lips.

Alastair had arrived.

Consciousness returned in small degrees to Piper. The noises penetrating her fog weren't those of the battle she'd recently fought. If she didn't know better, she'd think it was a soft snoring. She moaned as she turned her head toward the sound. The sight of her father dozing in the chair beside her bed brought welcome relief, along with a heavy dose of chagrin. Once again, he was playing nursemaid. She'd be lucky if he didn't lock her in a tower and throw away the key.

"As hard-headed and resilient as we Thornes are, you must stop pushing the limits, child." Alastair emerged from the shadows on the far side of the room.

She shivered at the eeriness of his ability to read her thoughts. "Noted."

"Your life will be significantly shorter than the average bear if you continue on this course."

"Thank you for charging to my rescue again, Cuz," Piper said with a wide smile. "I'm assuming you kicked the big baddies' asses?"

He snorted and tugged the cuffs of his dress shirt. "Need you ask?"

She sat up and hugged her knees. "No."

"Actually, it wasn't me alone. Bridget was happy to dispatch Moira with a solid punch or five."

A laugh bubbled out of Piper, and she nodded her approval. "Good. I hate that bitch."

"I'm going to assume you mean the duplicitous Moira," Alastair said dryly.

"Who else? Please tell me she's rotting in a jail cell. Or Hades. I'm happy if she was cast to the farthest reaches of hell. I'm not picky."

He chuckled as he cupped the back of Piper's head and leaned in to kiss her brow. "Never change, child. You're perfect exactly the way you are."

"Thank you," she whispered past the sudden lump in her throat. She suppressed the urge to ask why, if she was so perfect, was she so abhorrent to the male population. But she'd already decided it would be her and her munchkin moving forward.

Her hand flew to her abdomen. "My baby?"

Alastair's surprised expression was comical. His disconcerted gaze dropped to her belly. "GiGi didn't mention…" He shook his head and smiled. "I'm sure he or she is fine. My sister would've detected distress if your child was harmed." He hiked up his slacks and perched on the edge of the bed. "I suppose congratulations are in order."

"Thank you." Her gaze darted to her father. "How long have I been out? He looks exhausted."

"You slept through the healing—about three hours. Hoyt just dozed off about ten minutes ago. He's been cleaning up the last of this little mess."

"So it's done now? No more attacks?" He didn't immediately respond, and she could tell he was troubled by an, as yet, unnamed problem. "Just spit it out, Alastair. Please."

"Cian was dosed with a poison. He hasn't woken up since he

passed out. Spring, GiGi, and Rebecca are all trying to determine what he might've ingested to put him into such a deep stasis."

"*Stasis?*" Piper's hand flew to her mouth as Alastair's words sunk in.

"Yes."

She fought back the threatening tears. Although she didn't want Cian to die, his welfare was no longer her concern. He'd made his choice.

"I hope they can help him," she said in a deadened voice. "He…" She shrugged. What was left to say?

Alastair clasped her hands between his larger ones. "He cares for you, child. When you feel up to it, you should visit him. If only to say goodbye. You'll regret it if you don't."

Alarmed and feeling the urge to hurl, she stared into Alastair's kind, understanding face. "You think he's going to die," she whispered in horror.

"No one knows the Goddess's plan, Piper. But I've lived with many regrets in my life. I wouldn't wish that for you."

She nodded absently as she let his warmth seep through their connected hands to chase her coldness away.

With a last comforting pat, he climbed to his feet.

"Thank you, Cuz," she said again. "Next to my dad, you're the best man I know."

"If you believe me to be one of the best, you have a low bar." Alastair's laugh rumbled from deep within his chest and the rusty sound made Piper grin. "Be happy, child. Whatever you decide."

"That's *my* plan."

He grinned. "I'm sure Isis can't fault that. Free will and all."

In a blink, he was gone. As the atmosphere around her returned to normal, she thought about what he'd said. She probably should check on Cian before she left for home. She supposed she owed him for the gift he'd unknowingly given her.

With one palm cradling her abdomen, she rose to her feet. A simple snap had her dressed and ready to slay dragons. Or in this case, say goodbye to her stupid hopes and dreams.

"Dad." She gently shook her father's shoulder. "Why don't you go to bed? It's late."

"Pip?" He bound out of the chair and hauled her close for a bear hug. "You really need to stop scaring your old man like that. No more fighting or near-death experiences, all right?"

"Promise."

With a final squeeze, he released her and took in her appearance. "You look determined."

She snorted a laugh. "I suppose I am. I'm going to see Cian one last time. To check and make sure he's okay, and to see if Bridget needs anything, before I head home."

Understanding came to Hoyt and he nodded slowly. "Need company?"

"No. This is something I should do on my own. Besides, Alastair said our crew is with Cian. I'm fine." She swallowed hard and forced a smile. "I'm just going to say goodbye. I want the comfort of my own place, Dad."

The seriousness of his expression hurt her heart, and she had no doubt he understood her pain. Maybe not to the degree she was hurting, but still, he would give her the space she needed to heal.

"I suppose this is the perfect time for me to say that you do your mom and me proud, Pip." His gruffness spoke of his strong emotions, and once again, their deep and abiding love for her could be felt.

"Thanks, Dad."

As Piper gazed down at Cian's deathly pale visage, she realized this was the first time she'd ever seen him this still. He was always in motion. Always charming his way out of trouble —or charming his way into it.

"We won't give up," her mom told her from the opposite side of the bed. "Cian's strong."

Piper didn't bother to look up as she nodded. "I know. He's in good hands with you three."

She memorized each of his features: the sharply shaped brows, his full unsmiling mouth, the high cheekbones, and firm jaw. She ran a finger down his beautiful, straight nose, noting how well it healed after she'd broken it. Her lips quirked as she remembered his outrage when the rock had cut him.

"We had a fun run, Cian O'Malley. But I suppose it's time it ended."

His brows twitched, as if he were fighting a frown, but he remained asleep.

"I did love you, you know," she whispered next to his ear. Unable to help herself, she touched her lips to his. "Don't linger in stasis, okay? Your family is counting on you to come back to them."

Turning away, she caught sight of Bridget. Her distraught look crushed what was left of Piper's heart. Rushing over, she hugged her tight. "He's going to be fine, Bridget. He's a fighter."

Piper felt the movement of Bridget's nod against her shoulder, and the need to offer comfort where she could, overwhelmed her. "You're a wonderful sister to him. He's lucky to have you."

"He's an eejit, but he's ours all the same."

Soul-battered, Piper was amazed she could still laugh. "Thank you for everything. I've settled my bill online and secured Spring's promise to recreate your Granny's potion again whenever you need it."

"You need not have paid that. This wasn't the vacation you

were hoping for, and I feel badly about it." Bridget touched her hand. "Will you keep in touch?"

Piper knew the question was straightforward and offered from the heart. She didn't know how to respond. How would she keep her baby a secret from Cian if she allowed Bridget into her world?

"Yes," she lied. She gently squeezed Bridget's fingers then strode from the room before anyone could recognize the falsehood for what it was.

Piper made it back to her room without shedding a single tear. As she picked up her bag to teleport home, movement in the shadowed corner of the room caught her attention.

"Aeden?" She set her suitcase and purse on the bed. "What's going on, fry guy?"

He charged across the room and wrapped his skinny arms around her waist. A sob tore from his throat and she had a hard time not joining him in his grief.

"Is this about your uncle?"

Aeden nodded jerkily.

"He's going to be fine, kiddo."

The boy lifted his face to study her, as if he was searching for the truth in her words.

Piper brushed back the shaggy blond hair from his large, wounded eyes. She imagined this was what Cian looked like as a child. Squatting down, she lightly pinched his chin between her thumb and forefinger. "Listen to me. Cian is a fighter, Aeden. His body is sleeping as it processes the poison, but that's all."

His lower lip trembled, but he didn't speak.

"My family is here to help him through this. My mom's a brilliant doctor, and Spring and GiGi are powerful witches. If anyone can heal him, it's them."

"What about you?" he rasped.

"I can cast the occasional spell, but curing others isn't my gig."

"But you're *the Mighty Thorne*."

Aeden didn't know the pain brought on by his innocent words.

"I don't think I am, kiddo. I'm just a witch who doesn't know what she's about most days."

"You *have to* prick Uncle Cian's heart."

"Who told you that?"

"The Goddess."

Had she visited this boy and told him Piper needed to use magic on Cian?

"Are you talking about Isis?"

He shook his head. "Anu."

"Anu?" The only Anu she'd heard of was an Irish goddess, and Piper knew next to nothing about her.

"Yes."

Great, a new deity to contend with!

"What else did Anu say?"

Aeden dug into his jacket pocket and withdrew a twig with small black berries. "She said you would know what to do with this."

"Did she mention what these were?" Piper tried to keep the panic out of her voice. If the berries were what she thought, they were deadly. "You didn't eat any, did you?"

The boy shook his head as his eyes grew wider and more fearful.

"Okay, sweetie." She rose to her feet and guided him to the bathroom. "Wash your hands thoroughly, all right? These are supremely toxic."

Aeden did as she bid and held up his palms for her inspection. With an attempt at an approving smile, she ushered him toward Cian's sickroom. "Come on. We have to tell GiGi what we're dealing with here."

Five minutes later, they were discussing alternative

methods of healing. While they all knew what these hybrid witchbane-moonseeds were, none of them had ever encountered them.

"We know standard moonseeds are toxic," GiGi said. "Some Désorcelers Society botanist had felt the need to create a hybrid using these little suckers."

"Potentially fatal wasn't enough? They had to make them uber deadly?" Piper asked incredulously.

"Something like that." GiGi shared a worried glance with Spring. "What do you know about them, child?"

"Not much. I have a cure for moonseed poisoning, but not this."

Helplessness multiplying, Piper wanted to scream. "What if we combine the cures? Like whatever you'd normally use to counteract witchbane and moonseed, then blend them together?"

Spring shook her head. "It doesn't work that way. You could shock his system and finish him off."

"Aeden said a goddess gave him the twig, and that I'd know what to do." Piper touched Cian's pale, cold cheek. "I don't. I've no idea how to fix him."

Aeden surprised her when he tugged her sleeve. "You're *the Mighty Thorne*," he repeated from earlier. "You have to prick his heart."

A sick sort of hope caused her pulse to gallop. "I have to prick his heart! It *is* a literal translation!" She cradled his adorable little face and kissed his nose. "You brilliant, brilliant angel."

His mouth curled into a hesitant smile, and he shuffled back to the corner.

Piper belatedly wondered if he was more comfortable in the shadows, away from everyone's reach, like Alastair. Once Cian was out of the woods, she intended to broach the subject with his family.

"Aeden has a direct connect to Anu." She gave them a brief rundown of what she knew about the Irish goddess. "I think this means we'll need a syringe with a needle long enough to reach the heart muscle. Apparently, I'll need to administer the cure, whatever that might be."

"I think you should peruse the O'Malley's grimoire since it responds to you. Take Bridget and see if she can translate whatever you don't understand." GiGi then addressed Spring. "With your photographic memory, I imagine you can recall the antidote for witchbane poisoning."

"I'll pop home and check my notes just in case. Can you confer with Uncle Alastair and see if he's familiar with any of this?"

"Consider it done." GiGi hugged her before she teleported off.

"I'll search my medical books and see if there is anything on moonseed poisoning," Rebecca said. "It shouldn't take long. I'll have your father and my assistants help." She brushed her fingers over Piper's brow like she had when Piper was a small child. The gesture always provided comfort in the past, but today Piper was too worried to be swayed by her mother's assurances.

"Who will stay with Cian?" She wasn't comfortable leaving him with no one to stand watch.

Bridget touched her arm. "You stay, Piper. I'll bring our book to you."

The room was eerily silent after everyone's departure. Only Aeden remained like a tiny wraith in the corner, ever watchful and perhaps a little fearful.

"Is this also the sacrifice for *the One*, I wonder?" she murmured. "Does this count as a two-fer?"

Aeden didn't answer and Cian couldn't.

"Well, Cian O'Malley. I'm here to save your life, so you'll have to deal with me one last time."

Cian didn't recognize the park he wandered through. On the pond, ducks paddled about as if they'd no care in the world. Birds sang melodic little tunes only they knew the lyrics to, and deer grazed in the distance, unafraid of the intruder in their midst. There was an air of wrongness, as if he shouldn't be here. As if, it wasn't real but an illusion.

Where were the people? And how the hell had he gotten here?

He hated this place. It in no way resembled Ireland, and he'd no desire to be anywhere else. Determined to find a way home, he took off in another direction but ended back where he started.

Minutes turned to hours, but the sun never shifted in the sky.

Definitely off.

With a guttural yell toward the heavens, he stomped to a stone bench and plopped down.

"You have no patience, Cian O'Malley. Perhaps you'll learn some as you wait."

Jumping up, he spun to face the woman sashaying toward him.

She was easily the most beautiful woman he'd ever seen. Her hair was a shimmering blue-black, and her all-knowing amber tiger eyes were kohl-lined. She wore a sheer, white dress that reflected the perfect amount of light to provide modest coverage of her natural assets. The dress draped over her left shoulder, held together with a jeweled clasp. A gold scorpion bangle balanced the look and graced her upper right arm. In her hand, she held a long staff with a dark yellow stone cradled by the branch at the top.

Elements of her watchful expression reminded him of Piper. More than that, she actually *looked* like Piper to a large degree. Her skin was a shade darker, more olive in color, and Piper was more full-figured, but they shared a similarity of features and those eyes were the same, minus the makeup.

"Who are you?" he demanded. "And how have you trapped me here?"

Wicked laughter curled around him and drew him in. He appreciated a woman's uninhibited laugh, and his desire to share in her merriment was strong, but he held himself back. He would not give in to whatever enchantment she was weaving.

"If you look to your heart, you'll recognize me." She glided past him with a not-so-subtle sway of her hips, but it was as if the gesture was ingrained and not deliberate.

"I'm afraid I don't, love. But based on your beauty and blinding glow, I'd say you are a powerful witch. Why have you trapped me here?"

Again, she laughed. "Witch? No."

"Enchantress?" His heart beat harder. Please, don't say goddess, he silently begged her.

She cast a sardonic glance over her shoulder at him, and her lips twitched as if she fought a smile. "I'm sorry to disappoint you, Beloved, but I'm neither witch, nor Enchantress, nor Guardian. I'll leave it to you to deduce what option is left."

"Goddess." He closed his lids against eyes that wanted to weep.

He was dead.

"It's a pleasure to finally meet you, Cian O'Malley. I'm Isis."

"Yeah. I'd like to say the same, to be sure, but I'm a wee bit distraught by the knowledge I'm dead." He blinked and ran a hand through his hair. At this rate, his ghostly form would be bald soon.

She did smile then. "You're not, you know."

"Dead?"

"Correct. You're in a deep stasis." Lifting her arm, she brandished the staff. The pond turned gray and an image began to form—a picture of him on his deathbed with Piper beside him, her hand clutching his to her breast. "It's not a snapshot, as you'd call it. It's in real time. This is what is happening as you and I watch," Isis explained.

Cian was too choked up to speak. The sight of Piper's distraught, helpless expression was too much for him. The shadow in the corner shifted, and he wanted to call out a warning. But after peering closer, he recognized his nephew.

"Is this also the sacrifice for the One, I wonder?" Piper murmured. *"Does this count as a two-fer?"* Aeden didn't answer her and she didn't appear surprised, merely saddened. *"Well, Cian O'Malley. I'm here to save your life, so you'll have to deal with me one last time."*

"What does she mean by that?" he demanded. "Why does it sound like she plans to leave me?"

"Because she does. That sweet child has had many disappointments in her lifetime. She doesn't trust you won't be another." Isis gave him an artful look from beneath her thick lashes. "After all, you chose the black-hearted Moira over her."

"Now that's a feckin' lie! I…"

But he had to a degree. Out of the blue Moira had shown up, contrite and loving, begging his forgiveness, and although Cian hadn't been taken in by her tragic appearance, he had essentially called Moira his fiancée, knowing Piper had been burned before. Piper had gotten a good look at his face, had heard the hesitation in his voice, and bolted. Before he could run after her, Moira had latched onto his forearm and kept him from giving chase.

"I'd have gone after Piper later, but it was as if the moment Moira touched me, I couldn't." Staring into the pond, he guessed there was more to it. "What did she do to me? A spell?"

"Yes." Isis held out her hand, palm up. "Expose your arm to me, Beloved."

Unsure why she'd cared to see his bare skin, Cian frowned down at his covered forearms. "Which one?"

Her brows shot up, and he felt like the dimmest creature on the planet. Of course, she meant the one Moira had touched. He barely refrained from smacking his forehead with the heel of his palm.

"Right." After he rolled up his sleeve, he shifted closer to Isis.

"Two punctures. Did you not feel them?" Her touch was soothing as she stroked the affected area.

Scowling, he nodded. "Yeah. She told me her ring had a sharp edge."

"It actually contains a secret compartment." With no more than a sparkling swirl of her finger, Isis produced a replica and showed him how to press a hidden latch to expose the lancet.

Jaysus, Mary, and Joseph! He'd been a spy for fuck's sake. How had he not figured it out right away? Poison was a woman's weapon. He should've known to watch for it.

"Moira poisoned me," he said grimly. "Not once, but twice."

"The first was a potion to slow the toxin. The second was the toxin itself," Isis confirmed.

"But why? What did she have to gain?"

"I cannot reveal what I know. Circumstances can be altered

by Fate's design. But I can tell you that all will be revealed in due time, child."

"Will Piper forgive me? Can you tell me?" he asked raggedly.

She used her staff to point to the pond. "She loves you. A woman will forgive a man almost anything if she sees the truth in his heart."

Underneath her glamour spell, he caught a glimpse of Piper's tear-ravaged features.

Isis had given him the gift of insight.

She graced him with a tender smile. "What is *your* truth, Cian O'Malley? Do you know?"

"Yes. I do."

"I'll leave you to ruminate on what you've learned. You'll know when it's time to return."

"Thank you, Exalted One. You've shown me more kindness than I deserve."

She cast him a beaming smile, and the sun flared brighter above him. "You're a charming rogue, Beloved. You'll blend well with the Thorne family."

"If Piper will have me," he countered with a sad sigh.

"Show her your truth when you return. Then she'll reveal hers."

His head whipped around from where he'd been staring at Piper, but Isis had already disappeared. "What truth is she hiding?" he called out to the empty park.

The wind picked up and it sounded remarkably like her naughty laughter, but she didn't answer.

"Moira's ring."

"Excuse me?" Piper had been lost in her own mind for a short while as she waited for the others to return. Aeden's halting voice had jerked her from her morose thoughts. "Moira's ring? What about it?"

"The Goddess wants you to know the ring is the key."

Piper jumped to her feet and rushed to Aeden. Squatting in front of him, she gripped his hands. "She's speaking through you now?"

He gave a hesitant nod.

"Is Cian with Anu?"

Aeden shook his head. "He's in the Otherworld with the other goddess. *Your* goddess."

"Isis?" Piper's heart nearly stopped, before resuming double time. Isis watched over those in the Otherworld. If Cian was there, reviving him might be more difficult. "We can bring him back?"

"Yes, and use the ring for the an... the ant..." He gave her a helpless look.

"Antidote?" she suggested helpfully.

"Yeah. Mind the tip."

The desire to hunt down Moira had been a strong one. Piper had ignored her instinct, but perhaps she shouldn't have.

"Where is Moira now, Aeden? Do you know?"

"Alastair does."

"Of course. he does. I should've known." She smiled up into Aeden's too-serious face. "You really are a hero, you know. I adore you."

His fierce hug knocked her on her butt, and she allowed him the contact he needed to draw whatever strength he could.

"You're going to be okay, Aeden. I'll make sure of it."

"I miss my mam," he whispered brokenly.

"I'll bet she's with the Goddess, watching over you. I'll bet she's so proud of you and your part in helping Cian."

"She's not there," he cried. "She's not, or I could talk to her."

Piper wasn't sure how it would be possible for him to do that, but she wasn't going to say it aloud. If his mother wasn't in the Otherworld, there was only one other place she could be, and it didn't bear thinking about.

"I have to go, Aeden. It's important we save your uncle, but I don't want to leave you like this."

After he heaved an achingly sad sigh, Aeden drew back. "I'm okay."

"You're sure?" Guilt tore at her, but time was of the essence.

The seconds ticked without a response from him, then finally, he gave her a firm nod.

"Will you stay with Cian until Bridget returns, kiddo? It won't be but a minute, but I have to go find Moira's ring."

"Yes."

Giving in to the desire to hug him again, she pulled him close. "You're so brave. Thank you."

She touched her tanzanite stone.

"Alastair, where is Moira being held?"

"A Council cell. I believe Ryker is with her. Why?"

"She has something I need."

"Meet me at the upper garden of my home. I'll take you."

She envisioned the landscape of Alastair's estate. Her cells heated to burning, and when she arrived, it was to see Alastair striding out the double doors.

"Is this to help your young man?"

"Yes."

"Come, child. I doubt we have time to lose." He held out one of his scarred hands. With the other, he drew a symbol in the air, and as she watched, a crack in space opened between the garden and the Witches' Council grounds. Keeping a tight grip on her, he tugged her through the veil between locations.

Most people wouldn't recognize the difference between a teleport and stepping through a fold—the difference seemed subtle—but only the most formidable of magical beings had the ability to open a portal like he had. It was a rare gift, usually given from a god or goddess. Since it was thought by many that

Alastair was Isis's favorite, it wasn't a guess who'd favored him with his unique talents.

"I've never been on WC grounds. Do you know where to go from here?" she asked.

Not bothering to answer, he gripped her elbow and ushered her toward a building on the other side of the paved courtyard. Council members lingering in the public area shot them odd looks, ranging from alarmed to resentful. Or rather, directed them at Alastair—and all from a respectable distance.

"You aren't well liked, are you?" she asked in a hushed voice.

A wry smile twisted his lips as he held open the door for her to enter the prison. "They fear me. It brings with it distrust and hatred."

"I'm sorry."

"You have no need to apologize, child."

"It's for me that you're here, having to deal with their pettiness." She touched his arm, hoping to convey her deep-felt apology. "I know you are an empath, Alastair, and I can only guess how much their viciousness must hurt."

"I learned a long time ago to tune all of it out unless I'm in a dangerous situation." He shrugged. "Think nothing of it. It's actually useful to have them fear me."

How he could be so blasé about the constant barrage of negative energy was beyond Piper's comprehension, but he was Alastair Thorne and was a majestic island unto himself.

"I'll warn you, don't allow Moira to get into your head, Piper. I've known her kind. She's a master manipulator and will do or say whatever is necessary to hurt you."

"Because of Cian?"

"No. Or not completely, from what I can tell. She's after something greater, I believe." He grimaced. "For the moment, I don't know what that is, but I intend to find out."

"Ryker cares about Cian. I'm sure he'd be willing to help you figure it out."

"I believe Rafe has also had a run in with Moira before. I'll be sure to check with him, after this."

"Rafe? As in Liz's Rafe?" If Piper dragged Liz's husband back into the world of intrigue and danger, her cousin would *kill* her.

Alastair chuckled. "One and the same."

"Great," she muttered.

"I won't tell Liz that Rafe's future involvement stems from this. It'll be our secret."

"It's all right. I'd rather she know the truth. She might make my death swift and painless."

Alastair's wide grin always made Piper happy when she witnessed it. Rarely seen, it was like sunshine through a storm and brought with it hope and lightness.

Ryker met them in the corridor. "If you've come to question Moira, she's gone."

"What?" Piper couldn't believe her ears. "I thought she was behind bars?"

"I stepped out for a minute. That was all it took." He released a frustrated growl. "Before you ask, the security tapes have been wiped. Any spell I used to recreate the jailbreak showed an invisible entity knock out the guards and shut down the power grid of the cellblock housing her and Seamus."

"Those cells were supposed to contain a foolproof charm." Alastair's expression said he wanted to spit nails.

Piper knew the feeling. Her last hope of saving Cian had casually strolled out the door under a cloaking spell. "I need to get back to the O'Malleys. Maybe Spring and GiGi have come up with something to help."

"I'm sorry, Piper. We'll find them, though." Ryker radiated determination, and it gave her hope.

"Let me know when you do." She touched his arm. "Be careful, Ryker. Moira has a poison-dispensing ring at her disposal, according to Aeden."

"Aeden spoke to you?"

"Why is everyone always so surprised?" she asked.

Ryker exchanged a speaking glance with Alastair. "The boy hasn't spoken to anyone but his father in months, and those times are getting fewer and farther apart. The family suspects he's developed a physical issue. Probably a manifestation of the trauma he's suffered."

Alastair gave her a questioning look. "How does this boy know about the ring? Did he see it?"

"No. He has a direct line to Anu. I think he might be psychic." Piper's heart hurt for the boy. If Aeden was indeed psychic, he could potentially lose his mind as well as his voice if his family magic returned. The fact was that psychic witches tended toward madness. After an extended time, they couldn't differentiate between reality and the movie in their mind. The stronger the witch and the cursed second sight, the faster they spiraled.

"Aeden's problems are for another day," Ryker said. "But we have Moira's ring."

Afraid to hope, she swirled her hand for him to continue.

"When she was arrested, we stripped her of her powers and any objects that could potentially be charmed." He gestured to Piper's tanzanite ring. "Anything man-made can be infused with magic."

Unable to contain her joy, Piper flung herself at Ryker.

He caught her with a light laugh and returned her hug. "I take it you're happy we have the ring secured?"

"Exceedingly. Where is it?"

"Come on, I'll take you to the vault. I believe Councilwoman Sipanil will ensure my entry, since I'll be the one overseeing Moira's and Seamus's recapture."

Within minutes, the ring was in a protective metal lockbox and clutched tightly against Piper's chest. "I don't know how to thank you, Ryker."

"Save Cian."

"That's the plan. You be careful," she urged.

Alastair gave her a one-armed squeeze. "Ryker's always careful."

She gave a disbelieving laugh. Those two lived for danger.

"Here." Piper handed off the box to GiGi. "Your husband wanted me to relay his fervent request you save his friend."

"He's so demanding," GiGi quipped. "I'm going to visit Spring and see if she can reverse engineer this. Go open that fickle O'Malley grimoire. It's been dark since you left and none of us can get it to wake up." She leaned in and lowered her voice. "Bridget's beside herself." The serious statement betrayed how worried they all were.

Piper needed to share whatever strength she had left, if only to see Bridget though this. "I'm on it."

She gave Aeden two thumbs up and an encouraging smile.

He didn't return it, and looked as if he wanted to bolt at any second.

Bridget met her halfway across the room. "Here. See what—*oh!*"

The book immediately sprang to life and flipped pages at a mind-blowing speed until it settled on a hand-written spell that looked like it was four-hundred years old or more.

"What's this say?" Piper turned the book so it was facing Bridget and tapped the vellum page.

"It's an extraction spell." She shrugged her confusion and shook her head. "I don't know what it's intended to do."

"Extract the poison from Cian's system would be my guess." Without intending to, Piper silently checked with Aeden. He nodded, and she felt better to have Anu's sign they were on the right track. "Okay. So it looks like I'm shoving a huge syringe into Cian's heart muscle and withdrawing the poison while chanting this spell. No problem."

Bridget turned an alarming shade of green, and Piper imagined that her own face was a mirror image. The idea of stabbing him was stomach churning.

"Can't be wrong if both the book and the Goddess agree, right?" Bridget asked faintly.

"Right." They shared a sickly smile. Piper firmed her spine and shoved aside her squeamishness. "Can you read it word for word to me, so I can repeat it as we're performing the procedure?"

"If it means saving my brother, I can."

"You're a rock star, Bridget." After inhaling a cleansing breath, Piper handed off the grimoire with a firm command to the book to stay awake as they cast. "If you abandon us mid-spell, I'll burn your ass in a bonfire. Got it?" The symbols on the cover flared bright and settled in a soft glow. "I'm going to take that as a yes. And thanks."

Her mother disappeared and returned a minute later with a tray of items in sterilization bags.

Piper almost laughed. "You're the best mom. You know that, right?"

Rebecca blushed prettily as she smiled. "I'd like to think I am, but I wasn't always there for you in your formative years, sweetheart."

"That's not true, Mom. You totally were. You've always put family first."

"I'm glad you think so, but we can debate it later. Cian's vitals are concerning and I don't like the color of his skin and lips."

Rebecca conjured surgical scrubs and lab coats for them both, drew on gloves and made Piper do the same—*because poison!* In doctor mode, she went about preparing the room for their extraction procedure.

On the opposite end of the spectrum, Bridget prepared a casting circle and set candles in place. "Do we wait for GiGi and Spring to return?" she asked when she finished.

Piper turned to the only one of them with medical experience. "Mom?"

"I don't know if we have the time." Rebecca once more checked Cian's pulse. "I say we try the extraction and worry about administering the antidote as soon as those two can whip one up."

"Okay." Instinct told her to help Cian as quickly as possible. "Let's do this. And if I pass out or anything weak like that, don't worry about me. Finish the spell."

Rebecca laughed lightly and knocked shoulders with her. "You're my daughter. I have every faith you'll be strong when it matters."

"Didn't Dad cry over the birth of his prize piglets? I might've gotten more of *his* DNA."

Aeden giggled, and she shot him a wink.

"I don't know what your level of expertise is, Bridget, but please don't break the circle once it's cast." Piper nodded to Aeden. "You either, little man. No matter what you see or hear, you need to stay where you are, all right?"

"If you get scared, you can shut your eyes and cover your ears, Aeden," Rebecca told him with an encouraging smile.

"We're going to do everything we can to save your Uncle Cian. I promise."

The boy swallowed hard and nodded. His murky-green eyes were swimming with tears and Piper's heart hitched.

"Does Anu have any last words for us, fry guy?"

He shook his head.

"Okay. I'll take that as a good sign." She wanted to hide her nervousness from him, but she couldn't. If he was indeed a psychic witch, he'd know she was trying to cover up her feelings anyway. "Thank you for all your help, Aeden. You're one brave boy. And when this is over, I'm going to introduce you to root beer floats."

His tears dried up, but he still looked so damned heartbreakingly serious that Piper wanted to promise him the moon and stars if only to make him happy again.

"Goddess, hear our plea, and assist us in our time of need," they all chanted together.

Bridget then read the Gaelic spell as Rebecca assisted Piper in positioning the first syringe above Cian's chest. Her mom shifted to hold him in place with the full weight of her body.

As Piper repeated the words, she slammed the needle into Cian's heart muscle and tried not to panic as his body bucked underneath Rebecca.

"*Mom?*"

"Hold the barrel and pull back on the plunger. Do it now, Piper!"

Bridget continued with the spell, and Piper obediently repeated it word for word, trying to make sure the inflection and pronunciation didn't vary. All the while, she drew out thick black goo from Cian's heart.

"Again!" Rebecca said urgently. "Swap the barrel for a new one. Leave the tip and hub in place."

Piper worked quickly and it took four and a half more

times to remove the bulk of the poison. "How is there so much of it?" she cried as she filled yet another tube.

"It multiplies in the bloodstream. It's the nature of a magical poison," Rebecca explained. "But look, it's diluted and not as black. There was blood in that last barrel. Do another."

Her mother had the right of it, and the black sludge only filled a third of the final barrel. A cloudy yellow fluid followed the poisonous gook, and Piper shot a look at her mom. "Is this normal?"

With a short, humorless bark of laughter, Rebecca asked, "What about any of *this* is normal, sweetheart?"

"Right. So, do I keep drawing out the yellow stuff, too? Is that the original poison?"

"Yeah," Aeden said from his corner. "Draw unto blood, Anu says."

"Thank the Goddess for our little conduit there," Rebecca muttered.

After a lifetime of worry and sweat, the blood flowed freely through the syringe, and Piper felt confident she could remove the needle. "How do I close the hole when I'm done?" Silently, she hoped her mother would take over so she wouldn't shame herself if her shaking legs gave out.

Sensing her need, Rebecca released Cian and came to stand beside Piper. "I've got a sure-fire spell for that one. Quickly remove the tip, and I'll be ready."

They worked like they'd been colleagues forever, and their transition went smoothly with Rebecca stepping into place to voice the enchantment that would weave Cian's wound together.

As Rebecca performed her magic, Piper locked onto Cian's gray face. With each second that passed, his skin returned to a normal hue, and the blue tinge left his lips.

They closed the circle after Rebecca declared the procedure a success.

"It's going to be wait-and-see from here on out," she informed them as she pulled her gloves off by the edges in one practiced move that trapped any contamination inside.

Piper followed suit.

"I'll take this back to my lab and have my best team deconstruct and reverse engineer it," Rebecca said. "When GiGi and Spring return, have them administer their antidote as a backup, then call me. I want to make sure we are all working together and everyone has the cure should it happen again."

She muttered a few choice words about "dirty rotten Désorcelers and their underhanded tricks" as she gathered her instrument tray.

"Is there anything I need to watch for, Mom?"

Rebecca looked at Cian and a slow smile spread across her face. "I don't believe you'll need to," she said. "Welcome back, Mr. O'Malley. You had a lot of people worried."

Piper had hoped to be gone before he woke, but unfortunately, she'd never had great timing. She backed up so Bridget and Aeden could crowd beside him.

Although clouded with pain, his irises still reflected a bright emerald green and his gaze sought Piper. When he held out a hand to her, she gave him an impersonal smile and stayed where she was.

He stubbornly remained in the same position and wouldn't look away. His will was as unfaltering and determined as she'd ever witnessed, and he didn't move until she finally placed her palm in his.

A tingle ran up her arm as he entwined his fingers with hers. She wondered if this was the first line of the prophecy fulfilled. Did it mean his minuscule amount of magic was multiplying?

"Thank you, Piper me love." His voice was gravelly. With disuse or gratitude, she couldn't be sure.

"Of course. We all wanted you well, Cian."

Those penetrating eyes peered at her, as if he could see through all the layers of pretense. They missed nothing. Uncomfortable with feeling exposed, she tried to pull away. For someone who was knocking on death's door not ten minutes before, he was surprisingly strong and hearty.

"Let me go," she hissed. She didn't want it to appear like a tug of war to those around them.

"No. You and I need to talk. I'll not wait another minute to tell you what's in my heart."

She heard the door close and realized it was just the two of them. "Those traitors are like rats abandoning ship," she muttered.

His rumbling laugh erased the last of her worry for him.

"Piper, I owe you an apology and an explanation of the other day's events."

She cut him off with a wave of her free hand. "You don't. It's all good. All's forgiven. I'm—" *Babbling like a pin-headed goose,* as her father would say.

"All's not forgiven, and it shouldn't be. Not yet, anyway." With a firm tug, Cian pulled her to lie atop him. He released her hand to cup her face between his palms. "I'm sorry, Piper. For saying Moira was my fiancée, and for ever making you feel like I didn't love you with everything that I am. This heart of mine belongs to you and you alone."

The words to accept his apology were locked in the back of her throat. How could she trust him this time? She'd been played so frequently in life, she didn't know the truth when she heard it anymore. At least, not from men.

He studied her as she made up her mind, and in his eyes, Piper was certain she saw the love she'd longed for, along with patience and gentle understanding. His tender expression left her raw and aching.

"Why did you claim her as your fiancée, Cian?" She barely managed the question.

"Because she was. *Once.* My promise hadn't ended with her death. It should've. The honorable part of me believed I needed to formally break it off before I committed fully to you."

She wanted to yell, to tell him his archaic beliefs were stupid, but she couldn't. "Did you?"

"Break it off? Sure, and I did. The second you left the room, I told that horrid she-devil that she was nothing to me and if she ever set foot on O'Malley property again, she'd be answering to Alastair Thorne as well as your da and Ryker."

A grin Piper couldn't stop, curled her lips. "You were going to sic my dad on her?"

"I'm not a proud man. I know my magical limits."

Not wanting to add undue pressure to his chest, Piper rolled to the side.

He seemed to take the move as a rejection, and the teasing light left him as he turned on his side to face her. "Isis assured me you were a forgiving sort, if I told you the truth of my heart."

Was it possible Piper was too much of a pushover?

"Was she wrong, love?"

"Why didn't you come to my room after you sent Moira away?"

"Would you believe an enchantment kept me away? She warned me to watch me back, and I was fool enough to believe she wouldn't try anything as soon as she did."

"Were you able to see it all from the Otherworld?"

"All?"

"Like everything that was said or done here on the earthly plane while you were in stasis?" Did he know she'd conceived a child? Had he see how pathetically heartbroken she'd been when she'd made the decision to raise their baby alone?

"No. Not all. Isis swung her special stick and the water showed all your efforts to save me. I witnessed everything from the moment you sat beside me and said your goodbyes until I woke up."

So he didn't know about the baby. It was still her secret gift from Isis.

"Is there something I should've seen, Piper? Something that would make a difference between us?"

"No." And she spoke the truth. She had no intention of letting a pregnancy decide her commitment to another. She'd only stay with Cian if she believed he truly loved her and intended to put her first. Baby or no. "I won't pretend I don't love you or that I wasn't deeply hurt, but I think you need more time."

"Why would I be needing more time?"

"I want you to be sure of your feelings, Cian." She pressed her fingertips to his mouth when he would've argued. "I swept into your life with a load of trouble directly on my heels. It's been a whirlwind, and you've not had a spare moment to process everything." She couldn't help herself, and she caressed his lips. "Two months. You think about everything, put your household to rights, and come find me in two months. If you still want a relationship with me, we'll talk."

"No." His tone was harsh and his expression had hardened to granite. "I've not realized it, but I've spent my entire life looking for you, Piper Kelly Thorne. And now that you've tangled yourself in my heartstrings, you'll not snip the thread and float away. You're tied to me now. Forevermore."

"That seems bossy as fuck." She found his stubbornness thrilling.

He softened enough to grin. "And it's probably going to be the last bossy word I'll get in, between you and Bridget." She couldn't miss the plea in his eyes as he said, "Don't leave me, love. Stay and fight for what we've started. Live with me in that old crumbling building where you kissed me stupid and started the thaw of my poor wee heart."

"Oh, Cian. You make it impossible to say no."

"Good." He began to lean in, but stopped short. "Can you conjure me a breath mint so I don't cause you to faint when I kiss ya?"

She laughed and sat up. "Who said you're allowed to kiss me? I've never seen you wipe the Moira cooties from your mouth."

"Gargled with pure alcohol, I did. You'd have been right proud of me, darlin'. Those pints of plain destroyed every last trace, to be sure."

Piper narrowed her eyes and pretended to scowl. "Your accent grows thicker and more pronounced when you're trying to pull one over on me."

He laughed, and she felt the warmth all the way down to her toes.

It was suddenly essential for her to lay it all out for him. "I need you to be that guy, Cian. The one who loves me beyond reason, just as I love you. I want it all. The romance, the friendship, the loyalty until the day we die." She released a ragged breath and conjured two peppermints. She held out her hand. "If you can't be that guy, if there's a chance you're going to tear me apart, don't give me hope."

With great deliberation, Cian sat up, and his burning gaze locked with hers. He scooped up both mints, and Piper's heart began to hammer as he popped first one into her mouth and the other into his.

"I'm that guy."

EPILOGUE

Isis smiled as she watched Cian tumble Piper back onto the mattress and claim her mouth in a passionate kiss.

Yes, he'd be *that* guy. The one who would always dance with his love beneath the stars, the man whose soul burned white-hot only for her until the end of time. He'd be the one who would stay up to watch her sleep because he couldn't believe his good fortune. And he'd be the perfect father to their hoard of children.

Isis didn't feel one smidgeon of guilt for plucking the daydream from Piper's mind the day she'd rebuilt the old keep. The girl had made clear her thoughts as she welcomed Isis's gift and used it to create the perfect home for her future family. The very least Isis could do was work with Fate to make sure one of her descendants received their heart's desire.

"You know nothing is assured."

Isis didn't need to look behind her to know who had joined her. "Anu. Welcome. And yes, I'm aware."

She waved her staff and the scene on the pond's surface shifted to show the three who conspired to stop the O'Malley prophecy from coming to fruition.

"Yours, I believe."

Anu joined her and winced when she saw the group Isis indicated. "Should I end them?"

Isis smiled and shook her head. "Your offer comes from the right place, and I appreciate your willingness to assist me. However, if we remove the playing pieces from the board, the prophecy will be aborted."

"Ah, so you've already consulted the Three to glimpse the future. What threads have they woven into the tapestry of the O'Malley family's life?"

The Three were also known as the three Sisters of Fate. They were responsible for all future events. The gods and goddesses could dabble with Fate's design to a small extent, but in the end, the final outcome was for the Three to decide.

"I wish I knew. The Three only shared enough for me to understand Moira and Seamus needed to be free to run amok and set the wheels of the next part in motion.

"And the third? How does he play into this?"

"Oddly, I can't seem to get a read on him." Isis frowned as she peered closer. "Do you find that as disturbing as I do?"

"Exceedingly." Anu studied the blond man who towered over Seamus and Moira. "He's familiar to me, but I can't place him."

"Let's watch and see how this plays out. Perhaps we'll give little Aeden the help he needs if the time comes."

"You've always had a soft spot for children." Anu's smile was warm and admiring. "You're descendants will be a welcome addition to my island."

"Thank you, Blessed." Isis hugged her. "Shall we continue to work together on this one?"

"I'd like nothing better."

They shared a smile and turned back to watch the scene reflected on the pool surface as it unfolded.

Seamus and Moira stood in front of Ronan's chair, arguing about who was to blame for the current failure. The bickering was driving Ronan mad. If they didn't stop soon, he was likely to murder them both.

His phone burned a hole in his pocket, and he removed it to read Rebecca Walsh-Thorne's message from two weeks ago. The only one he'd received from Bec in over a decade and a half, despite his waiting impatiently.

"See that Piper doesn't come to harm while she's in Ireland."

He'd promptly texted back.

"Not my call."

Rebecca's reply was immediate and stung like the dickens.

"You owe me that much for what you did."

Ronan guzzled what was left of his red wine and stared moodily at the screen.

What he did, yes. He'd tried to seduce her away from her husband and child twenty-two years ago. For all of a moment, he thought he'd had done it. Thought she'd loved him as he loved her. But no. Her heart had been given to Hoyt Thorne and she had no room for Ronan.

Well, if Bec ever saw him again, she'd murder him dead, to be sure. He'd failed to keep Piper safe. Despite his command to leave Piper untouched, Seamus and Moira had gone off script and harmed Bec's daughter at every opportunity.

Ronan was a piss-poor excuse for a watchdog.

He eyed them sourly as they continued their quarrel.

"You're a fecking *eejit* is what you are!" Seamus roared at Moira. "You didn't trust I'd take care of Piper meself, and you had to show your hand as you tried to prove Cian still loved ye above all others." An evil, gloating grin spread across his face. "But he doesn't, does he?"

The sound of Moira's slap rang out.

The scarlet hand imprint on Seamus's cheek was no more than the idiot deserved.

As the ring leader of their trio, Ronan had his work cut out for him.

He should've killed them the first time they defied him.

"Enough!" he barked and slammed his fist on an end table.

With a surly exchange of glances, Moira and Seamus complied.

Ronan lifted his hand and let flames dance along his fingertips. "The next one who defies my direct order will roast in a hell of my making, do you understand?"

Seamus audibly gulped as Moira studied the polished points of her two-inch nails.

"Moira. Do you understand me?"

"Yes," she hissed, and the boiling fury in her glare would singe a lesser man.

"Cian O'Malley is now off the table, as is the Thorne woman." He rose to his impressive height of six-feet-five and stared down at his two impulsive cousins. "I mean it. If Piper Thorne gets a hangnail, I'll visit it on you both tenfold. Am I clear?"

They nodded, and Ronan was positive they'd have this conversation again. Preferably before they not-so-accidentally killed Piper with their harebrained schemes.

"We need to prevent the next part of the prophecy," he told them, to gain their focus.

"Why can't we just take out the brat?" Moira whined. "Once we do, we've ended it for good."

"*No,*" Ronan snapped. "The boy was *never* to be harmed." He snuffed out the fire by fisting his hand, then proceeded to punch Seamus in the face.

Seamus flew from his seat, landed in a heap, and curled into a ball. After a time when he sensed no further threat, he scurried up, clutching his broken nose. "I'm sorry, Ronan. I've said it again and again."

"I'll remind you both one last time. We don't make war on children and we don't use blood magic." Ronan crossed his arms and turned his steely silver gaze on the two of them. "You've already disobeyed me when you caused the accident that killed Roisin, Seamus. And *you!*" He pinned Moira with a look. "You defied me with the poison and your fucking blood magic. It will *not* happen again. I will kill you both where you stand should you ever try."

"Rona—" they began to whinge in unison.

"*Shut up!*" He hollered.

The stone walls of their family castle shook and a wealth of dust particles rained down on Seamus's and Moira's heads. The two of them ducked and covered.

With a snort of disgust, Ronan beckoned his men from the shadows. "Take them to the south tower and lock them in. Perhaps a few weeks of reflection is what they need to understand I'm deadly serious."

"No!" Real terror shone in Moira's eyes. "Please, Ronan. Please don't lock me in that room."

The tower rooms had been their punishment from the time the three of them were small children. Stripped bare of all but a hard mattress and a bucket for pissing or shitting, the eight-by-eight space was enough to send the strongest-minded into the mouth of madness.

Ronan hated the place himself, but he couldn't risk either of his cousins killing anyone else. The intent had been to scare Piper into leaving or to convince Cian to send the woman away. Ronan hadn't counted on O'Malley falling in love—not after what Moira had done to him in the past. Her betrayal had been one of Ronan's best laid plans, and she destroyed it when she resurrected herself and showed up in Cian's salon.

Which reminded him…

"How did you get past the wards, Moira?" he asked in a tone as soft as silk. Sure, and he had his suspicions, but she would answer for her mischief before the day was out.

"I don't know what you're talking about." Her panicked eyes darted sideways as if to seek Seamus's help. Her plea-filled look was in vain. Seamus was a coward on the best of days.

Ronan gave her a chilly smile. "Right." Without breaking eye contact, he motioned the closest guard forward. "Search her. Be careful of poisonous rings and be sure to confiscate whatever you find."

Moira's eyes were huge in her deathly pale face. "Ronan—"

"I suspect you borrowed what wasn't yours to take, Cousin. I'll have it back now."

It took less than a minute for the security guard to pat her down, but he shook his head in answer to magical items Moira might be packing.

"Where is it, Moira?" he growled.

"My guess is the Witches' Council," Seamus inserted slyly. "They took her ring, too."

Rage detonated in Ronan's brain. The missing piece had been given to him by Rebecca during their brief affair. One that allowed him to slip by the Thornes' wards. It was the only thing he had to remember her by, and now it was gone. His desire to maim tried to overwhelm him. With careful control, he tucked the emotion behind a mental wall. He'd deal with Moira in due course.

"This was orchestrated down to the last note and has been in play for the last *seven* years, Moira. If you believe I'll let you or Seamus fuck it up again, you're delusional. I want the O'Malley magic, and I'll get it. With or without you."

—————

THANK YOU FOR READING CIAN & PIPER'S STORY. IF YOU'RE LIKE me, you don't want to see them go away. Well, they're not. Going away, that is. You'll see them woven throughout the rest of the books in my new series, *The Unlucky Charms*! Turn the page to read an excerpt of Carrick O'Malley and Roisin Byrne's love story, *Whiskey & Witches*.

When the Golden Son sacrifices for the One,
Only then can the curse be undone...

Chapter One

Aeden O'Malley was playing in the yard when the blonde witch showed up. Even at the ripe old age of seven, he knew what she was. Her light was brighter than most, and he also knew this was a sign she was magically stronger than others like them.

"Hello," she said, her pleasant smile reminding him of his mother. Everything reminded him of her. But she was gone now. Killed in a car accident when he was only six.

Killed by evil.

As the witch moved to pass him, Aeden jumped to his feet and barred her way.

Her smile eased into a frown, and she looked beyond him to the door of the cottage, then back down at him. "Are you all right, Aeden?"

He wanted to demand why she was here, but his vocal cords refused to work. His throat was damaged after he inhaled all the smoke from the flames that had burned the car his mother had driven. Six months later, he stopped speaking to anyone but his da due to the pain. A year later, all he could manage were the occasional grunts, and once or twice during a nightmare, a scream.

Tears welled in his eyes, and he pressed his lips together.

A soft light entered her incredibly blue eyes, and she reached out a hand as if to stroke his cheek.

Jerking back, he scowled and slapped her hand away. He didn't want her kindness. Didn't need it when he had a family to look out for him. Turning away, he scooped up his toys and raced for the front door.

"Aeden?" she called, and there was sadness in the sound.

He paused just as he reached the entrance to his da's home. Something in her voice compelled him to turn around.

"I can help you." She smiled. "If you'd like."

He didn't want her help. Didn't deserve it. He was the reason his mother was dead. But he couldn't tell her that. Couldn't tell anyone.

Aeden ran.

Roisin Byrne sighed deeply. Perhaps she should approach Carrick again and offer her services as she had after the tragic accident that left his beloved son mute. Maybe he'd be more receptive to her cures this time around.

Movement in an upstairs window caught her attention. As if she'd conjured him with her thoughts, Carrick appeared. He stared down at her, his corded arms crossed over his impressive chest and a dark scowl on his devastatingly handsome face. Today, he only wore a simple t-shirt, and even from this distance, Roisin could see how the material loved his body, conforming to all the well-defined muscles.

Oh, how she remembered the beautiful contour of his chest and abdomen!

Damn, but the man was grand. Always had been, always would be. Too bad he had no place in his life for her.

She gave a little wave, causing his frown to deepen. Without meaning to, she grinned. But the cheeky smile fell from her face when he ran a hand through his dark hair and turned away in dismissal.

Tears welled up, and she violently wiped them away. She was an eejit for wanting the family she couldn't have.

A tingling in her face was the only indication she had that her glamour spell was wearing thin. She released the clip holding her hair and arranged the corkscrew curls to shield most of her scarred visage. Careful to keep the ravaged side of her face away from oncoming foot traffic, she traveled the road until she came to the dirt path leading to her cottage.

She'd only been home five minutes or so when banging on the front door commanded her attention.

Carrick.

It had to be. No one else would dare confront the witch of the woods. Not in her own home anyway.

"Open the door, Roisin!"

The demanding tone grated on her nerves. Who the hell did he think he was? *He* had rejected *her.* Now he thought to come here and what? Take her to task for talking to Aeden? For trying to reach beyond the poor child's pain and help him heal?

"Go away, Carrick. I'm not accepting callers today," she hollered from the other side of the wooden panel.

"Jaysus, woman, you'd try the patience of a saint! *Open the fecking door!*"

A little devil danced on her shoulder this day. "Only if you ask me nicely. I'll be expecting a please from you, I will."

She imagined she could hear his teeth gnash together. To be sure, she heard his frustrated exhale.

"*Please,*" he gritted out.

Suppressing the bubble of laughter was difficult, but she

managed. When she could speak without inflection, she said, "Please, what?"

"I swear to the Goddess," he muttered. Raising his voice a hair louder, he called, *"Please, open the bloody door!"*

She turned the knob and stepped away, presenting her back. "It wasn't locked."

"You'd try the patience of a saint."

"You're getting repetitive, Carrick, my love. I'd make a concerted effort to find another way to insult me if I were you. It shouldn't be too hard." Without bothering to spare him a glance, she limped to the stove and spooned soup into two bowls. She slapped them on the table and followed it with a loaf of freshly baked bread. "Eat. You look like you haven't had a decent meal in ages."

She sat to his right, so he didn't have a direct line of sight to her scarred side. After a long, tense moment, he joined her at the table. They ate in silence. She got lost to another time when the two of them had broken bread together. A time when love and laughter were the themes of the day. When they had lovingly fed each other and followed each bite with a delicious kiss.

"You have to stop coming by, Ro. You're frightening Aeden."

She struggled to keep her voice steady even though her heart was breaking. "I've never let him see the marks."

"When you appear like the way you do, you remind him of his mother."

Her stomach clenched in knots. "Is that such a bad thing?"

Carrick set his spoon down with a loud clatter. "Yes, it is. For *both* of us."

Blinking furiously, she nodded.

"I'm sorry, Ro. I have to do what's best for him."

"You mean what you *think* is best for him."

"He'll never accept you. Not like this."

She glanced up in time to see the pity in his eyes. Rage

clouded her vision, and the plates on a nearby shelf rattled to express her most profound emotion. "Get out of my house, Carrick, and never come back."

"Ro—"

"Get out!"

The ground rumbled, and his face grew pale.

"Is this what happened that day? Did your anger take over?" he demanded.

Her fury faded into a black void of grief. "I don't know. I don't remember much." But she did. She remembered almost everything, although she'd never say, not to him anyway.

Roisin climbed to her feet with great care. If she moved at a faster pace than a snail, her back would pinch, and it would take the devil's own magic to make the muscles respond to her commands. Carrick jumped up to assist her.

"Don't touch me," she snapped, her voice raspy and raw. "Never touch me."

"I was only trying to help."

"I don't want your help."

She shuffled to the other end of the kitchen and reached for the bottle of the elixir she'd concocted for Aeden. Her back spasmed, and she couldn't prevent a cry of pain. She'd over-done her exercise today.

Warm, strong arms encircled her from behind, and for a brief, heavenly second, he held her to his chest. She didn't have more than a heartbeat or two to savor the feel of his touch before he scooped her up and settled her on the kitchen bench.

"Stubborn to the last." There was a hint of affection in his statement. When he squatted to look into her face, her hands came up to shield her face. "Your scars don't matter to me, Ro. They never have."

"Sure they do. They matter enough that I can't be part of your life. Part of Aeden's."

His face turned to stone, and he stood. "He has horrific

nightmares of that day. It's caused him to shut down, Ro. I'll not subject him to anything that could trigger more trauma for him."

"Right." She tried to tell herself he was being a good da, but it got more challenging every day. "Take that potion and go, Carrick." She pointed to the bottle she'd tried to reach. "I'm tired, and I need sleep." What she really meant was that she was exhausted from the age-old argument. All she'd ever receive from him when he wasn't shoving her away were scraps of affection. She was tired of that, too.

No more.

She refused to meet his probing gaze and kept her eyes trained on the stone floor.

It seemed as if an hour passed before he moved out of her good eye's peripheral.

"What is this?"

"It's for his throat. I've been working on the proper recipe for months. This should help."

His large hand came down on her shoulder and caused her to jump.

Damned blind eye!

And damned stealthy male!

"What's the dosage?" he asked as he held the bottle to the light and squinted at the contents.

"A spoonful morning, noon, and night until it's gone. And should he regain his voice, he's to continue until there's none left."

"What if he hates the flavor?" he asked dryly. "You don't know what it's like to make that child take—"

He clammed up when she glared. Their gazes remained locked until a redness dusted his cheeks. "Right. Sorry."

"I flavored it to taste like his favorite sweeties. He'll take it without complaint," she told him. From her pocket, she pulled a note. "He might not be able to speak this aloud, but have him mouth it, at least. He needs to concentrate on the words and the intent behind them. It will give the potion a boost."

"He's an O'Malley. He has no power."

"Oh, you O'Malleys hold more magic than you realize. But the spell is from my family's grimoire. It'll work."

A mist of tears covered Carrick's dark green eyes, and Roisin was positive she heard her heart crack for the second time that day.

Once, those eyes used to be a brilliant emerald color. But in the months since he'd lost his wife, his eyes had turned to the shade of the forest. Eyes were a witch's tell. The lighter and brighter the color, the happier or more content they were. Carrick's told the tale of his pain.

"I don't know how to express my thanks, Ro."

"Meg. I'm Meghan now. Roisin is dead, remember," she said snidely. "And I'm not doing any of this for you. I'm doing it for Aeden. And only because I don't want him to know his da is a fecking eejit."

She bit her lower lip as she struggled to her feet. Having Carrick hover over her was causing her neck to lock up. With her standard shuffling walk, she crossed to the door and pulled it open. "Goodbye, Carrick."

He paused to stare down at her. His hand lifted to her destroyed cheek, and she flinched at his touch. As he trailed three fingers along the network of scars, she forced herself to give him a stern look from her good eye.

Wordlessly, he dropped his arm and left her alone.

A sob caught in her throat, and she sank to the ground with her back to the closed door, giving in to her grief. She knew it would be hours before she could move again.

https://bit.ly/whiskey-witches-amzn

Also, if you haven't already subscribed to my newsletter, *www.tmcromer.com/newsletter*, or joined my Facebook reader group, *Cromer's Carousers*. I encourage you to do so. It's the best way for you to stay current on upcoming stories. After I'm done with the O'Malleys, I'll be introducing the next generation of Thornes, and you won't want to miss it.

Books in *The Thorne Witches* Series:
SUMMER MAGIC
AUTUMN MAGIC
WINTER MAGIC
SPRING MAGIC
REKINDLED MAGIC
LONG LOST MAGIC
FOREVER MAGIC
ESSENTIAL MAGIC
MOONLIT MAGIC
ENCHANTED MAGIC
CELESTIAL MAGIC

Books in *The Unlucky Charms* Series:
PINTS & POTIONS
WHISKEY & WITCHES *(March 2022)*
BEER & BROOMSTICKS *(July 2022)*

Books in *The Holt Family* Series:
FINDING YOU
THIS TIME YOU
INCLUDING YOU
AFTER YOU *(Sept 2022)*

www.ingramcontent.com/pod-product-compliance
Lightning Source LLC
Chambersburg PA
CBHW071239190726
48292CB00007B/2360